INVISIBLE COUNTRY

ALSO BY ANNAMARIA ALFIERI

City of Silver

INVISIBLE COUNTRY

ANNAMARIA ALFIERI

Thomas Dunne Books
Minotaur Books
New York

This is a work of fiction. All of the characters, organizations, and events portrayed in this novel are either products of the author's imagination or are used fictitiously.

A THOMAS DUNNE BOOK FOR MINOTAUR BOOKS.
An imprint of St. Martin's Press.

INVISIBLE COUNTRY. Copyright © 2012 by Annamaria Alfieri. All rights reserved. Printed in the United States of America. For information, address St. Martin's Press, 175 Fifth Avenue, New York, N.Y. 10010.

www.thomasdunnebooks.com
www.minotaurbooks.com

Design by Meryl Sussman Levavi

Library of Congress Cataloging-in-Publication Data

Alfieri, Annamaria.
    Invisible country: a mystery / Annamaria Alfieri.—1st ed.
        p. cm.
    "A Thomas Dunne book."
    ISBN 978-1-250-00453-6 (hardcover)
    ISBN 978-1-250-01496-2 (e-book)
    1. Murder—Investigation—Fiction.   2. Paraguay—Fiction.
I. Title.
    PS3601.L3597158 2012
    813'.6—dc23

                                              2012005479

First Edition: July 2012

10   9   8   7   6   5   4   3   2   1

In memory of my father, Samuel Puglise,
a World War II combat Marine
who came home a pacifist
and taught me to hate war

Between 1864 and 1870, the small landlocked country of Paraguay fought against three major South American powers—Argentina, Brazil, and Uruguay—the conflict known as the War of the Triple Alliance. . . . At the war's end . . . Paraguay's cities were in ruins, its economy destroyed, its male population reduced by upwards of 90 percent.

—Alyn Brodsky, *Madame Lynch & Friend*,
New York 1975

☀

In representing the courage, the fearlessness of death of the Paraguayans as so extraordinary, my statements are fully supported by every one, of whatever shade of opinion, who has written or spoken of this singular people. . . . The story of their sufferings and of their heroism should not perish with them.

—George Frederick Masterman,
Seven Eventful Years in Paraguay, London 1870

☀

Paz Y Justicia (Peace and Justice)

—The Coat of Arms of Paraguay

DRAMATIS PERSONAE

MARISCAL FRANCISCO SOLANO LÓPEZ, dictator of Paraguay
ELIZA LYNCH, his mistress
COLONEL FRANZ (called François) VON WISNER DE
MORGENSTERN, Hungarian nobleman

✦

COMANDANTE LUIS MENENEZ, minion of López
GILDA LEÓN DE MENENEZ, his wife

✦

SALVADOR LEÓN, head of the area's leading family
ALIVIA, his wife
XANDRA, their daughter

✦

PADRE GREGORIO PEREZ, pastor of Santa Caterina

✦

RICARDO YOTTÉ, close ally of López and Lynch
MARTITA, his sister
ESTELLA, his sister

✦

JOSEFINA QUESADA, village seer
PABLO, her grandson

✦

MARIA CLAUDIA BENÍTEZ, devout parishioner

✦

MANUELA ARAGON, village blacksmith

✦

HECTOR MOMPÓ, SATURNINO FERMÍN, GASPÁR OTAZÚ,
three old men of the village

✦

TOMÁS PEREIRA DA GRAÇA, Brazilian cavalryman

PARAGUAY 1869

They faced the edge of a cliff. The deep river gorge in front of them, with rocks and water far, far below, resembled nothing so much as a palisade along the coast of Ireland, which she had left almost twenty-five years ago. From thence to Paris, where after years of surviving on her looks, she met Francisco Solano López, the son of the dictator of Paraguay, a toad of a man with no neck and execrable manners, but limitless wealth. He saw in her everything he lacked: beauty, charm, style, and in return for her company he offered her so much more than freedom from want. With him she could have luxury and adventure, even a chance at becoming an empress like her friend Eugénie. And so she came here to the heart of South America, where he would be the great leader of his people and she his consort.

The mountains were rugged here in the north, streaked this chilly morning with mist that clung to the ridges and obscured the peaks. Harsh terrain. Not at all like the benign and verdant valley where they had last pitched their lovely white tents.

The enemy had driven them to this forbidding place. The war, which was supposed to have raised them to be the rulers of the continent, was lost, had broken her heart and his mind.

"This is as good a place as any," the great Mariscal López who was going down in defeat said to her in French. It was a statement, not a question, but his eyes searched hers for approval.

She nodded. Her gray mare backed away from the edge. She reached forward and patted the beast's neck to calm her. López thought the four trunks on the wagon behind them contained the treasure of Paraguay and hiding it here would protect the gold and jewels from the ruthless invading army that pursued them. He imagined that what he was about to do was sane, though he was mad. Perhaps he had always been mad to think he would become an emperor. She, Eliza Lynch, who was to have ruled with him, knew the trunks contained only rocks. The real treasure was elsewhere, entrusted to people who promised to protect her interests. She had used all her seductive powers to arrange it. Now she could only hope her plans would turn out. But recent life had taught her the limits of what even her iron will could achieve.

"Mark the spot," he said, again in French.

"I have," she answered.

He wheeled his stallion around. "Bring up the wagon," he barked, this time in Guarani, to the two men who were their only companions that day.

The driver beat a rawhide whip on the backs of the poor bullocks that had dragged their heavy load to this desolate spot. The creaking of huge wheels on wooden axles sounded like a wounded cat. López ordered the two men to unload the four heavy trunks. They sweated and grunted with each one but did with dispatch as they were bid.

"Cast them over the side," López ordered. He watched as they toppled the trunks, one by one, over the edge and out of sight, down the cliff, those precious possessions they had carried with them in their desperate retreat through the rough cordillera. Over they went, still nailed shut and bound with heavy leather straps, into the gully below where only jaguars walked.

As the last trunk fell, López drew his pistol and pointed it at the men who stood at the edge, their shirts soaked with sweat. "Now jump."

Uncharacteristically, they did not obey at once. The taller one looked inquiringly at his commander.

The mariscal, who held the power of life and death over everyone in Paraguay, aimed his pistol. A shot cracked over their heads. "Now! Jump!"

Without a word, the two men embraced and, still clinging to each other, went headfirst off the precipice.

PARAGUAY 1868

From his pulpit, Padre Gregorio looked out over a sea of lovely spider lace mantillas. His congregation was almost entirely women. Only seven males of this village still lived: three old and bent rogues, who were here in the church, snoozing in the back row; a wounded and spent shell of a former boy who would never function as a real man; Salvador, the midwife's husband, who had lost a foot at the Battle of Curupaity; Ricardo Yotté, the scion of a noble family who had become a close companion of Eliza Lynch, the consort of the dictator, Francisco Solano López, making him one of the most powerful men in Paraguay. Last in the priest's heart, Comandante Luis Menenez—the local governor—tall, proud, and petty, who inhabited a place safer than that of almost anyone in the country, so sure of his convictions, so secure in his unstinting support of López. The comandante looked up expectantly from the front row. His usual benign expression, the padre knew, masked a wrath that might descend on a priest just for saying what this priest intended to say today. The government dragged men of the cloth to prison as fast as it did rebels and slackers.

"My children," the priest, barely thirty-two years old, said forcefully into the thick humid air above the heads of the congregation, "today we must speak of a grave matter. An infinite and rending sorrow weighs on all our hearts. The violence that has so long plagued other parts of our continent has now devastated our once-tranquil Paraguay. You have all felt great pain and great loss. Paraguay is like a tree struck by lightning, burnt and withered. Night seems to have fallen.

"But we must look forward to the sunrise. Though the embers of enmity and conflict burn on, the war's great battles seem to be over. It is time to put aside weariness and sorrow and begin to rebuild our country. To do so, we must overcome one great obstacle. Here in Santa Caterina only one of ten men remains. It must be the same all over our beloved Paraguay. You can see what this means. If we go on following the church's laws of only one wife for each husband, our numbers will die out entirely. I and the good Padre Juan Bautista before me have taught you the marriage laws, the sanctity of your bodies, the commandment against adultery. We have enjoined you that you risk eternal damnation if you do not live chastely.

"I have prayed and fasted, struggled to find a way for you to cling to these laws, but I can see no other way, my children. We must, for now, give up these holy precepts." He raised his voice and let it ring out over their heads with a conviction he prayed would convince them. "To repopulate our nation, you must accept the necessity to conceive—outside of marriage— the children who will be our future. Unions I cannot bless before this altar, I am sure God will bless in private. Pray to our Holy Mother. She will know you are not committing foul acts of the flesh, but making sacrifices to save your race. She will intercede for you at the throne of heaven. She will understand that these beautiful flowers of womanhood must find a way to bring new souls to Paraguay, so the tree of its life will grow up again from its roots. *Paraguay para siempre!* Paraguay forever!"

The faithful in the church, silent as they ordinarily were, buzzed with surprise, puzzlement, shock. They sang the responses for the rest of the mass in a state of distraction, until Padre Gregorio placed the chalice in the tabernacle, closed its black wood and silver door, genuflected, and turned to his congregation. He held out his thin, elegant hands. *"Pax vobiscum."* He raised his right hand to bless his flock, but they did not go in peace. As he left the altar for the vestry, they filed down the main aisle, singing the recessional with unusual energy, and were hardly out the tall front doors of the church before they began exclaiming.

A knot of three or four women, straight-backed and barefoot, their traditional white homespun clothing hanging from their thin bodies, whispered together excitedly. The name they spoke most frequently was "Ricardo Yotté." Yotté—young, elegant, securely connected to the most powerful people in the country—was the first choice of several of them to father their future children. Energized by their prospects, they quickly retreated to Alberta Gamara's café at the north end of the plaza.

Cross-eyed, leather-faced Gaspár Otazú separated himself from his elderly male companions and dusted off his quasimilitary shirt, complete with epaulettes askew and one brass button. He sidled up to the lithe and winsome Xandra León, doffed his military cap, and leered at her. Within seconds, her parents—Salvador, the wounded war veteran, and Alivia, the village midwife and healer—ushered her off toward their family's estancia just outside the village. Gaspár then approached Manuela, the lady blacksmith, who also politely rejected the old man.

Comandante Menenez, after eyeing Xandra León as if she were a pastry in a shop window in Buenos Aires, took his small, smartly dressed wife Gilda by the arm. They spoke to no one. The señora comandante opened her frilly white parasol and marched with her tall, stern husband directly to their stately Spanish-style house, which faced the church across the square, the most prestigious location in the town.

"That priest is taking his life in his hands," the comandante said into Gilda's delicate little ear.

❦

Ordinarily, Padre Gregorio quickly changed out of his vestments and hurried to chat with his parishioners at the front door of the church. Today he shied away, slowly removed the chasuble and alb, hanging and folding the sacred clothing—green for the Sundays after Pentecost. Pentecost, when the Holy Ghost infused the spirits of the apostles. Had the Holy Ghost inspired him? Or had the counsel he had just given his flock come from some base and willful place within his own soul? He could not at this moment deal with their astonishment, their need for guidance through the waters he had roiled. He would exit through the back, would wait to see the villagers in the coming days, a few at a time, and deal with them quietly. Cowardly as it was, he left the vestry through the dim belfry. The only light in the tower slanted down from the unglazed windows high above his head. His foot hit something on the floor. He tripped and nearly fell. A sack had been left there. He opened the back door.

Bright, early September sunlight streamed on to a scene that tore his breath from him. The sack was a man's body, lying on its side. He turned it. Good God! How could this be? The young, handsome Ricardo Yotté's dark eyes stared blankly. Impossible that this man could be dead. But there was a terrible gash in his head, the white of his skull showing under pink flesh.

The padre's breath came back in gasps. Yotté's pomaded black hair was crusted with blood around the horrifying wound. The skin of his face was ashen. His lips slack. None of the man's considerable power remained.

The priest looked up into the tower. Had Yotté fallen? But what could he have been doing up in the belfry? The priest put his fingers to Yotté's neck, feeling for a pulse, though the man was cold, surely dead. Then he remembered himself and ran back into the church for the oils of extreme unction. Yotté's soul—such as it was—must be a priest's first priority.

He returned to the body, uncorked the vial, and took a drop of the holy oil on his right forefinger. If Yotté's soul lingered, the sacrament might help him into the next world. The padre closed Ricardo's dead eyes and with the oil made the sign of the cross on the lids. The body still carried the slight lemony scent of Yotté's cologne. "Through this holy unction," the priest said aloud, "may the Lord pardon thee whatever sins or faults thou hast committed by sight." He repeated the words, anointing Yotté's ears—"sins or faults thou has committed by hearing"—then nostrils and lips. Fervent as he wanted his prayers to be, Padre Gregorio knew full well that Yotté's eyes and ears and lips had sinned, if not against God, then against many others. He had aided the dictator and his concubine in looting the citizenry of every last trinket of any value. He had reported anyone who lacked enthusiasm for the carnage López had perpetrated. He had embraced any scheme that furthered his own fortunes, regardless of the suffering caused to others. The padre bit his lip and forced his mind away from judgment. That was God's province. "Whatever sins thou hast committed through taste," the priest continued. Before he died, Yotté might have repented the evil he had done. His soul could still go to God. At least that was what a priest was supposed to think.

The padre took the dead man's limp fingers, intoning, "Whatever sins thou hast committed by touch." The priest's hands continued their motion, but his mind stopped. Beneath Yotté's usually carefully manicured nails, there was grass and mud, as if he had been clawing the ground. Then as he moved toward the dead man's expensive patent leather boots, intending to anoint his feet, he saw something that redoubled the chill in his heart: cuts in Yotté's elegant European shirt, with a small bloodstain near each slit. He raised the shirt. Under the fabric were wounds, as if from a knife. He counted six of them in the chest.

The padre sat back, stunned. Murder. It could only be. And in a country where in the past few years, tens if not hundreds of thousands had died in battle and of disease, this death seemed somehow personal. Mano a mano. That it was this man made it at once understandable and incomprehensible. Yotté was not only a henchman, but also a close friend of the dictator, Francisco Solano López, and a kind of courtier to López's consort—the beautiful foreigner, Eliza Lynch. Yet someone had murdered him. The comandante would have to be told. The priest now had another piece of dangerous news to deliver.

2

Still kneeling before the tabernacle after everyone had left the church, Maria Claudia Benítez listened to the congregation making a great noise at the front door, waiting for the padre to appear. But his voice never joined theirs, and they must have given up and drifted out into the tree-shaded plaza. She rose from her aching knees to go find and confront him.

She did not blame him for not showing his face after what he had said. How could he make such a terrible error? Telling the women from the pulpit that they should fornicate? If the bishop got wind of this, the padre would be—she did not know what the bishop would do. Rumor had it that López had imprisoned the bishop.

She had to save Padre Gregorio from himself. He was flirting with heresy. This could end his priesthood, which he always called his most precious possession, as if it were a jewel from the Indies or a treasure guarded by a cyclops in a cave. There was no sacristan left in the town, who in the old days might have befriended the priest. He had no one but her to talk sense into him. He was far above her, and not entirely of this world. He loved Paraguay as if it were his own country, but he was born in Buenos Aires, had studied in Rome. She was of this world, and because she knew it, saw things he did not, and she burned to help him do God's work. Too much familiarity would cause him to withdraw, and she would lose him. She must cloak her worry, act cheerful and respectful, as he would expect of her.

She dipped her fingers in the holy water, blessed herself, and walked out into the beautiful sunlit spring morning. The coldest months were over and though the nights still chilled, the warmth of the sun, so welcome in the morning, grew uncomfortable by noon. Today a hot wind blew from the north.

Several people lingered in the square under the shade of the violet-blooming jacaranda trees, speaking with animated expressions.

All skin and bones, old Hector Mompó came running toward her. Or at least as close to running as a man of his age and frailty could manage. Like many poor peasants had always been, he was practically naked, sporting only a double apron of dressed leather, an old straw hat brim, and heavy silver spurs bound to his horny bare feet with rawhide thongs. Nearly eighty, he would have been a young man when the first dictator Francia required all the males in Paraguay to wear hats so they could doff them when they passed militiamen or government functionaries on the roads. Hector—like many of the peasant class—wore a brim without a hat. He caught up with Maria Claudia at the church steps and swept the brim off his bald head with a cavalier's gesture, bowing low. "At your service to do Pai Gregori's bidding," he said with a twinkle in his eye.

Maria Claudia, suppressing a guffaw, managed to blurt out, "You will be in my prayers," and hurried on.

Across the grassy square, Alberta Gamara chatted with a group of women near her tiny café. An ugly cucuru toad hopped into the shade of a tree. The toads and Alberta were the only creatures in the village that had not grown thin during the war. Everyone knew the toads stayed fat eating the myriad insects, but no one knew how Alberta did it.

Near the flagpole, white-haired and mustachioed Saturnino Fermín, wearing his habitual, ancient three-cornered hat, and the cadaverous, wrinkled, and cross-eyed Gaspár Otazú, in his mock military shirt, spoke intently together. They paused to greet small, wiry Josefina Quesada as she passed, towing her maimed and broken grandson, Pablo. The old lady stopped under an orange tree to light a cigar. Three of the many villagers who revered her for her gift of prophecy approached.

Maria Claudia turned away. Their old Indian practice of believing in dreams and visions bordered on heresy. But then, curious about what Josefina would say, she stopped to listen. Padre Gregorio would need to know how people reacted to his announcement, and this oracle would greatly influence their response.

"Before the Jesuits came," Josefina said, her voice, like that of many of her countrywomen, low and gruff from many years of constant cigar smoking, "our people had no marriage laws. The Spanish had taught the Guarani the rule of one woman for one man. Before they came, people lay with whomever they wanted. Sex was no different from eating or sleeping. Girls gave their love freely and were admired all the more. But we cannot easily return to the old practice. Our blood may see the good, but our hearts have been taught to leap to jealousy. People will be born because of what the padre said, but people may also die because of it." She pushed her unruly gray hair back from her handsome, weathered face, and with her bony old hand took the empty sleeve of her uncomprehending grandson and pulled him slowly toward the Yotté family's luxurious house at the edge of the village.

Maria Claudia removed her mantilla and folded it. Josefina was probably right. People could not easily return to those old ways. The Spanish conquerors had found the local people humble and amiable, easily converted. Today's Paraguayans, although they still spoke their old language, worshiped the Spaniards' God with great fervor. Go back to the old beliefs, birth bastards without shame? She certainly could not.

She forewent her usual Sunday morning visit to the graves of her mother and father and prayers for Fidel Robles, who had no grave. He had been her husband for eight days before he went away to die. She tried to remember him for something other than fumbling lovemaking and boyish dreams of military glory that marked the whole of their time as man and wife. She crossed the cobblestone patio to find the padre.

As soon as she opened the small, arched sacristy door, a strange acrid scent and the sound of the priest praying in a low voice slowed her steps. An apprehension she could not name chilled her blood. Without thinking, she covered her head with her mantilla and moved toward the light inside the belfry and the sound of the praying.

Padre Gregorio, kneeling next to a man lying on the floor, implored with his eyes without unclasping his hands.

"Who is that?" she heard herself ask.

The padre blessed himself and stood. His face was pale as paper. "Ricardo Yotté. He is dead." He bent and picked up the vial of holy oil that lay next to the body.

Her shoulders stiffened with fear. One glance took in

Ricardo's face, arrogant even in death, hair and clothing disheveled as it never had been in life. She wanted to move closer, but could not. She had known him as a child, when she went to his house to play with his sisters. "What happened to him?"

The padre shook his head. "At first I thought he had fallen from up there." He glanced up at the bell tower. It held no bell. Theirs, like all the others in the country, had long ago been taken away by the dictator's English engineers, to be melted down for cannons. "But there are stab wounds in his chest. He was murdered."

"Oh, Lord!" She saw immediately how dangerous this was. "We will have to tell the comandante." She did not have to look into the padre's eyes to know the alarm in them. Luis Menenez, the commander of this village and the territory around it, had been second only to Ricardo Yotté in his power and devotion to the dictator. With Yotté gone, he would ascend to become the most feared person in the area. Incurring his wrath could mean torture, death, even for a priest. "I will say I found him," she said.

"Do not be absurd. I must tell Menenez the truth. But first, I want Alivia León to look at the body. There are strange things about this. She is more than a midwife. With all she knows about the human body's sicknesses and cures, she is the only one left in the village who might explain what happened here."

"Someone will have to tell his sisters," Maria Claudia said. The Yotté girls had been her closest friends. She hated the thought of delivering the dreadful news, but she should be the one to do it.

The priest's face, already grave, twisted with grief. "Those poor women. First their father, then their mother. Now this. How will they bear it?"

※

Alivia took a slow pace along the calle León to her family's estancia just across a stream from the edge of town. Her daughter Xandra had gone off to care for César, the horse she suddenly seemed so obsessed with feeding. Alivia's husband Salvador—where had he gone, hobbling away despite the pain of his lost foot? Of late, he mumbled excuses and disappeared. Perhaps he had started taking Padre Gregorio's advice before it was given. She twisted her gold wedding ring. Salvador had never been that kind of man, but war had changed him. Along with his foot and far worse, their sons, he had lost his capacity for joy.

Alivia was tired. "Souls for Paraguay," the priest had said. She had brought Paraguay four souls, if she did not count the two infant boys who lay in the cemetery. She had given her country her three sons that had lived past infancy. Juan, tall and studious and so thin. His hands so like her father's. He had reached a man's height but never had a chance to fill out. When the tocsin sounded, he was among the first to march off, saying he would defend her and his country from the invaders. Salvador followed soon afterwards because he could not allow his son to fight if he himself stayed at home, as if staying home were an option for any man.

Then went handsome Aleixo, the strongest of her boys, so robust in his enthusiasm, so graceful and quick. He was the one she was sure would survive. But he had not.

In the end, they took even poor little Mariano who was only twelve. His voice had not even changed. She had hidden him on the roof. Ricardo Yotté had come with soldiers and demanded the boy he knew must be on the property. He had known all the village boys from birth. He laughed when Alivia pled with him and laughed even harder when the boy peed himself and water dripping from the eaves on a clear day gave him away.

She stopped a tear with the back of her hand. She had lived after they died, though she did not think she could. Paraguay had taken their souls and their dear bodies. Not even their bones came back. She had nothing left of the sons of her heart.

The padre wanted the women to bring more souls to Paraguay. She was past her time for bearing children, but even if she could have more sons, she would not. Why have them? So that some insane despot could lead them off to horrible deaths from wounds or disease?

But in her heart she knew if she could, she would gladly bear another son. Not for Paraguay. For herself and for Salvador, who had not one son left to carry his name. He never spoke of his loss. Nor did she, not only because the dictator forbade mourning as unpatriotic, but because she could not bring her pain to Salvador and add it to his, which was already too great. His amputated foot tortured him. Still, every morning he strapped on the wooden foot he had made for himself and walked out to work in the fields.

Her body was useless to give him another son. She longed to be again that young woman Salvador had fallen in love with. After their first child, Juan, was born, she had wondered if he would still want her. The first time they made love after the birth, she had felt timid, somehow shyer than their first night. For some weeks after the baby came, they had abstained. Salvador's joy in the birth of his son had transformed him for a while from a quiet man into one who talked and talked— about the boy's future, about his love for her. It seemed during those first weeks that because he could not express himself with his body, he was forced to use words: joy and plans flowed from him. Then came a night when the period of abstinence was over. She felt the hardness of him, and it frightened her a little. It could hurt more than on their first night. But he was gentle and slow and caressed her until the pain of not having him inside her was greater than the pain she feared, and she grasped him to her. They made love again and again by candlelight, looking often right into each other's eyes.

"A traveler told me once," he said as dawn was breaking, "that up in the Amazon there is a tribe of people who believe that the seed of the father not only starts the baby, but builds it up throughout the pregnancy of the mother."

"What a silly idea," she said. She was about to remind him that she was a midwife like her mother and would never believe such a tale.

He put his finger to her lips. "No," he said, "this is going to be my way with you. To make you pregnant, and then to make love to you over and over, as many times as I can. So that the babies will come out healthy and beautiful."

And happy, she thought, if the mother's happiness has anything to do with the baby's. Joy had flowed in her that morning, even to the tips of her toes.

The last one living of their beautiful, healthy babies was the second to live beyond infancy, Xandra, that young woman running across the campo to the horse hidden in the forest. Healthy and strong, she ran like a colt—her arms round and graceful, her thick, black hair loose and trailing behind her like the mane of a Thoroughbred.

Perhaps Salvador's love while she was pregnant with Xandra had made the girl strong. But happy? Xandra was easily agitated, especially during the past few days. She pretended gaiety, but she was troubled. How could she be truly happy? At nineteen, she must long to have a husband, a lover, children of her own. But there were no men. Should she have a baby with whatever man was available? She deserved the love of a real husband. Someone to thrill her in her bed, to support her in her weakness; someone who needed her strength.

If Xandra followed the priest's dictum, who would she choose? Old Josefina's grandson, poor Pablo, had gone to war like her little Mariano when he was only twelve. At fourteen, he was alive, but he would never be well again. He might survive for years, but father children?

Would one of the old ones have her tender, young daughter? Practically naked, lecherous Hector Mompó? The timid Saturnino Fermín with his silly three-cornered hat? Gaspár Otazú in his homemade military garb? They were too old even for the war. Babies they might be able to make, but husbands, never. No bony wrinkled old man could make her fiery daughter's bed happy.

There were only two other men in the village besides Salvador, but the thought of either of them with her daughter made her stomach burn. Ricardo Yotté—

A shouting behind her spun her around. Maria Claudia, ordinarily so decorous, was running and waving. Alivia hurried toward her and in breathless gasps, Maria Claudia said the very name Alivia had been thinking: "Ricardo Yotté!"

"What?"

"He is dead. Murdered. You have to come. The padre needs you."

Well, that bastard Yotté was dead. It seemed something to celebrate, except that someone would have to pay dearly for his death.

3

 Salvador León left the church straight after mass, embraced his thin, careworn wife, mumbled a vague "something to take care of," and left her with the others waiting to greet the padre. He put on his straw hat and rolled his blue poncho under his right arm, leaving his left hand free for the cane that bore the weight he could not relinquish to his false foot. He had a long walk to the hiding place.

The sun, high now, had burned off the morning chill. His good white shirt of heavy cotton that Alivia had so handsomely embroidered for him was already soaking up sweat brought on by the heat and the anguish of his leg and of his mind. A spicy scent in the air told him the wind came from the Mato Grosso up across the Brazilian border. No rain today. The heat meant a long siesta, which he would welcome. But even though it was Sunday, after the midday rest, he would work in the fields. No visiting with friends, sipping yerba maté, and gossiping about their aches and pains, their crops, their neighbors' business. No time and no friends left to gossip with.

His way veered left. As he walked, Alivia, moving much faster than he, followed the road to the right, along the calle León, to home. Their paths diverged, and the metaphor in that growing separation hurt as much as the pain of his missing foot. She carried herself with such dignity, erect as always, as if there were a bundle on her head, resolute even in her crushing sadness, though exhausted to the bone from the years of toil keeping herself and Xandra alive. Unlike his own, her thick hair was still mostly black, but the haunted look in her great, dark eyes showed the ravages of the past three years.

It always seemed as if Alivia were the aristocrat and he the peasant, instead of the other way around. His father had objected to her, but nothing could have kept Salvador from her once he had fallen in love with her beautiful face and warm smile. Eventually, because he could not help himself, he became Alivia's lover, and far from getting her out of his system, making love to her bound him to her. Her sweet body, her strength, her warmth. The taste and the smell of her. He wanted to drink her in, to consume her. He defied his father. "I will stay with her and only her, with or without marriage." It was a challenge. He was an only son. They were the most prominent family in the area. The old man would have no legitimate grandsons to carry the family's position forward. But his proud father did not give in, expected Salvador would eventually relent and marry a girl of his own kind. "Fuck her, support her brats if you must, but I insist you marry a woman of substance," his father had said. By "substance" he meant of pure Spanish blood.

The old dictator Francia—El Supremo—rescued them. Help from the most unlikely place. The decree said that within Paraguay, no penninsulare, or member of the white elite, would be allowed to contract marriage with another member of that same class. They could marry only mestizos or mulattoes or

Indians. They called the decree the *bando* because it was announced to the sound of fife and drum. Salvador's father and those like him were indignant, saying Francia was out to break the power of any family that might challenge his absolute rule. But Salvador and Alivia danced and sang, drank aguardiente, and made love for two days to celebrate. Then they were married in the church, under the eyes of his bitter father.

Salvador continued along, walking on a carpet of fallen petals until he came to the cross that marked the spot where his father had fallen from his horse. No one knew whether the old man's heart had given out or if the horse was perhaps attacked by a snake or a jaguar. The horse had come home riderless, and they had found his father here. Salvador had followed the old custom of marking, with a rough wooden cross, the spot where a person had died of an accident or violence. On the cross were carved the words, *"León cué,"* Guarani for "León was here."

Salvador knelt down to whisper a prayer. "I am sorry, but you were wrong," he said aloud to the cross before him and to the memory of that proud, intransigent old man. "She has more real substance than any woman I have ever known." He took a knife from the waist of his baggy pants, cut some flowering oleander, and draped the pink blossoms over the arms of the cross. If they erected a cross in every place where a Paraguayan had died in the past three years, there would be vast tracts of the country where no one would be able to walk for all the crosses.

He wished he could tell Alivia about the pain in his heart, but his thoughts clung to the war whose horrors he tried in vain to forget and could not reveal to her, of boy soldiers crawling away from battle dragging their shattered limbs, or their half-naked little bodies lying dead in the mud. He must not put into her mind pictures that would torment her, with visions of their sons suffering so. And never, never could he confess to her the dark secret he kept, of the depths to which he had sunk to survive the war.

Why, when so many had died, had he come through? Why had he not perished in place of one of his sons? Why . . . when he deserved to die.

He leaned heavily on his cane to rise and brushed the red dust from his knees. He passed along the red clay road that soon entered a deliciously cool wood where the branches of the towering old trees met overhead. From them hung lianas and bougainvillea, covering the limbs with pink and purple flowers.

His path followed a stream where hundreds of butterflies fluttered over ferns along the bank, each species clustered together—black ones that wore emerald and ruby eyes on their wings, great red ones the size of his hand, small green ones with nearly transparent wings. They flew about and drank from the stream but never crossed into one another's territory, each group content to stay within its own borders. There were no wars among the butterflies.

He went to a nearby, hollow tree where the woods broke out into a grassy plain. He reached in and took out a canvas-wrapped pot of honey. He picked a few wild oranges and with them and the honey and some chipa, the dry cornbread he had hidden deep in his pocket, went to feed the mad boy he had tied up inside a jungle-smothered cabin hidden among the thick trees and vines.

⚘

Padre Gregorio fetched candles from the church, lit them, and placed them on either side of the corpse of Ricardo Yotté. He knelt near the dead man's head and tried to pray for the repose of Yotté's soul, but not even a priest could banish the resentful and hateful thoughts that connected themselves to the history of this sinner. So many people in the village had reason to detest Ricardo, who in his quest for power had sacrificed their needs to his own. Some burned with envy because he had gotten for himself that which they desired but could not achieve: wealth in this time of want, power that came from his service to the dictator; or merely because he ate sumptuous meals while ordinary people lived on the brink of starvation. In the confessional, the padre had heard of many sins people had committed because of, or with this man: of betrayal, of adultery, of lies told to avoid Yotté's wrath or curry his favor. And there must have been some who did not confess because they did not see the sin in despising Ricardo Yotté.

"Padre?"

He looked up to see Alivia León standing in the dark doorway to the sacristy. He stood and motioned her to come in. Maria Claudia entered behind her.

Without a word, slight, wiry Alivia looked down at the body, took it under the arms, and dragged it into the shaft of light coming through the doorway that led out to the campo. The corpse's foot disturbed a candlestick, and the priest and Maria Claudia both reached out to catch it from falling. Their hands touched accidentally.

Alivia knelt and examined the wound on Yotté's head. She picked up the dead man's hand and peered at his fingernails.

"See that dirt?" the priest asked.

Alivia nodded.

"Look at his chest."

Silently Alivia unbuttoned Yotté's shirt and looked closely at the wounds and then again at his fingers. She turned and examined the floor of the belfry where a thin layer of dust had been disturbed by her moving the corpse. Alivia picked up some of the dust on her finger and examined it. "No one has cleaned here in several days."

"Domingo Ypoa used to clean it every day," Maria Claudia offered. They all knew Ypoa had long since died of dysentery, along with thousands of others fighting in the swamps around the great fort downriver at Humaitá.

"I swept it myself a few days ago," the priest said.

Maria Claudia's hand went to her mouth. "But I would gladly have—"

He waved off her comment. She clasped her hands together in front of her skirt and stood stiffly, her head bowed: a posture of humility, but somehow she seemed injured.

Alivia went back to Yotté's head and looked again at the deep gash. She touched the dried blood in his hair. She lifted his head, which lolled in her hands like a broken doll's. She peered at the nape of his neck and turned the body and examined the back of his tan velveteen jacket and black cashmere trousers. The priest watched her fingers admire the softness of the fabrics.

Alivia rose to her feet and brushed off her skirt. "How long has it been since anyone came into the church through this belfry?" she asked.

"Since they took away the bell, there are few reasons to come here. The door has no lock, but I am the only one who comes this way. I cannot remember coming through since"—he had to think—"Wednesday, maybe even Tuesday."

"This man has been dead less than a day, probably only a few hours," Alivia said. "It has not been so hot, so it is hard to tell, but I would say five or six hours at the most. And he was not killed here."

"How do you know that?" the priest asked.

She pointed to streaks in the dust between where the body lay and the back door of the belfry. "His body was pulled in that way. Besides, wounds of the head bleed profusely. Even a little cut will let a lot of blood. The head wound killed him. If the blow had been dealt here, there would be a pool of blood, or it would look as if someone had cleaned it up."

"But the wounds to the chest," Padre Gregorio said.

Alivia shook her head. "If he had been alive when those wounds were made, his shirt would be soaked with blood, but there is only a very little bit of blood by those wounds. Some of them have no blood at all. The cuts in the shirt match the cuts in the skin. The only real blood is on the back of the shirt collar."

"He was stabbed after he was dead?" The priest was incredulous. "Why would anyone do that?"

The two women looked at each other. "Hatred," they said in unison.

Across the plaza from the church, Comandante Luis Menenez was sitting down to an early Sunday lunch of chicken *puchero*. With devastation and starvation all over the country, he could still find a tender pullet and plenty of rice for his larder, while the rest of the populace subsisted on boiled manioc, palm nuts, wild oranges, and greens gathered in the campo, or they starved to death. The comandante had his connections and privileges. Even when the war was still raging, as long as López still held power over the country, Menenez could depend on periodic saddlebags of food that arrived with orders from the mariscal's headquarters. All he had to give in return was his obedience, his reports, and occasionally to personally bring a miscreant to the dictator. Sometimes, when he had not seen López face-to-face for a few weeks, he arrested someone just to take a prisoner to headquarters, to remind the mariscal of his loyalty and service.

His food deliveries had become sporadic lately. He had had to confiscate today's chicken from Saturnino Fermín, who wept like a baby when the comandante found it in a box in the crotch of a tree behind the old man's shanty on the outskirts of the town. "For the war effort," Comandante Menenez had said when he took the bird. He did not bother to arrest the old fool. He could always take him later if he needed to.

He smiled down at the tureen. This chicken actually was for the war effort, if one included in the definition having a strong, well-fed leader to control this sector of the country. The entire south had fallen to the invaders. López, his entourage, and what was left of his ragtag army had fled north with the enemy in their wake, bypassing Santa Caterina. But Luis Menenez still controlled this area in the name of López, and he intended to keep it that way.

He took his place opposite his bland wife, Gilda. "What does that do-gooder priest think he is saying?"

"He means well."

A typical remark. She picked at her food as she picked at life, never approaching anything with gusto. Elegant, he had thought her before their marriage, with her tiny frame and graceful movements. He had chosen her because she was a León—half sister to Salvador—head of the most important family in the district. He had thought his brother-in-law would make a powerful ally. But rather than taking advantage of his bloodlines and connections, Salvador had chosen to serve as an ordinary soldier. He had come back missing a foot and now he planted crops with his own hands as if he were a peon like Alivia, his lowly wife.

At least Gilda was still ambitious, even if she lacked fire. Not even the priest's repeal of the marriage laws irked her. The comandante squared his shoulders. "That priest is a fool. Chaos will result from his stupid announcement."

She raised her eyebrow, a characteristic gesture. "We have had chaos for more than three years."

He pointed his fork at her in warning. "Careful what you say. Orderly society requires that people strictly follow rules or be punished if they do not. Obedience to authority must be maintained if Paraguay is to have a glorious future."

She looked at him askance. "Glorious future? Really, Luis. I am very afraid the future you hoped for has escaped our grasp." She placed her snowy white, lace-trimmed napkin next to her still full plate. "Please excuse me. This wind from the north has given me a headache." She got up and left the room.

The comandante wolfed down the rest of his meal, then took her plate and finished what she had left.

As he mopped up the last of the gravy with a crust of bread, a new thought occurred to the señor comandante. The priest's speech could easily be interpreted as critical of the war and therefore treasonous. He could arrest the padre and bring him to López as proof he was in charge of this district.

Paraguay needed strong men more than ever. The first dictator, Francia—called El Supremo—had controlled everything, closed the borders to bar outside influences that might lead Paraguayans to want more freedom. Freedom that would only result in anarchy. Now this silly priest, with his liberal notions, was tearing down one of the most important proscriptions. Think of the number of bastards that would be conceived. The

comandante knew how chaotic a child's life could be when his
father and mother were not married. But he banished this personal thought for the larger, national issue he preferred to pon-
der. Mariscal López disregarded these very same rules. He never
married, but instead fathered bastard children—especially with
his Irish courtesan, that rapacious woman he had brought back
from Paris. Oh, the attraction was obvious. La Lynch was most
elegant. That beautiful figure. She flattered López with parties
lasting a week to honor his birthday. She treated him like an
emperor. Only a strong man could resist such adulation. López,
like many short, homely men, fell victim to an ambitious
woman. Not that any sane man would express such a thought.
López's own brothers had been thrown in prison as suspected
traitors. The comandante knew enough to keep his opinions to
himself.

He went to the mirror over the sideboard. He ran his fingers through his still black and thick hair and smoothed his
luxuriant moustache, the badge of the highborn Spanish blood
coursing through his veins. He may have had some Indian
blood, but it did not dominate. Where it did, men's faces were
practically hairless. His hair showed his worth as a person.

The dictator too sported a full black beard. But he was
flawed, and the war had turned to a shambles. The comandante's complete loyalty to López could no longer secure his
future. Nor could he change sides. He was bound to the dictator so tightly that any hint of disobedience would mean certain
death.

Menenez turned away from his looking glass and from
these threatening thoughts. He had to concentrate on how best
to deal with the things he could control. That meddling priest
was an Argentinean. He could be suspected of spying for the
enemy. Uncovering a ring of Argentine spies might boost the

comandante's reputation. Yes. That priest was opening a possibility. Menenez's mind was just beginning to warm to this idea when a knock at the door brought the object of his ruminations into the room.

The tall, slender priest doffed his broad-brimmed hat and held it over his heart. "Señor Comandante, I must ask you to come with me. Ricardo Yotté has been murdered."

With trepidation, Maria Claudia neared the house where Ricardo Yotté had lived with his younger sisters, Martita and Estella. Their old aristocratic family, like most of their ilk, rejected Eliza Lynch when she first arrived from France. But Yotté eventually became the loyal companion of the dictator's beautiful mistress. No one understood why a young man far more attractive than López had been allowed such access to the lady. He had spent almost all of his time in the capital—Asunción, a hard three hours ride away—to be near La Lynch, seeing her nearly every day, if he were to be believed. One imagined López would have kept a potential rival at a distance. Perhaps the dictator believed no one would ever have the nerve to cross him. But someone had. Not by making love to Señora Lynch, perhaps, but by murdering one of their closest supporters.

Yotté's sister Martita, Maria Claudia's old schoolmate, had confided that Ricardo was never alone with La Lynch. Still, he bragged in Santa Caterina about their friendship. He impressed some with his access to power but scandalized others by boasting about a woman they thought a harlot.

Ordinarily, Maria Claudia might have chatted with Martita and Estella after mass that morning, but she had been too distracted by Padre Gregorio's announcement.

She approached the big, carved wooden door of their villa, near the little river that separated the center from the estancia León. In years past, she had frequented this house but not since the deaths of Martita's parents and her brother's subsequent rise. She had grown to hate Ricardo, who marched into people's houses and confiscated their possessions "for the war effort," he said, but how could her father's carved ivory pipe or her mother's embroidered silk shawl help the war effort? Ricardo just took anything fine or desirable. She despised him so intensely that she could not have hid her feelings from his sisters, so she chose to stay away.

The door was missing its old bronze knocker—sent to the foundry at Ybycuí like all metals that could be cast into cannons. That factory for arms had been built eighteen years ago, when she and Martita were first starting school. This war, the government said, was being fought because the allied enemies had invaded their country, but if this war was unexpected, how could the old dictator—López's father—have known Paraguay would need a factory to make weapons? Despite their protestations of being completely surprised, the Lópezes must have been planning for this war for decades. She shook her head to banish the thought that all those people, including her gentle young husband, had died for a lie.

She pounded on the door and wondered how she would express the awful news. Could she say Ricardo was with the angels, as one did to comfort a person on the loss of a loved one? Would angels welcome a man who rounded up boys of ten and twelve and marched them off to be maimed and killed?

Maria Claudia raised her fist to knock again, but the door swung open and Josefina Quesada, the old servant and clairvoyant, who had been nursemaid to the girls' mother as well as to the Yotté children, bowed and gave Maria Claudia a wary look. In her left hand she carried her perennial lit cigar. Behind her cowered her war-ravaged grandson Pablo who never left her side. *"Buen día,"* she said in a hoarse whisper. She held the door only partway open, asked no questions, nor allowed Maria Claudia to enter.

Maria Claudia swallowed hard. Her throat felt as if it would close up rather than allow her to speak words of shock and injury. She should have kept closer to these bereft girls after their parents died. What would it have mattered if the other villagers thought she was in league with Ricardo because she remained friends with his sisters? It would not have been true. But she had chosen to save her reputation and so kept her distance. "I have urgent news for the señoritas," was all she could get out.

Josefina's watery eyes narrowed, but she let the door swing open. "They are in the garden."

Maria Claudia hurried through the airy hall and the music room to the garden door. Unlike the simple layout of rooms built around a central patio typical of the finer houses in this village, this one was built in the European style. She expected to see the sisters dressed in white, sitting at the round table on the garden terrace, as she had sat with them so often, gossiping and teasing. Instead Martita, wearing a plain homespun skirt and an overblouse, both of dull gray cotton, was turning over the turf near the back wall of the garden. Her forearms and hands and the front of her skirt were stained with the reddish muddy soil. Her sister Estella sat hugging her knees on the ground nearby. Her dress was finer, but also muddy, as if she too had been digging.

Though older, Martita was the smaller, with a homely but pleasantly round face and big almond eyes fringed by thick lashes that had been the envy of the girls at school. She wore her hair as always, parted in the middle with a single braid wound around the top of her head to make a little platform for the things she always carried. All Paraguayan girls, regardless of their class, carried bundles on their heads from time to time, but Martita had hardly ever been without one. At school the girls had teased her, said that was why she was so short: that the heavy bundles she always carried had stunted her growth.

As soon as Martita saw Maria Claudia she dropped the spade she had been wielding. Before this accursed war, no lady of her station would have been caught planting and tending a garden, nor would she ever have worn such common clothing or gotten so dirty. The hurt pride of her class consciousness shone in the flush of shame on Martita's face.

Maria Claudia put her hands together as if in prayer. "Please forgive me for intruding," she said softly. "I must speak with you. It is very important."

Martita rubbed her hands on her already mud-stained skirt and grabbed Estella by the arm and pulled her up. Before the war, Estella had been plump and beautiful. Now she was thin and pale and barely spoke. Martita dragged her sister toward the house saying, "We must change."

Maria Claudia opened her mouth to object, but the two girls ran inside. She heard Martita scolding Josefina for letting a guest in when they were in such disarray. Maria Claudia regretted even more that she and the sisters had drifted apart. I abandoned them, she thought, because I disapproved of Ricardo. But what he did was not their fault.

She sat at the table under the arbor. They had played cards here as children. Her finger traced the open design of grapevines in the ironwork. People's lives were like these shapes, twisting and turning, coming together and moving apart.

"What is it?" Martita spoke from the doorway. She and

Estella had changed into matching, clean but not pressed, white lawn dresses. They took seats at the table.

"I need to tell you—you must prepare yourself—" Maria Claudia twisted her hands in her lap. "It is about Ricardo."

Martita's big dark eyes turned wary; Estella's mouth twisted. "What shameful thing has he done now?" Martita's voice was filled with stony resignation.

Maria Claudia reached for her friends' still dirty hands. "I am so sorry, Martita, Estella. He is dead."

Estella wailed, a sound that seemed to well up from the earth below her feet and grew in pain and volume as it poured out of her anguished mouth. Josefina came running and gathered the girl in her arms. *"Ayee!"* the girl wailed again. "Now we will die."

Josefina rocked her. "No, *querida,* no."

Tears streaked Martita's soiled face. Her fingers gripped Maria Claudia's. "Tell me what you know," she whispered.

Guilt assailed Maria Claudia again. "Oh, my dear friend, the padre found him in the belfry. He was—" she broke off, unable to say "murdered."

"Say it," Estella demanded.

"Alivia León saw the body. He was murdered."

"Eeee!" Estella wailed again, writhing in Josefina's strong grip.

The old duenna rocked the girl. "His soul will linger," she crooned. "The old gods and the new one will protect you."

When they were children, Josefina had taught them the old Guarani religion: that the Indians had already believed many things the Spaniards preached when they arrived—that the soul lived on after the body died and then flew to a land in the sky. The old Guarani, however, believed the soul did not go immediately to the heavens, but hovered nearby, an invisible presence, sometimes for years, before it went to the stars.

"How can his soul protect us?" Martita demanded. "He brought us riches and food when everyone else was starving, but he also brought us shame. We will live with shame till we die."

4

Sweat trickled down Xandra's sides. Without slowing her pace, she undid the red sash from her waist and used it to tie up her heavy hair and keep it from slapping against her back. She had told her parents she was going to take care of the horse, but she ran to Tomás. He had been so gentlemanly with her, so correct, nothing like what was written in *El Seminario*: that the invaders, especially the Brazilians, were devils and rapists. The newspaper said nothing about long, muscular legs, golden brown eyes, of silly teasing jokes or a sweet Portuguese accent that sounded like whistling a song, or a man too polite, maybe just too weak, to try to kiss a girl.

Today, she would kiss him. The padre said it was okay, even though the nuns had taught her, when she was too young to understand what they were talking about, to guard her virginity.

From the moment she saw Tomás, she felt tender feelings for him. The day two weeks ago when she found him, she had been walking this path toward the place in the deep woods where she had hidden her father's favorite stallion from the army. A huge white *rubicha* vulture circled overhead, terrifying her. César! The horse was dying. Oh, *dios mio*. Could a jaguar have gotten him? She ran toward the spot where she had managed to secrete César, along with a rooster and a few laying hens.

As she entered the clearing that day, she saw immediately that the horse was fine. He lifted his great, dark head and trotted toward her. She put her hand on his powerful neck, and he nuzzled her.

She moved toward the chicken coop and saw something that stopped her forward movement and her heart: tall, fine brown cavalry boots, encrusted with mud, lying on the ground next to the lean-to, as if they had been dropped in haste. Her skin moist from the heat of her walk turned suddenly chill. She moved cautiously toward the open part of the shed.

The boots were still on the man, who lay staring at her. His light brown eyes, full of gold flecks and pain, made her heart hold its breath. She hid her fear and confusion with pretended anger. "What are you doing here?" she had demanded. "I will kill you if you try to take the horse or even one chicken."

He smiled wanly, and those golden brown eyes sparkled. "Then it is good that I am too weak to steal anything. Are you the goddess of this forest? Do you have a magic cure for this fever?"

He was a foreigner. He spoke, not in Guarani, but in Spanish, but even his Spanish he spoke with an accent. Portuguese? All these lonely months and years she had longed to meet a beautiful stranger, and here he was, but a Brazilian— the enemy.

"Angry goddess," he had said in his thin, weak voice, "could you not bring me a sip of water? I have been lying here dreaming of the cool mountain stream I knew as a boy. I am so thirsty."

"You are an invader. I should kill you." But for all the fury she put in her voice, she had known immediately that she could never harm him.

"This fever, I think, will do that for you. Please do not think of me as your enemy, but as poor lonely Tomás far away from home."

A lost boy, like her youngest brother, who had marched off when he was still such a baby. She took the bucket for César's water to the spring under the little wild orange trees. She rinsed it and filled it with sweet, cool water. An orange blossom fell into the pail. The perfume of the trees surrounded her. She scooped out the flower and held it in her wet hand. She should report the presence of this enemy so near the village. But to whom? Not that pig of a comandante. There was no militia here. She had not heard of a battle nearby. How had this soldier come to be here?

She walked slowly back to the lean-to, suddenly fearful. What if he was fooling? Not weak? But strong enough to overpower her? He had a pistol in his holster. He might take César, whom she had kept so carefully hidden for more than three years. Surely he would steal the horse if he could. He might be gone already.

She ran back, her bare feet catching in the fallen scarlet liana vines, the water sloshing in the pail, wetting through her skirt and petticoat, but when she came back to the clearing, César stood peacefully, flicking his jet-black tail to shoo the flies from his flanks. She walked round the lean-to to face the stranger again. His eyes, though still open, had not seemed to see her. He moaned and spoke. "Swimming in the sea . . . Guanabara . . . I must go into the water."

Delirious. The fever was taking him just as he had said, and she had been dawdling in the forest with silly thoughts about abduction.

She grabbed a drinking gourd from its peg and filled it. She knelt beside him and felt the heat of his skin burning up. She carefully opened his lips with two of her fingers. They were soft and warm. She poured a little water between them and after he swallowed, a little more and a little more, but still his breath came quick, unsteady. His eyes closed. He babbled. *"Quero isto? Coxim? Faça favor. Coxim. Faça favor."*

She took off her white petticoat, the only one left, which she had mended many times. She said good-bye to it and tore it into rags. Slowly she bathed his face and neck in cool water. A short, narrow golden brown beard framed his jaw. She removed his shirt and bathed his beautiful chest. The water turned the golden hairs dark. Her brothers had the Indian trait—almost no hair on their faces and bodies. Her brothers. All dead. Even skinny baby Mariano. He could have been killed by the likes of this man. Sure as she was that she should kill him now, she continued to bathe him, and the heat of the fever seemed to enter and spread through her own body. The sickness would probably take him anyway. Her hand trembled as she removed his trousers. She rinsed the cloth in the cool water and with it stroked his long, muscular legs. She dried him with the soft cotton of her petticoat. She let her fingertips touch the beautiful, golden brown hair of his calves. His breathing subsided, but hers quickened.

Finally he slept peacefully. With regret, she withdrew her hand. She dressed him again, took the machete into the forest and picked a wild pineapple, which she cut up and left beside him with the water.

She had returned the next day with molle resin mixed

with chicha stolen from her mother's store of medicines. For five days, in constant fear of being discovered, she had gone to nurse him. He had lucid moments when the fever abated, but it always returned and cast him again into a fitful stupor. Finally, a few days ago, in desperation, she took César and risked exposing him, herself, and Tomás by riding six leagues to Valenzuela. She kept off the roads, tied César to a tree in the woods, and got from her mother's sister the powerful healing fruit of the mammon tree. She brought the rare melonlike pear to the clearing and with it saved the life of her enemy. This morning she would make him her lover. Even if she had never been with a man, she knew what desire felt like.

She wanted to run straight to him, but she had gone that way too often. As she had throughout the war, she varied her path through the woods. If she went the same way every day, she would make a trail that would betray César and the chickens. Despite the heat of the sun, she took hard detours through brush and around trees, her bare feet squishing on marshy spots and her skirts tangling in brambles. It was more important than ever that she protect her hidden treasure, now that it included Tomás.

She entered the clearing and began to sing "Las Cosas," a song that would let Tomás know she had come alone and he was still safe. César lifted his great, beautiful head, neighed, snorted, and with ears erect and his mane and tail flowing, trotted over to the fence. She ignored the horse and ran to the lean-to, raising her voice in song, expecting to see smiling eyes.

The lean-to was empty. She was happy Tomás was at last strong enough to walk. She had cured him, and that made her feel like a heroine. He was hiding somewhere to tease her. "Okay," she said in a loud voice, "I'll play your childish game."

Her search began with giggles that soon turned to frantic

shouting and ended with tears. Everything of his was gone. His boots, his red sash, his hat. He had left without a good-bye.

※

In a cabin behind a natural wall—thick trees intertwined with lianas, creepers, and bushes—Salvador retied the ropes around the boy's skinny wrists, careful not to constrict the blood but making them tighter than before. The young body was still bony and gaunt, his thick black hair lank and unwashed, but the boy was filling out a bit, getting stronger. Salvador would have to ask Manuela, the blacksmith, to make something of metal to hold him, if she had any iron. His heart twisted with images of the shackled prisoners the dictator kept in misery up north in Peribebuy. He did not want to be a dictator to this poor wretched soul. "I do not know how you freed yourself, but I will not let you go again."

The boy's eyes blazed with anger, but he said nothing. He had not spoken since a few days after Salvador had brought him here and imprisoned him to protect himself and others from the boy's rage.

The boy had escaped from López's prison for his own men. When he first came home, he had growled like an animal, threatened to kill anyone who came near him. If he had not been starving like most Paraguayan soldiers, Salvador would never have been strong enough to subdue him. Now he was gaining strength. There were calm moments when the only emotion he displayed was greed over bits of food. But then after he had eaten, rage overwhelmed him again. He beat his heels against the floor like a two-year-old having a tantrum.

Salvador put his hand on the boy's head and wished his touch could calm his brain.

He put a bowl of water on the floor, though it shamed him

to force a human being to drink like an animal. "I will come back with more food soon," he said. "Try to say your prayers." He always made the same farewell and for weeks now had prayed for nothing but that the boy might not bring punishment on them all.

Salvador locked the cabin door and bore away in his heart the affliction of this secret, carried it along the banks of the stream back to the road. As always, the beauty of the land offered some comfort: the wild diversity of the forest where orchids bloomed on the tree trunks and bees buzzed among the webs of twisted vines, where the bright green trees of early spring met overhead, as if they wanted to protect and comfort him.

Once the red clay road turned toward home, it left the soothing shade, and he had to content himself with a stately honor guard of acacia trees that led all the way to the entrance of his house.

He had walked down this avenue the day he returned from the war, exhausted, famished, nearly naked. His compatriots in the trenches had often fainted for lack of food, only to be declared traitors by their leaders because in their starvation they were failing to defend their country from the invaders.

They had started out proud in their uniforms—white cotton trousers, scarlet blouses with blue facings, and wide white belts that held their cartridge boxes. They had drilled and marched, and because they were dressed like soldiers, they thought they were an army. Full of faith and fully dressed—except that most of them had no shoes—they marched off to war, as if they were going to a fiesta. They soon discovered that only a few had cartridges in those boxes and almost none had rifles. Through the long years, their trousers had torn to shreds in thorny thickets. They had ripped apart their filthy blouses to staunch the wounds of their comrades. Along with their clothing they had lost their belief in their invincibility. How glad he was that he had been content to be a corporal, rather than taking a commission as one of his education might expect. Officers had to force the men to spy on their brother soldiers. They had all learned to fear one another even more than they feared the enemy.

He was wounded one sunny, cloudless day at Curupaity. At high noon, General Díaz had ordered them through a narrow pass, and like good soldiers, through smoke that stank of hell, they went, screaming, *"Independecia o muerte!"* Independence or death! They ran right into the arms of six thousand of the enemy. Suddenly a howitzer shell exploded overhead. Smoke stung his eyes. Another mortar, and a tree came crashing down. He dove into the underbrush as blue-shirted attackers came hollering toward him. He struggled to reload his rifle, but before he could get off a shot, another mortar exploded, and hot metal seared into his ankle. The shock knocked him to the ground.

He woke up screaming and flailing. A man with a thick foreign accent held him down. At first Salvador thought he had been captured, that the Brazilians were killing him, but this cool and reserved foreigner turned out to be an English doctor the mariscal had brought to Paraguay. Were it not for him, Salvador would have lost his life, or at the very least his whole leg. As it was, he lost his foot and a part of his mind there in that place of darkness, pain, and stench with men shrieking under the knife. "Don't cut," one had screeched in the night. "Please don't cut anymore." Salvador could do nothing but lie there with two other half-dead men, in a bed meant for one, and listen to the moaning of the wounded who lay outside on the wet ground with no bed at all, to the buzzing flies, and to sweat and pray and curse and weep.

He had come home. Without his foot, he had managed to walk the narrow roads through the vast cemetery that was his country. He saw, as if in delirium, his life—like a river. In his youth it had bubbled and grew, sometimes turbulent, full of energy and hope, rushing toward the future, but as soon as it was full and seemed to have settled into its path, it had hurled itself over the precipice of a great salto—the war—and shattered itself on the rocks below.

He had survived. In those early days of combat, when all he wanted was to get through it and go home, he had feared he never would. Then, after he had committed the sin that cost him his soul, when he deserved to die, he could not.

Now, on this bright, hot Sunday morning, when even Padre Gregorio seemed to have taken leave of his senses by redefining sin, Salvador reached the end of the tree-lined road and neared his house, leaning more and more heavily on his cane. If only there were another man in the village who had been to the war, someone he could talk to about it. But there was only his accursed brother-in-law and that spy Yotté. They had not experienced war. They marched in parades wearing silly, over-decorated uniforms as part of López's honor guard and traveled back and forth to the capital, getting rich while others fought and died, doing their duty in terror and remorse.

He crossed the little bridge onto his property and entered his house through the front doorway. The long one-story building was of whitewashed adobe with a thatched roof and a colonnaded portico across the front. The arrangement of rooms was simple. Beyond the front door, a short passageway led to a wide hall running the length of the house. This main room contained a dining table and at the other end four old ox-leather chairs. Here in the days before the war, at siesta time, his children and any guests hung their hammocks from the broad beams of the ceiling. With windows on three sides, it was cool, even on a day like today.

He called out, *"Hola. Hola, Alivia. Hola, Xandra,"* as he walked through to the back of the house where the big hall opened onto the veranda, also covered with a thatched roof and an awning of grapevines. The windows of the house had only shutters; none of the outside doorways had doors. At one end of the veranda was a brick fireplace for cooking. Alivia was not there, which surprised him, even worried him a bit. A creamy aroma drew him to the hearth, where Alivia had left a platter of pastel mandi'o to keep warm. They were made of boiled mandioca and cornmeal, and today in honor of Sunday each one contained a slice of hard-boiled egg from their secret chickens. He took two and wrapped them in the scrap of cloth he kept deep in the pocket of his trousers for taking food to the boy.

"What are you doing?" He jumped at Alivia's voice behind him. She stood in the hall doorway, looking more fatigued than if this had been a workday.

He straightened up and held the packet behind him. "I confess," he said, knowing his guilty look would betray him. "I ate a pastel. The war has made me a sneak thief." He tried to keep his voice light.

She came to him and put her hand on his shoulder. "You are hungry. We are all hungry most of the time. The food in this house is yours. You cannot steal from yourself."

He put his arms around her, moving the packet behind her. "Our food has more to do with you than with me."

Her head reached only to his chin. She kissed his shirt

over his heart and turned to lift a cauldron of vegetables from the table and place it on the fire.

He slipped the pastel into his pocket. "Where were you?" he asked, and immediately saw she might have asked him the same question.

She turned and looked into his eyes for a second, and he saw that she realized it too. "I had to go back to the church."

Something in the timber of her voice chilled his scalp. "What happened?"

She took his hand and drew him to one of the chairs away from the fire. She sat opposite him. "Ricardo Yotté has been murdered."

Instinctively, he jumped up. He could do nothing but stare at her. Suddenly he remembered the boy had been loose. He must not let any of the questions that assaulted his brain issue from his mouth.

"The padre found him in the belfry after mass. His head was bashed and his chest was stabbed six times."

"He was murdered twice?"

Her lips turned up in a wry smile. "The blow to the head killed him. The stab wounds came after his heart had stopped. Whoever killed him was eaten up with anger."

His scalp turned cold. "In church, this happened?" He found himself pacing back and forth between his chair and the fire.

"Not in church. There was no blood. His body was taken there after he died. He was wearing that kind of French-style clothing he liked, made of smooth, elegant cloth that must have come from Argentina, if not from Europe. His collar had blood on the back, and there was mud and grass streaked on the tail of his jacket. I was thinking on the way home that his body was dragged across a damp grassy area. It looked as if it was dragged by the shoulders, the way the mud stains were. But there was no mud on the back of his pants. It is all very strange."

Salvador was afraid to even think about what might have happened. The boy in the cabin had raged against everyone, but against Yotté more than anyone else. Could he ask him if he had done it? Could he expect a boy who never spoke a coherent sentence to answer such a question? "Why do you think the murderer took him to the church?"

She shrugged.

He hid the suspicion trembling in his brain. "This is bad for the whole village," he said. "It will mean retaliation, and the wrong people are likely to be the ones to suffer."

"More sorrow, more death," she said, as if she were predicting another rainy day in a wet week. She got up and went to stir the bubbling pot of wild greens.

"Who could have done this?" he asked, though he feared he already knew. He had to protect the boy, who certainly would have wanted to kill Yotté. War had taught even the gentlest men to kill, and anyone with a Paraguayan sense of justice would want to kill a man who profited when others suffered and died. But if the boy did do it, no one must ever know.

"Who would have had the nerve to kill him?' she said distractedly. "Many people might have wanted to. Yotté betrayed so many to gain his position with President López and Señora Lynch. He reported Saturnino Fermín's daughter as a traitor even though all she did was express her grief when her husband died in the battle of Tuyutí. They arrested her, and Saturnino has never seen her again." She looked around as if there might be someone to hear and lowered her voice. "I could have killed him for taking away my Mariano."

"He took away Pablo too," Salvador said. Ricardo had spotted Josefina's grandson, with his cousin Jorge, sitting on the branches, high up in an acacia tree at the back of the campo behind his grandmother's house. Everyone in the village knew no boy would be safe if Yotté had the nerve to take the grandson of the woman who had wet-nursed his mother and changed his dirty diapers.

Salvador tried to find comfort in the thought that the boy in the cabin was not the only suspect, but fear prickled insistently under the skin of his back. He could not shrug it off. "Hard to believe," he said, "that anyone had the nerve."

"Nevertheless, someone did."

"Remember when he brought Señora Lynch to our church to take the jewels from the Virgin?" The statue of Our Lady in the village church had been revered as miraculous for more than a hundred years. People adorned it with emeralds, diamonds, and rubies set in gold to honor God's mother for the favors she bestowed. Salvador bit his lip. "They replaced the Madonna's precious jewels with dross."

Alivia smiled. "They would say they took them for the war effort."

"They took them long before the war."

"And who would listen to our protests? Where would one go for justice these days? There are no tribunals, no judges to decide what is right and what is wrong. Besides, Our Lady does not need jewels on earth. She reigns with her son in heaven. Why should we care?"

"I care," Salvador said. "Yotté helped La Lynch rob our church."

Alivia put down her big wooden spoon and came close. "You thought her attractive when she first came to this country. We all did—her elegance, her beauty, her sophistication. That golden hair, like that of the Virgin in a holy picture."

"Not that there is anything holy about her."

A smile flickered on Alivia's lips. "Still, in spite of her past, she seemed otherworldly—something between a woman and an angel."

"You traveled four hours to Asunción when she called on you to help her sick child."

Alivia clasped her hands together as if she were praying or confessing. "I would help any woman with a sick child," she said and turned away toward the cooking. "That child of hers died. I could not help her. That baby was their only daughter. Whatever else Eliza Lynch is, she is a mother. I know what it means to lose a child."

He gripped the back of the chair he had been sitting in. His wife, trained by her mother and grandmother in the old medicines of the forest, followed their dictum that a healer must heal without regard to the worthiness of the sufferer who came for help. "La Lynch will want to see the murderer punished, and her word will be law."

"Someone will pay, whether he is guilty or not," Alivia said. She took a few grains of precious salt from the crock on the mantel and dropped them into the stewed vegetables. "I want to talk to you about something else. Padre Gregorio is right. There is not much of an army left to take our food. The few surviving soldiers are way up north. If we get to keep our harvest this year, the village women will want babies."

"So?"

She took some plates and forks from a shelf where they had dried after washing. "What about Xandra?"

"Xandra? What about her?" His mind was still distracted by the suspicion the boy had murdered Yotté.

"I cannot bear to think of her having babies without a father, but look at her choices in this village. Saturnino Fermín is still too shy to talk to a woman even though he must be seventy. Gaspár Otazú is very willing, but he goes around sporting that silly imitation of the comandante's uniform that would endear him to no one, especially not Xandra. Besides, he cannot even look at a woman with both eyes at the same time. Hector Mompó? Do you want that practically naked old reprobate to have your virgin daughter?"

He knew she was serious, that the idea should outrage him, but he could not help but laugh. "I am sorry, but the very thought of it is absurd. Besides, if Hector convinces even two of the many women he was soliciting this morning, he will be dead of exhaustion by sunset."

She did not smile. "Yotté is dead, so she has nothing to fear from him, but there is another man in the village." She looked at Salvador, waiting.

She could not mean poor, injured Pablo. "The padre?" He could not believe she meant the priest.

She blew out a breath of exasperation. "Certainly not." She continued to set the table. "Your sister's husband."

He slumped back in his chair. *Dios!* The comandante, as he insisted on calling himself, would want Xandra, as he wanted to possess everything that was beautiful and precious.

Salvador slapped his hand along the side of his face. He had allowed his sister to bring that man into the family. When his father died, leaving his second wife a widow with the three-year-old Gilda, he had felt responsible for the girl, and even for her mother, though he could not like the woman and never understood how his father had married such a self-indulgent, silly person. Gilda had grown up to be more like her mother than like their father. It seemed, no matter what he advised, she did the opposite, especially after her mother died and Luis Menenez, not yet comandante, came sniffing around. Alivia said Luis was after the land, but that made no sense. The estancia belonged to Salvador, not to Gilda, and he and Alivia had three strong sons to inherit it.

Perhaps if Salvador had liked his skinny, willful sister more, he might have refused her permission to marry the man who, though smart and ambitious, came from an ambiguous background and had a reputation for cruelty. But Gilda was stubborn and insisted she would marry Menenez. Salvador knew what it meant to be denied his heart's desire, though he could not imagine his sister's passion for Luis was anything like his for Alivia. Against his heart, he had said yes.

Alivia wiped her hands on a cloth. "I will not have that bastard near my daughter." She said it like a vow before God Almighty.

"Xandra would not want him," he said. "She has always disliked him. I myself have scolded her for being impolite to him."

"A woman's scorn can fan a man's desire. And men can force women." She held a cloth over her fingers and moved the pan of pastels to the stone-topped table.

Two contending thoughts gripped at Salvador: that not even Luis would do such a thing, and that Xandra was in danger. "We must send her to the convent in Bólen. There, at least, she can live her life in peace." Away from the world, she would be safe from the lust of that grasping bastard. "That is final. We will send her to the convent."

Alivia turned to him with fury in her eyes. "What are you talking about? She is our only child now. How can we send her away?" Her tired, beautiful face was full of disbelief.

"I am only trying to protect her."

"I will not be without her. Do you never want to a have a grandchild?"

"You would rather have her defiled?" he shouted. He had not shouted at his wife since the war began.

"Stop it! Stop it!" Xandra was screaming and sobbing behind him.

He spun around. She was gripping her red sash as if she were going to strangle someone with it. She turned her head from one parent to the other so vehemently that her thick black hair flew out. Alivia reached out her hand to the girl, who looked at it with scorn.

"Why are you fighting about my life? Yes, she should go to the convent. No, she should submit to some stinking old man. Who are you talking about? This is my life. What about me?" Tears welled up in her eyes. Her mother dropped the cloth she was holding and hurried toward her, tried to take her in her arms. Xandra struggled free and ran from the house.

Alivia looked at him, this time with a glance full of blame. He held up his hand and shook his head. "I will go to her," he said.

5

 Maria Claudia finished her Sunday meal: a thin gruel of boiled cornmeal. She sucked on the wooden spoon as if it could nourish her with faint flavors of Sunday dinners of the past: chicken *pucheros* and *sopas* that she had stirred with the only spoon she had left. The metal cutlery had all been taken—to make bullets. Bullets for men who inexplicably wanted to kill other men they did not even know, just because their leaders said they must. She looked up at the crucifix on her wall. "Even you. They killed even you."

She wrapped the last of her palm nuts to take to the padre. He would be seeing to Ricardo's funeral with no time to forage. He could not be allowed to go hungry. They all needed their priest. She pressed aside how much she needed him. He belonged to all the village.

She went to the mirror Fidel Robles had so proudly given her as a gift for their wedding. As always, she did not know what to think of the woman who looked back. She was not plain, nor very pretty. Her hair was not dark, not light. Her gaze was steady, but her heart was as empty as her stomach. She took the packet of palm nuts and walked to the priest's house, using the rosary in her pocket to count Pater Nosters and Ave Marias, trying to cover the loneliness in her chest.

The plaza lay silent at siesta time. She crossed quietly, not wanting to encounter the other women who had leered at her expectantly after the padre's disruptive sermon, as if she would immediately run to lay with any man available. She tried to feel herself invisible and then realized that much of the time that was exactly how she felt. She had read stories about people making themselves invisible in order to spy unseen. The invisible people in stories felt powerful, but she just felt devastated with solitude.

As she passed under the thick orange trees and started across the stone-paved road in front of the church, a rider on a large gray horse sped into her path. The horse reared. The hand she raised to protect herself from its hooves still held her rosary. She heard a scream and jumped aside, her heart pounding, and realized the scream had been her own.

The rider cursed as the horse bucked, but then the man got control of the beast and trotted on. She backed against the trunk of a jacaranda tree and tried to catch her breath. Then, just as suddenly as the horse had appeared, the padre was there, looking into her face and saying her name. "Maria Claudia, are you all right?"

"Yes. Yes."

"I heard you scream."

She clasped her hands over her heart. Invisible. If only she were. "There was a horse. I must have been distracted. I did not hear it. A messenger from the government."

"He must have been going to the comandancia. Come. Let me make you a maté." He gestured toward his house.

She walked in front of him through the archway to his patio.

"Please sit down. You are pale. You have taken a scare." He went inside.

She sat under the vine-covered pergola where she had seen the padre writing his sermons. Here is where he thought up that idea about the babies. The church wall loomed on the other side of the small patio. Its only windows on this side were high and like almost all the windows in the town un-glazed, covered only with beautiful wrought iron to keep out the parrots. In Buenos Aires, where the padre was born, he had once told her, all the windows had glass, even in the houses of ordinary people.

He came back and handed her a maté gourd. "Drink this." It was a command.

She put the bombillia between her lips and pretended to sip, but she knew the tea would be too hot to drink. "The rider was not going toward the comandante's house. He was speed-ing right though the square."

The priest shook his head as if he did not believe her and said nothing. His eyes followed the skim of a hawk flying over the peaked roof of the church.

"I spoke to the Yotté sisters," she said.

He took a chair opposite her. "I have asked Saturnino to dig the grave. Manuela has managed to make enough nails for a coffin. We will bury him on Tuesday to give his sisters time to get used to the idea."

"Where is his body now?"

"Josefina and Saturnino moved it into the vestry. It will stay in the church where it is cool and the ants won't get to it."

"Who do you think killed him?"

"I could not say." His voice was flat, as if he meant that he would not tell her even if he knew.

"Suppose it was the comandante," she asked, not knowing where that idea came from. It just fell into her head, like an orange falling from a tree.

"That is highly unlikely. He and Yotté were allies."

She did not tell him that with the war going so badly, old allies could quarrel. She did not even suggest that the comandante might see Yotté's success befriending Señora Lynch as a threat to his own power. Nor did she press him, since he thought so little of her theory, to offer his own. He usually ignored or rejected her ideas, and she always backed right down. It made her chest feel even emptier. "This is so dangerous," she said. "What did the comandante say when you told him?"

"He went white and then red and said nothing. He did not even come to look at the body. He immediately took his pen and wrote to Señora Lynch. When I tried to discuss what I knew, he waved me off, saying he would make his own investigation."

That sent a chill through her heart. "Then perhaps he did it himself."

"No matter who did it, Menenez will find someone to blame, most likely an innocent person."

"Yes, but who?"

When she got no answer, she told him what else she knew. "Martita and Estella expect to starve. I saw them trying to plant a garden, as if they knew the first thing about growing food. All Josefina does is fill their minds with superstition."

"Alivia will help them," he said, as if Alivia were some kind of food magician.

She could not stop herself. "Alivia cannot feed everyone. She has herself and her family to think of."

He twisted his mouth, as if he thought her impertinent or stupid. He pushed his chair back with a jolt and stood up.

She stood too and put the packet of palm nuts on the table. "I brought these for you."

"I do not want you to give me your food." His voice was harsh.

"I found a big tree full of them deep in the forest," she said. "I had too many. These are extra."

He looked into her eyes. "Are you going to confess that lie next Saturday?"

✿

Xandra ran weeping through the forest. "I hate my parents," she said to a bright toucan that flew up as she approached and the yellow green lizards that scurried out of her path. "They never listen. They always think they know what is best for me." But she was not a helpless baby they could pick up and move at will from mother's shoulder to cradle. Girls were not what they had been before the war—like her father's spoiled sister Gilda, who had been fawned over and overprotected, never allowed to lift a finger. Since the war, Xandra had worked alongside her mother, literally like a mule, pulling the plow. She had figured out how to hide the animals. She had built the corral for César and the coop for the chickens. Hardly any women were old-fashioned ladies anymore. Even her once careful and compliant mother, having taken charge for all the years of the war, now clung to her own opinion and no longer always gave in to her husband, who should have been the head of the family.

When Xandra arrived at the clearing with tears drying on her cheeks, she found it too quiet. Even the little animals were still. Then suddenly, César neighed loudly and raised himself up on his hind legs. The chickens! They started putting up a ruckus: the hens squawking and the rooster screeching.

She ran toward them to see what was happening. Tomás? Could he have returned? Why was the horse suddenly so agitated?

A feeling on her skin stopped her. Then she saw why. A jaguar, his spots nearly invisible in the dappled sunlight, crouched, still as a stone, facing the little fence around the chicken yard. She had forgotten to put the flock inside the coop when she left after finding Tomás gone.

She stood stock-still. "Do not run if you see a *yaguareté*," her father had always told them. At the sight of this one, she froze, not because she was consciously following his advice, but from terror: she could not have moved if she wanted to. A shimmering insect landed on the sleeve of her blouse and bit her right through the cotton, but she did not so much as twitch. Only her heart moved—it thudded against her ribs.

The rooster continued to screech and flapped madly.

"Get away from them!" Xandra shouted.

The cat did not even look at her.

She looked around for a stick, a rock, anything she could throw at the cat. There was nothing.

Inside his enclosure, César neighed and reared again. The cat pounced on the chickens, and though the rooster pecked and scratched, the jaguar killed and tore apart a hen in one swift movement. The flock was in tumult. Now, Xandra thought, I should strike while its mouth is full. She backed slowly, silently, toward the horse's bridle, which hung from the corral fence, her heart pounding out of control. She never took her eyes off the jaguar.

He pounced again. This time the rooster, who fought desperately but lasted only seconds.

She grasped the bridle and wound it around her hand like a whip.

The cat killed another hen and gobbled it up.

Xandra breathed in. She could picture what she should do: run at the cat, slash the air in front of her with the leather bridle, with the metal parts hitting the ground. She should do it, try to save what was left of her precious chickens. If she had a machete, she would kill the cat and take his beautiful skin for the brick floor in front of their hearth. But the machete was in the lean-to where she could not get it and her father's words repeated themselves in her head, "Do not move. Do not move." He had always warned that the most dangerous thing was to get between the beast and its young, or its food. If she went for the cat now, it would think she was trying to steal its lunch. You are taking mine, you bastard, she thought, but she stood like a statue, hardly breathing while the jaguar took two more hens in its mouth and slinked off into the forest.

After a few minutes, she went and mourned over the devastation the cat had left behind. The sight of bones and bloody feathers broke her down. She wept harder than when she had found Tomás gone. Nothing. She was not allowed to have anything. In the months past, she had looked at the chickens over and over again, wanting to eat them, but had left them to lay eggs. Now the cat had eaten the chicken leg she had only dreamed of. It was her own fault. If earlier she had closed them in the coop properly, they would have been safe. She could not stop crying, even as she took the quivering remaining two hens and put them inside. There were a few eggs in the nests.

Over her sobs, she heard someone approaching through the forest, someone creeping up slowly. Someone who would find César and take him away! Fear stopped her tears. Silently she took the saddle off the makeshift fence and strapped it on the horse, put the bridle over his head. She put her foot in the stirrup and stood on one leg, ready to mount and speed him away from whoever would want to take him. But then a happy thought arrested her. Tomás could be retuning. She listened with every pore of her skin, watching the trees at the edge of the clearing. The air was so still the leaves and the red-flowering vines hung limp from the branches.

The noise came closer. It would not be the jaguar. He had gone in the other direction. Besides, they never made a sound, only appeared as if materializing on the spot. Whoever this was made entirely too much noise, almost as if he wanted to be heard. Her heart pounded. Tomás! Anyone else would have been quieter.

Then she heard a familiar, near-perfect imitation of the knocking of a *carpeintero*—a woodpecker! It was her father, making the old signal they had used when he played with her and her brothers in the forest long ago in their old life before the war, that time of hope and plenty, when fear was something one played with and giggled over. Now they had nothing but fear and broken hearts and loss and empty stomachs.

Her beautiful, gentle father, whom she loved with all her heart, whom she had feared would never return from the war, entered the clearing from the west, gaunt with the pain of walking on his missing foot. His kind eyes were full of love for her, and she screamed at him, "Stay away from me! I hate you!" She mounted the horse and made to jump the stockade fence.

Her father whistled and called out, "Halt, César." The horse planted his feet and though she kicked him, he did not move.

She put her head on the beast's warm neck and wept.

"*Querida,* please." Her father came near and crooned to

her, reaching through the fence and putting his hand on her ankle. "Come down. Speak to me." He tugged at her foot.

Guilt and anger warred in her heart. "I will not. Why are you here?"

"I want to hear what you have to say." He held her ankle and waited with that irresistible patience of his. He never had to yell or insist the way her mother did. He never pushed. He just waited. No one—not the most recalcitrant of the villagers, who used to follow him as their leader, not even her stubborn brother Juan, not even her mother who was stronger than anyone—could resist doing the right thing while Salvador León patiently waited.

She slid off the horse into his arms and wept into his shoulder. "A *yaguareté* took almost all the chickens. I left the door of the coop open. I was—I—" She could not tell him why.

He patted her shoulder. "Oh, *mi querida,* are they all gone?"

"Five. Only two hens are left and five eggs."

They went and looked at the remains of the jaguar's lunch.

"He got the rooster, eh?"

She nodded.

"Well. I guess that must have cost the cat a few hairs on his nose, as mean as that old buzzard was."

She could not help but smile. The rooster had pecked her hands and drawn blood so many times when she came to take away the eggs. "He fought valiantly."

Her father looked at her as if he had never seen her before. "You were here when the cat was here?"

"Yes."

"What did you do?"

"As you taught me. I stood still."

He shook his head. "God, you are brave."

Her heart swelled with pride.

He picked up an iridescent brown tail feather from among the rooster's bones. "I just hope the old boy did his job with the eggs we have left. Then at least, we can let them hatch, and maybe we will get another rooster from five chicks. And hopefully he will not take after his father."

It reminded her of having babies. "I will not get pregnant by any man who happens to be around." She pulled away and dried her eyes with the sleeve of her blouse.

"You do not have to."

"Padre Gregorio said—"

Her father made a dismissive gesture. "I am sure the padre did not mean for a young girl like you to do something that disgusts her."

"It would."

"That is because you are such a fine girl."

"I am a woman."

"Yes, I can see that, *querida*. I can see that."

"At the beginning everyone said the war would soon be over. No one says that anymore." A deep sigh shook the last sobs from her chest.

"People are afraid to speak their fears and disappointments. You know the government takes any complaints as treason?"

"That is wrong, Papa. People cannot help how they feel." She rubbed her eyes. The sky above was clear and blue; the air aromatic and heavy. "What is the war really about anyway?"

"It is very hard to understand. I have never talked to anyone who understood it completely. The mariscal said that the Argentineans and the Brazilians and the Uruguayans signed a pact and invaded our country, which is true, but before that ever happened, we struck the first blow, by invading the Mato

Grosso in Brazil. There was a big celebration in Asunción when we won that battle."

"Why did we attack Brazil? I have never really understood"

"I have heard many explanations. They wrote in *El Seminario* that we had to stop the Brazilians from interfering with Uruguay. I guess if they can interfere with Uruguay they might interfere with us. We had to show our strength."

"And this happened all of a sudden?"

He shook his head. "Wars never start all of a sudden. The mariscal must have seen it coming. Otherwise why would he have built that huge fort of Humaitá down south, near where the big rivers come together?"

"Has Brazil always been our enemy?" She tried to sound only curious. Though Tomás was gone, she was desperate that his country and hers not be enemies forever. How was she supposed to feel about him? He went away. Would he ever come back? Her heart did not know where to go.

"Oh, no," her father said, "Brazil was the first country to recognize Paraguay after we declared independence from Spain. In fact, not very long ago, the mariscal offered to marry the infanta, the emperor of Brazil's youngest daughter."

Xandra made a face. "Why would a princess want to marry a fat man with beady little pig eyes?"

Her father put his forefinger to his lips. "Quietly, *querida*." But then he smiled broadly. "As a matter of fact, her father turned him down. I think he was very insulted."

"The mariscal or the emperor?"

"Both, I suspect."

"And now we hate one another."

"Countries are not people," he said. "Their relationships are based on many things. Brazil and Argentina, because of

their great rivalry, need Paraguay and Uruguay as buffers between them."

"But now they are united against us?"

He shook his head. "None of it makes sense by itself. Paraguay had things they did not: the railroad, the telegraph, those
English engineers who spoke bad Spanish but built good forts.
And López"—he looked around again—"he sees himself as a
great general, like Napoleon, which he is not."

"But even Napoleon lost in the end." She hung her head.
She hated this whole story.

Her father lifted her chin. "I am impressed you know that."
He brushed back a lock of hair that had fallen over her eye.

"I have heard that Paraguay invaded Brazil because we
wanted their land, to have a port on the ocean."

His look challenged her. "What kind of an idea is that?"
He sounded shocked.

She needed it to be true. She needed Paraguay to be wrong.
"I also heard that the mariscal was such a bad leader our powerful neighbors had to come in to change the government."

He stiffened. She bit her lip, but too late. It was what Tomás
had told her.

"Where did you hear such a thing?" her father demanded.

She stared into the distance until she could not stand his
silence anymore. She told him the truth. "I talked to a soldier
who was passing through here."

He did not take his suspicious eyes from hers. "Through
the village?"

She hardened her heart. "Is it true then?"

"Tell me about this person who told you all this."

"He is gone," she said, and she wished she could weep
again. "I will not tell you more."

He took her hand with that irresistible patience of his, and waited.

⚘

Late that evening, a rider, having traveled at top speed for nearly three hours, brought an envelope to the white tent in Peribebuy where Mariscal Francisco Solano López had settled his consort, Eliza Lynch, after they abandoned Asunción to the Brazilians. When her maid Carmencita brought the message saying it was from Santa Caterina, the señora snatched it up in her alabaster hands. Her sky blue eyes scanned the few lines scrawled on the paper. "Get von Wisner. Immediately," the Irish courtesan said to Carmencita in perfect Guarani.

Once the maid had gone, La Lynch walked to the ornate mirror that hung from a rope over a French ormolu sideboard. Her darling son Juan Francisco had overseen the moving of her things and made sure her quarters were as elegant as possible, despite the rustic simplicity. Her boys—even little Leopoldo, who was only six—understood how important it was to keep up appearances. She looked carefully at her reflection and tucked a strawberry-blond wisp behind her ear. "More awful news," she said aloud to her own beautiful reflection. Ricardo Yotté was dead.

She went to her escritoire and withdrew the keys to her trunks from the drawer and fingered them. What now of the possessions she had hoped to rescue from this debacle? The treasure of Paraguay was in those trunks. She and López had dragged the wealth of the nation with them from the great fort at Humaitá to Yvaté and back to Asunción. In the rout and rush of abandoning the capital, without López's knowledge, she had entrusted the trunks to Yotté. López's capture or capitulation had seemed imminent. If the dictator perished while in possession of the treasure, the invaders would have taken it. She needed it for herself and her children. If by chance López survived the next month, she would have gotten the treasure back from Ricardo and López would not have been the wiser. Whatever the outcome, she was sure Ricardo Yotté would carry out her wishes because he was sly and brave and she had owned his soul for years now. She had kept him close against the time when it would become unavoidably clear that the war was lost.

Against all reason, López not only survived, but insisted on fighting on. He, who was to have been emperor to her empress, could not tolerate the notion of failure. She was forced to pretend to him that she too saw victory ahead. But as far back as Riachuelo, she had seen triumph as ever more elusive. In that first battle on the Paraná River, far superior Brazilian men of war had gained control of the waters and then poured men and materiel into Paraguay. There was no stopping them. She had clung to hope because they still had Humaitá at a perfect strategic point on a bluff on the east bank, high above a curve in the Paraguay River. Its enormous, heavily fortified walls rose up over ammunition stores, cottages, even a pretty little church. Down in the river, mines and three rows of great chains prevented the passage of enemy ships. The mariscal then had twenty-four thousand men to fight for them.

For a while, life there seemed more like a festival with fireworks than a battle station. She had walked out on the ramparts to watch as the Brazilian fleet tried to bombard the river. López raised the mast from a defeated Brazilian warship in the center of the camp. At her instigation, the troops erected a marquee around it, and they held a dance. How the soldiers applauded when the musicians played "La Palomita," and she danced for them.

But then, the Allies broke through on the river and overwhelmed them. When the shreds of her hope fell with Humaitá, she decided Yotté would be her savior. Now he was dead. If she could not get back her trunks of treasure, she would have to tell López she had entrusted them to Yotté. He might accuse her of the treason he so often saw in others. Losing his trust could lose her her life. Finding her way though this would be like the army fighting its way through the swamps.

"Halloo," François von Wisner called through the flap in the tent.

She dropped the keys back into the drawer and closed it. "Come," she called.

The Hungarian, who was now her only confidante, entered and bowed with perfect grace.

"I need you," she said to this man she knew would never have the balls to do anything really useful.

❦

Two days after the discovery of Ricardo Yotté's body, Comandante Luis Menenez left the graveyard where the dead man's sisters had held each other in an awkward embrace: the taller, younger one weeping copiously into the shoulder of her older, shorter sister, as the white-haired and appropriately somber Saturnino Fermín filled in the grave. Xandra León stood with them, her hand on Estella's shoulder. Those two were the same age, but Estella, who used to look like a juicy young thing, was now wan and pathetic. The comandante's niece by marriage, on the other hand, was spirited and athletic. She could be delicious under the right circumstances. His sex stirred at the thought of subduing that virago. But not now. He had a problem to solve that could not wait. It had been too long since he had done anything to impress López. Yotté had become such a favorite with La Lynch that it had been hard for Menenez to get the dictator's attention. For some time now, on every path the comandante took to gain López's admiration, he found Yotté ahead of him. Well, now Yotté was out of the way. But the next step would be tricky. He intended to look clever, brave, and useful by delivering Yotté's murderer into the mariscal's hands. And the first clever and brave thing he needed to do was to accuse the right person.

Heaven knew how long it would take to receive a reply to his letter reporting the bad news. The mariscal had only recently fallen back to Peribebuy with what remained of his weary and broken army. The comandante lifted his military cap and ran his hand through his hair, damp from the heat. La Lynch would be in a fury over the murder of her puppy boy. To prove himself a faithful ally, Menenez would have to bring forward someone for swift punishment. He would start by interrogating the only man besides himself who had any power over the villagers: the priest.

※

The women of Santa Caterina, looking for seeds for their future children, might or might not have been interested in the two men who descended from a mule-drawn wagon at the door of the Yotté mansion late on the morning of Ricardo's funeral. It would have depended on the sort of man a particular woman found attractive. Both of these were well-fed, strong, energetic specimens. Their scowling faces, though, might have put some women off. The older one barely moved his thin lips when he spoke. The younger had sickly looking pale skin that might have been brightened by his green eyes but for their lack of fire.

As it was, none of the women was about that day to see the two men approach the mansion and be let in by Josefina.

Within, Martita answered their questions politely while Estella remained wide-eyed and silent. After about forty-five minutes, the men left, taking nothing with them.

⚜

The fake, ingratiating smile on Menenez's face put the padre on his guard. The priest had been sitting in the open patio of his small house next to the church. He had dipped the nib of his pen many times into his pot of ink, but had written nothing. Since the war began, paper was impossible to find. He had torn this piece from the flyleaf of an old novel, though it pained him to mutilate any book, even a profane one. By now this tiny scrap should contain the outline for next Sunday's sermon, but instead of concentrating on the counsel he should give his flock, his mind kept going back to the murder of Ricardo Yotté. Clearly, whoever dragged the body into the belfry wanted the padre to find it. Why? Did the killer intend to implicate the priest? He was fingering his pen and trying to think through the fear that pained his brain, when the man he feared the most came smiling through the archway from the plaza with his military cap still on his head.

"Your bold announcement last Sunday is causing chaos," the comandante announced as if he were declaring a new law. "Women are spreading their legs any chance they get. Panchita Robles and Alberta Gamara are talking about posting Saturnino Fermín's daily schedule in the café, as if he were some sort of prize bull. And that heathen Josefina is holding forth about old Guarani sexual practices. Outrageous."

"I am sure they are just joking," the padre replied. The comandante's words evoked sexual images and stirred urges the priest had vowed to eschew.

"Why would you make such an announcement?"

"To assuage their guilt."

"You are supposed to absolve their sins in the confessional. You cannot forgive them before they are committed."

"No God of mine would punish these women for wanting babies now that the war is coming to an end."

"Are you saying that Paraguay has already lost?"

"You yourself told me the Brazilians control the rivers and whoever controls the rivers controls the country. Nothing and no one can come and go from our country but that they allow it. How can we win under these circumstances?" As soon as he spoke, the priest knew he had made a potentially deadly error.

But the comandante did not pounce. Instead he paused, and after a moment said, "Still, you do not decide what is or is not a sin."

"I think I do."

The oily look of condescension on the comandante's eyes finally clouded into threat. "I actually came to talk about the death of Ricardo Yotté."

The priest indicated the chair opposite him. Clearly, the comandante wanted information, and the priest must at least appear to cooperate, though he had learned his only information in the confessional, secrets he would never reveal. Since the days when the old Dictator Francia cut the country off from the outside world, the clergy of Paraguay had been more beholden to their supreme leader than to those in Rome who spoke for the Supreme Being. Priests had been expected to—and regularly had—revealed secrets from the confessional. But he was not that kind of priest. Still, he smiled as if he regretted his inability to help. "I am sorry, Señor Comandante, but I have no information I can give you."

"You will become even sorrier if you do not tell what you know, Padre."

The priest's mouth went dry. "I?"

"You found the body. You were the only one who passed through the belfry on a regular basis."

"Yes, but—"

"You, Padre *Argentino*, know more than anyone except me about what happens in this village. You will have to collaborate."

The dryness in the padre's mouth spread to his throat. Not for years had anyone in the village referred to his Argentinean birth. "I cannot. I am a priest, not a constable."

"I have a strong feeling you know, or think you know, who murdered Yotté. You had better tell me, or the people of this village will be left without a priest."

The padre held his peace to hide his anger. And his fear.

"You are deciding if you should tell me." The comandante took off his hat at last and fingered the patent leather brim. He shot the priest an arch, expectant look.

The padre had to say something. He chose a truth. "The body was dragged into the belfry."

Menenez's dark glance turned even more threatening. "How do you know that?"

"I am sorry you did not look at the body yourself. I could have shown you how the dust on the belfry floor was disturbed with long lines leading from the back door to the spot where the body lay." He did not mention Alivia. He pretended it was he who understood Yotté had not been murdered in the church.

"You did not tell me this on Sunday."

"I saw it after I went back to the church after speaking to you," the priest lied. "When Josefina, Saturnino, and I lifted the body to prepare it for burial, I noticed the dust. I also saw streaks on the back of his jacket, as if he had been dragged across grass and mud." These were all Alivia León's observations.

"Mmm." The comandante scratched his neck. "That would mean whoever brought the body to the church was not strong enough to carry it, but had to pull it. That would eliminate you, Padre. You seem to have remained strong, despite the want in our country."

The priest could not help releasing a barb. "Are you suggesting the war has been a hardship for our people?" When neighbors reported one another for expressing such thoughts, Luis Menenez dragged them off to be tortured.

The comandante pointed a finger as if it were the muzzle of a pistol. "Beware, Priest. I have taken note that you based your misguided sermon on the dangerous notion that Paraguay's cause is hopeless. You have raised that subject to your peril."

A charged silence descended. After a moment, Menenez stood and positioned his hat slowly and exactly, so that the brim obscured his eyes. "Someone will pay for Yotté's death."

"Yes," Padre Gregorio said as evenly as he could. He was reluctant to direct the comandante to the casa Yotté. Those poor girls were still in shock over their brother's murder, and Ricardo was barely cold in his grave. But his sisters were the ones most likely to know something useful.

The priest held his peace, but Menenez read his mind. "I will find out what Ricardo's sisters have to offer." He turned on his heel and marched off.

"*Vaya con Dios,*" the priest called after him, as a prayer for the Yotté sisters, rather than as a blessing for Luis Menenez.

6

That afternoon, the comandante approached the
sunny patio of the casa Yotté and surprised Martita
and Estella by using the warm traditional greeting of Paraguayans nearing the home of friends. Though he and their brother
had ostensibly been allies, it had been a chilly and competitive
association. Yet here he was, warmly calling out, *"Ave Maria,"* to
Yotté's sisters out in the garden beyond the veranda.

"Sin pecado." Martita gave him the required response. The
Virgin was without sin, she thought, but the comandante certainly was not, but neither had her brother been.

"Por siempre," he continued with the formulaic entrance
exchange. He doffed his military hat as Martita took Estella's
hand and led her toward him.

"Adelante, señor." Martita completed the ritual, bidding him
enter, though he was already inside, and there was no way to
keep him out.

Estella curtsied and began to weep. "Go to Josefina," Martita said. "Ask her to bring a maté for our guest." Estella sped

off as if she were running from a fire. Martita indicated a chair at the patio table for the comandante and sat across from him. "My sister has been very distraught since the passing of our brother."

The comandante appraised her as if she were a melon in the market, without even a pretense of sympathy for their loss. "It falls to me the sad duty of finding the person who murdered Ricardo. I am sorry to pain you with questions." His voice made an attempt at sympathy, but his expression remained stern. "Can you tell me why someone committed this atrocity?"

"You should know," Martita offered, "that just a few hours ago two men came looking for something."

"Oh? What men?" The comandante rose and paced the space between the table and the patio's central fountain. He bristled with sudden energy.

Martita stood too. "They did not give their names. Just that they were emissaries of Señora Eliza Lynch. That the se-ñora had entrusted something to Ricardo that she required back."

The comandante's body tensed. "Did you give them what they asked for?"

"No, señor. We knew of no such items. They insisted on looking everywhere. Estella and I had to let them, as they were Señora Lynch's men. I watched them search the house. They were very thorough. They found nothing and then left in the wagon they came in."

The comandante fingered his moustache. "Items, you said. More than one, then. Did they say exactly what they sought?"

"No."

"And do you know what your brother had that belonged to Señora Lynch?"

Martita put her hand over her heart. "Señor Comandante,

my brother had many secrets. He never told them to me and my sister."

In the early morning, two days after Ricardo Yotté's funeral, Salvador slipped out of the bed where he could not make love to his wife and dressed silently, choosing a shirt of homespun without decoration. The woman he intended to seek would have more sympathy for a man in plain clothing. He looked up at the red dawn, wondering how much time he had before the threatened storm turned the roads to mud and made walking more torture than it ordinarily was.

This sky was the same shade of red as the battle flames the morning they invaded the Brazilian camp at Tuyu Cué. Starving as they were, they could not believe the riches they found in the enemy's stores: salt, flour, even brandy and cigars. They went wild, looting anything they could eat. Then came a sound like thunder—the hoofbeats of the Brazilian cavalry counterattacking. His closest friend, José Cépeda, was shot through the heart while his head was inside a burlap bag of sugar. At least poor José had died with sweetness in his mouth. Salvador wondered if every red sky, for the rest of his life, would bring him back to Tuyu Cué.

Hurrying to beat the rain, he made his laborious way to the village, thinking what it would be to ride a horse—to move about as easily as he did in his youth. But he knew he would never feel that young again. At the height of his strength, he had felt as if he could tear his way through stone walls. Now he despised his own weakness: drained as he was of bodily strength, of courage, of the will to go on living. Alivia was his only reason for staying alive. He tried to tell himself he had Xandra too, but the girl's heart was already gone from him. He did not know where she had given it, only that it was not his anymore.

Passing the forge, he tipped his hat to Manuela Aragon, one of about twenty village women who had been drafted into the ranks and sent to San Fernando, where she trained as a lancer and held the rank of sargenta. The women's brigades never fought. Their lot was worse: they dug the trenches, risked their lives to carry the dead and wounded off the battlefields and most of all, died of cholera. Manuela had come back to the forge of her dead father—a lady blacksmith, and a good one. Like Salvador, she had survived. That word "survived" at first had made him feel triumphant, even in the midst of devastation. But guilt soon overwhelmed him for he knew that he least of all deserved to go on living.

When, sweating and sad, he finally came to the open doorway of Josefina's little house just outside the wall of the Yotté garden, he called out, *"Hola, Josefina."*

Young Pablo appeared suddenly out of the shadows, startling the breath out of Salvador. The boy's eyes carried the same blank expression as the mad boy in the cabin. Salvador's chest filled with dread. Alivia had nursed this child with all her skill, tried all her cures. Nothing helped. Pablo had lost one of his arms in a fight with a Brazilian cavalryman. What monster would do such a thing to a skinny, frightened child? Now Pablo's eyes stared blankly from his dark, square face. He never spoke, and grief-stricken Josefina, who had only him left of all her family, had to force him to eat. The wounds on his legs still festered, no matter how much molle balsam Alivia applied to them. A fever in him continued to flare up from time to time. Alivia said the festering wounds would kill him one day. Salvador reached for the boy, embraced him, and kissed his cool smooth cheeks.

The end of Josefina's cigar glowed in the shadows behind her grandson. "May I come in, señora?" Salvador asked with all politeness.

"Come in, please, Don León." She offered a chair with a wordless gesture.

The room was small, with a mud floor, peeling whitewashed walls, and nothing but rafters overhead, up to the roof. Green beetles glinted here and there in the thatch. The house smelled of the sickness of the boy, like the odor of the miserable field hospital where Salvador had lain after he lost his foot—the smell of death and desperation. He forced his mind to the here and now and accepted the gourd of maté Josefina handed him without asking if he wanted it.

"What is it you have come to discuss? Is it which of the village ladies will benefit from your services? If you are going to make babies, you had better begin. Hector Mompó is already hard at work, so to speak." She laughed heartily and made herself cough. "That old goat goes about with his harp, serenading the women, and he says he intends to sleep in a different house every night." This time the coughing came before the laughter, but when she looked him in the eye, her expression turned serious. "You are not here about that, are you? It would not be like you. You want to speak about the murder of Ricardo Yotté; I warn you I cannot tell you who did it. You are not the first to ask."

He was not surprised that she guessed what was on his mind. Others in the village called her a sage or a witch because she frequently saw through people's words to what they were thinking. He believed she observed things others missed and used what she saw to understand people, which made his question all the more dangerous. She was capable of feeling his fear, even if she knew nothing about the hidden boy. Suppose she guessed? Suppose she told others he was hiding something? If anyone decided to observe him closely, his secret would be exposed.

"Has anyone seen a person in the village they did not recognize?" He forced his voice to be offhand, but he did not think it sounded that way to her. This conversation was a mistake, but it was too late to stop now.

"Like the messengers for the comandante?"

He saw her suggestion was disingenuous. "No. Someone who might have been suspicious?"

"Like an enemy soldier? Or a deserter from the army?"

His only defense against her peering eyes and knowing smile was to confess some fear that might explain the apprehension in his voice. He could not specifically ask if, on the day of Ricardo's death, she had seen or heard of a mad boy dressed in rags with murder in his eyes. "I am afraid of who will be accused of Yotté's murder. The comandante will not let it go unpunished. Yotté was too powerful with Asunción." He used the name of the abandoned capital rather than even say the names of the powerful people everyone feared to the marrow of their bones.

"He will choose the wrong person." She said it the way she said all of her pronouncements, as if it were an unassailable truth that came from the gods.

Salvador suppressed a sigh. Though Josefina much enjoyed her role as an oracle, he would never find out what she knew if she chose not to reveal it.

❦

That same morning, Xandra León also slipped silently from her parents' house, hid behind the tall causauria pine outside her bedroom window, and watched her father hobbling along the road into the town. Her father had a secret. He could be making love to the women in the town to produce those babies the padre had called for. The thought disgusted her.

Despite the red glow in the morning sky that carried a threat of lightning, which seemed already to be crackling on her skin, Xandra made her way to César. She had not exercised him in more than a week. They both needed to move. With the threat of a storm, foragers would stay out of the forest, making it safe to take the horse for a ride. She could hide in the lean-to if the storm actually broke.

She took César out of the corral, strapped on his saddle, and mounted him. She leaned forward to pat the white triangle on his forehead. She squeezed her knees against his powerful flanks and hugged his strong neck. "Take me away," she said into his ear, and the great horse bolted forward, picking up speed, lengthening his strides. As they neared a dense clump of cacti blocking their way, she leaned against his neck and whispered, "Go, go," and he leapt over the obstacle, flying like a great black eagle with her between his wings. What she really wanted was to soar over Paraguay and find Tomás. It would not be so difficult. Which way? South. The war had been moving toward them from down there. But lightning was flashing to the south. And she had not prepared for a journey. But that was not it. She was a coward.

The horse sailed like a leaf in the wind before a storm, happy and free, his mane whipping around her. She pulled the band of cloth from her head and tore off the red cords that held her long, thick braids. She loosened her hair and let it fly, black as César's mane, and free.

A rumble of thunder sounded in the distance. She turned César round, back toward his hiding place, so he would be safe before the storm hit.

When they ducked into the *picada*, the long, low green tunnel through the dense trees that lead to the hiding place, the horse slowed to a walk and snorted. She scissored her hands before her face to push away the dangling vines. Every once in a while she caught a glimpse of the darkening sky through the canopy of leaves and blossoms. To her right, among the creepers and thick ferns in the undergrowth, a wild agouti sat in silence until she approached. Then he ran into the path and barked at her like a puppy. A blue partridge startled her by flying up right in front of César, but the horse kept his footing. If she had Tomás's pistol she would shoot it and bring it home and roast it for dinner. She never looked at birds anymore just to enjoy their plumage. They always looked like a meal, even the toucans squawking in the trees overhead. When they fell silent, a woodpecker tapped its plaintive, hollow knock-knock-knock.

César skirted a *bañado*, a low spot where the smooth mud was treacherous. She turned him to the left and down a steep rocky hill, almost like steps. He walked down the incline as sure-footed as a mule, rocking her like a mother rocking a baby. She moved with him, tightening the grip of her thighs. She pushed away a branch wreathed in purple orchids, her mother's favorite flower. Before the war, people used to bring each other flowers. It was what they had most of, but it was what they offered one another, because the flowers were beautiful and gifts were not a contest to impress. Flowers brought a smile and could be kept in the house to remind everyone of the warmth of a visit. There were no visits anymore, not like in the old days of impromptu dances and laughter. None of the old friendliness—only heat too hot to bear and cold fear that froze the brain.

She would pick some orchids for her mother. Little things

to cheer her, she who never lamented, as so many other women did who had suffered less. Sometimes she hated that strength so intensely, yet all she wanted was to have such steel herself.

The conversation she had with her father yesterday about the war was the first since he came home. Xandra had imagined he had drawn away from her because of the loss of her brothers. He was a man, and even though he had never shown it, everyone said fathers prized sons more than daughters. But there was something else, something bothering him that he felt he had to hide. He spoke but seldom, and when he did the look in his eyes hardly ever matched his words. Since Yotté's death, he was more disturbed than ever—as if he were somehow guilty. Unimaginable that her gentle father could have anything to do with murder. But in the war he must have killed enemies. Her heart refused even to imagine it. "I do not believe it," she said to a green and yellow parrot perched on a swaying liana vine.

When César reached the clearing, she dismounted, took off his saddle, and pulled the bridle over his head so he could eat some of the luxuriant grass outside the makeshift corral, for he had long since gobbled up every blade within.

In the dense growth of the forest, a protected clearing like this was rare. Her brothers Juan and Aleixo had found it and called it the secret castle. They played here at being conquistadores who came in their armor looking for silver and gold in 1536. Strong and gentle Aleixo took the part of the Guarani; she and Juan were the Spanish. They pretended to ally themselves to fight against the hostile Agace tribes from across the big river in the Chaco.

Now, because she was too much of a coward to follow Tomás, she came here every chance she could to imagine him still here and speaking soft-accented Spanish. Although, like most Paraguayans, she spoke both Spanish and Guarani, she felt more comfortable in Guarani. But when she came to the clearing, she tried to think only in Spanish, as if Tomás could read her mind and would not understand if she thought in Guarani. She longed for his love, but he had run away. She was stupid.

She put the horse back in the corral and sat in the shade of the lean-to where Tomás had lain the day she found him. She should hate him for fighting with the invaders who had killed her brothers. They were gone forever. And so was Tomás.

What kind of person was she that she did not miss her brothers more than she desired him? She was like a liana vine that grew from tree to tree and did not put down roots. She should renounce Tomás out of loyalty to her family. But instead of thinking of her brothers, she came here and longed for him.

She lay down in the place where he had lain and looked out at the sky, feeling delicious desire, and tried to recall the smoky, musky scent of his hair that first day when she bathed him in cool water to drive away the fever. She felt hungry, hungry to touch him, and hungry for food.

She soon fell so fast asleep she did not hear César's neigh as someone approached.

When the landau arrived in the main square of Santa Caterina late the same morning, the threat of a storm had passed and the sun had come out. Alberta Gamara, leaning against the jamb of the open door of her café, did not notice that the Arms of the Republic emblazoned on the carriage door were faded and scratched, or that the wheels and the undercarriage were splattered with red mud. The faded glory of the vehicle did not diminish the excitement and fear created by the arrival of the personage everyone knew must be inside. Two guards, from the dictator's elite Monkey Tails—so called because tails of howler monkeys hung from their brass helmets—guarded the carriage but spoke to no one.

Only twice before had Señora Eliza Lynch herself traveled the more than three hours from the capital to their village. Once, those many years ago, she had come to Alivia, desperate for help for her dying daughter. The other time she took from their miraculous statue of the Virgin—well, it was best not to think about what she did with the Virgin's jewels.

By the time La Lynch's tall, elegant escort alighted and helped the lady descend, a small group had already gathered under the mottled shade of the blooming jacarandas. That day, all of Eliza Lynch's clothing—her dress, bonnet, gloves, boots, parasol—exactly matched the pale violet shade of the blossoms over their heads. Her hair was the color of setting sunlight and her eyes matched the sky.

At the sight of her, Gaspár Otazú, in the midst of a knot of gaping villagers, grasped the lapels of his quasi-military shirt and shouted out, "Viva Francisco Solano López, great mariscal, hero of the Corrientes! Victory to our leader!" He might have continued, but no one else in the crowd joined in his paean to the dictator.

The smile La Lynch flashed at them was genuine. She enjoyed showing herself to the people, even ones such as these. An old woman at the front of the crowd stared at her over a cigar she held between her teeth. The crone grasped the empty sleeve of a boy of about thirteen—wan and thin, with large, vacant dark eyes and bandaged legs.

Into Eliza's mind flashed the image of her own dear Juan Francisco, about the same age as this shell of a child. Her son, so handsome in his cadet's uniform, insisted on going to the battlefront at his father's side. Would her child end up like this half-dead boy? God forbid! There was no hope for the war. She would never become the empress of South America. But she was determined to find the treasure she came here to retrieve and with it take her sons back to France to live like the princes they were born to be.

She turned to the man at her side: Colonel von Wisner de Morgenstern, a true Hungarian nobleman. He would have made a perfect lord chamberlain for her imperial court, if she had gotten to have one. "Find out where the house is, please, François. Tell them I have come to condole with Ricardo's sisters." While he went to inquire of the fat woman in the doorway of the café, Eliza let the people under the trees bask in her elegance.

Von Wisner gave the directions to the driver and helped her back into the landau. This carriage had come up the river on the *Esmeralda* from Buenos Aires at the beginning of the war, with the last of her muslin and Paraguay's gold, which their agent Ejusquiza had withdrawn from the Argentine bank. Now the Brazilian warships blocked any luxuries from coming in and her from escaping. Knowing that their days were numbered, she had entrusted her only ticket out—that same gold and more—to Ricardo Yotté, because she knew only he had the cunning and courage to help her get out of this backwater.

She had first spotted Ricardo coming along the reception line at the inaugural ball in Asunción, when Francisco Solano López became president. Was that only six years ago? She had looked into Ricardo's intense, dark eyes and knew he was already in love with her and would champion any cause she offered him. She had observed other women assessing a new man—his height, physique, hands, hair, crotch. She cared nothing about such details. She watched men's eyes to see what part of her they feasted their gaze on, assessed how powerful the attraction was and what sparked it—her breasts, her eyes, her ass. For Ricardo, there was no such venal exchange. He drank in everything about her, and she saw hunger, not unlike what she had seen in the mariscal at their first meeting in Paris. Clearly, Ricardo Yotté wanted not just her sex, but her essence: her style, her grace, the Italian fabric and the French cut of her gown. He wanted not only her, but to be like her, to be admired for having the sorts of things she had—her taste, her sophistication. And Yotté would give her everything of himself in return. Now, despite all her careful cultivation of his absolute loyalty, she had been robbed of her champion and perhaps of all she had entrusted to him.

As they drove out of the square toward the casa Yotté, she waved her violet glove out the window at the peasants under the trees.

"Those people love you. You are a goddess to them. I saw it in their eyes," von Wisner said.

"They are savages," she said. "All the Paraguayans are. At the beginning of the war, when we won the battle for the Mato Grosso, they hung a necklace of Brazilian ears around López's neck, actual human ears!"

He took her gloved hand and kissed it. "The mariscal says we still have a chance. The enemy forces are all sick since the great battle at Tuyutí."

She gave von Wisner a doubtful look. "You know better than that. Tuyutí was a bloodbath for us, and just about all of our soldiers are sick or wounded as well. Dr. Stewart says that fifty die of cholera every day, while the Allies keep pouring fresh troops into Paraguay. We have no fresh troops. We have conscripted all the boys and even women, for heaven's sake." He should know by now that she was a realist, even if López was mad enough to fight on.

He squeezed her hand and looked out the window of the coach.

"Perhaps I should have given the treasure to Dr. Stewart, instead of Yotté. He's a Scot, practically a landsman of mine, or at least what passes for one this far from home. And he's clever. But I thought Ricardo was the one who would never, never betray me. I never felt as confident about any of the others."

Von Wisner gave her an arch smile. "Not me?"

"Oh, stop, François. You know that if you left, the mariscal would have immediately gotten suspicious. I intended to tell him Ricardo had gone after a woman."

He fanned himself with his hand. "And we all know I would not do that."

"You know very well the mariscal depends on you as much as I do. And I could manipulate Ricardo in a way I never could you." She let a deep sigh escape her. "All these months of boredom when we were surrounded at Humaitá, and then the sudden stark terror of barely escaping the invaders. The children were in such danger, crossing the river when it was in flood. That awful trek through the Chaco—horrible. And Francisco rushed ahead of the rest of us." He had had the only good horse. She chewed on the fingertip of her glove. "My heart abandoned him then." She took von Wisner's hand again. "You grew up rich and always knew money could not buy everything. I grew up on the verge of starvation. All those rich and powerful connections you have heard me claim are fabrications. There are no bishops and admirals in my family. Francisco Solano López's wealth seemed vast enough to accomplish anything." She gripped the edge of her seat as the carriage bumped over ruts in the road. "If I cannot recover the gold and jewels,

I am going to have to tell the mariscal what I did. I am terrified, François."

"You can control the mariscal," von Wisner said.

She smiled at the Hungarian, pretending that she agreed. López used to stand in awe of her beauty and superior knowledge of the world. Now she was able to manipulate him only with sex and by playing along with his self-delusion.

She looked into von Wisner's green eyes. "I almost wish the Brazilians had caught us when they took Asunción."

"They could have if they had tried."

"It would have ended the war—at least for me. Suppose the next time the enemy advances on us, we are captured."

"If they capture you, you will captivate them." He looked into her doubtful eyes. "The Americans are trying to negotiate peace."

She patted the beautiful green silk of his sleeve and pretended to be heartened. "You are the only man who has truly loved me."

"That is because my love is untainted by sexual desire," he said with a self-satisfied smile. "Other men want only to throw their hairy, slobbering bodies on your alabaster skin." He made a face that made her laugh in spite of her fear.

"I will have to make up a story for Ricardo's sisters. If anyone finds out how much wealth is in those boxes, there will be no protecting them without an army. And we no longer have an army."

Rich, red earth, damp from rains during the night, oozed between Alivia's bare toes. Moisture hung in the air. Huge drops of dew collected on the leaves of the bromeliads growing along the edge of the field and ran, like glistening pearls, down the high reedy grasses that grew in clumps under the tall palms. This was the first planting of maize that she and Salvador had done together, the first that might nourish their family and their neighbors rather than being taken for the army. In the old days, planting was an occasion for gatherings and celebrations, where the boys of ten and twelve dressed up as *curupí,* the old Guarani spirit of the crops. Not anymore. There were no more boys of that age. She clenched her teeth against the pain of loss. Today should be a moment of hope and closeness to her husband. He walked before her, leaning on the cane in his left hand and using the sharp stick in his right to poke shallow holes in the furrow. She took, one by one, kernels of precious maize and dropped them into the holes and stepped carefully on the planted seed to cover it just enough. So many of the villagers had eaten their seed corn during this past winter of want, but no matter how hungry she and Xandra had gotten, she always conserved enough to start a new crop.

After the farmhands went away to fight, she and Xandra had figured out for themselves how to manage the planting. The knowledge of how to do it had marched off with the workers to the sound of the tocsin and never returned. She and Xandra had produced enough to keep themselves alive and feed the worst off of the villagers. Stay alive, she had told herself. She still said it in her mind as she worked, the way she used to say her Aves to the Virgin in the old days.

Xandra had been so clever, had hidden the horse and chickens and sneaked eggs into the house in a water jug on her head. She had made stout leather bags, filled them with corn, and suspended them from trees in her secret forest— high up where the government would not find them and the ground animals could not get to them. Not even the black howler monkeys could get into the heavy tanned leather sacks.

When Yotté and his squad of soldiers came to confiscate the food they took all they found, but thanks to Xandra, they never found everything. Much as Alivia had thought she was saving Xandra, Xandra had also been saving her.

When Salvador returned from battle, she had imagined he would know more about how to grow food, but he had never taken an interest in the crops. He knew everything about the cattle. But they had no cattle anymore.

He paused, took off his wide-brimmed hat and mopped his brow. The sweat, she knew, came as much from the pain of his missing foot as from the heat of this muggy day. The sun was getting high now, evaporating the dew, making it too hot for this work, but tonight would be the full moon, which everyone knew was the proper time for planting crops that ripened above the ground. Just as two weeks ago they had planted yams in the dark of the moon. Corn had to be planted today.

Always a quiet man, Salvador had been silent since the war. His heart seemed to hold secrets and little else. What once passed between them in bed—the depth and intensity, the pure satisfaction of it—had bound them to each other in a way no words could. But this war-worn Salvador had not come to love her. She tried gently to encourage him. One of his secrets, she thought, could be a woman. Manuela, the blacksmith, perhaps. He went along the road that passed the forge nearly every time he went away from home. Yesterday she saw him in the square intently discussing something with Manuela as if they had a secret. He had said he was talking to the lady blacksmith about something he wanted her to make for him, but he would not say what it was. Alivia feared the truth too much to insist. Wives were not supposed to question husbands, but while he was gone, she had lost the habit of those old ways. Back then, he had never given her reason to doubt him.

"What do you do with the food you put into your pockets?" She looked down at the kernels in her hand, not willing to look in his face. She felt his spine stiffen.

"I eat it. The war has made me selfish."

"I do not believe you." She looked up, but he was facing away from her again, walking and poking his pointed stick into the earth. "You have always been generous," she said to his back.

"War changes men, Alivia." There was an ocean of sadness in his voice.

"It changes women too." She thrust her hand into the bag and pulled out more seeds and tried not to think of today's hunger that they could not be used to assuage. "The padre says Luis is looking for the murderer of Ricardo Yotté. The priest is frightened."

"My brother-in-law is dangerous. I am afraid of him too." He stopped again and this time they looked into each other's eyes. "I heard from Josefina that Señora Lynch was at the Yotté house looking for valuable government papers. Yotté's death must have had something to do with them. Gilda complained to me that the señora did not visit her and Luis when she was here. If Yotté's death threatens Luis's position with López, he will do anything to hold on to his power." He whispered the last thoughts, though there was no one near.

"I thought the comandante was secure in López's friendship," she whispered as well.

"The mariscal will not put friendship ahead of whatever Señora Lynch came all this way to find. He has executed his sisters' husbands. He has imprisoned his own brothers."

"How do you know this?"

"My brother-in-law, the comandante." He said the last two words with an irony bordering on hatred. "He wanted to frighten me." He turned to go on with the planting. "And he did."

"Are you going to make babies as the padre advises?" she asked to his back after a few steps.

He stopped but did not turn around. "You are beyond the age," was all he said and moved along the row, jabbing the stick too hard into the soil and making the holes too deep.

7

Comandante Luis Menenez paced the faux French drawing room of his house, back and forth between the tall glazed windows overlooking the plaza and the fake fireplace beside the door to the central hall. His wife Gilda, her lacework in her lap, perched on the settee and babbled on about her idol, Eliza Lynch. Everything about this room was a poor imitation of the drawing room at La Lynch's now-abandoned pink and white marble villa on the outskirts of Asunción. Eliza Lynch's furnishings were by far the most elegant in Paraguay. Theirs were a pale, tawdry imitation. Her walls were covered with peach-colored silk. Theirs were whitewashed. There, the dictator's consort had sat on chairs brought across the ocean from Paris. Here, the furniture had been carved—in a manner of speaking—by local men who had never seen a French chair in their lives. This clunky settee was upholstered in cotton embroidered by peasants in trite black and red. Eliza Lynch's settee was of fine Neapolitan brocade. Her lace came from Venice. This lace was made by the inept hands of his wife.

Like the room she sat in, Gilda was only a pale imitation. Unlike La Lynch, Gilda had no real style. No verve. No capacity for subtle thinking and strategizing about how to achieve one's goals. No grand gestures. She was not the woman to help a man achieve greatness.

Just now, she was going on and on about how La Lynch, whom she craved to imitate, had eaten cherries and held her napkin to her mouth to remove the stones. Gilda did not realize that that elegant spitter of pits had just threatened their future. Never truly secure, his path to glory had just become more uncertain. In fact, death awaited him around the corner if he lost the support of López before López won or lost the war once and for all.

"Why did she come here and not call on us? She did not even tell us she was coming."

Gilda waved a dismissive hand. "I told you; she went directly to the Yotté house. Josefina said she went to give condolences to the Yotté sisters. I gave Josefina some yams and salt in exchange for which she told me Ricardo might have been holding some important documents when he died."

Apprehension chilled his scalp. "Important documents I did not know about? I tell you, Gilda, something is seriously amiss."

"Well, you will just have to find out what. If you ask me, Señora Lynch was just in a hurry. She and I are great friends. I was one of the only women from a good family who befriended her when she arrived." She fingered the bobbins of lace, but did not attempt to weave them. "If she had time, she would not have missed visiting me." She looked him in the eyes. She dropped the bobbins, and her hands went limp again. "With all that is happening in the country, do you really think this is so important?"

"Yes," he said emphatically. "She did not come to give her condolences. She came for those papers. And if they were that important and I did not know about them, then . . ." He let his voice trail off rather than speak his worst fears.

Gilda put aside her lacework and stood. "Josefina said Señora Lynch did not find them."

"Mmm . . ." was all he answered. He took a cigar from his breast pocket and lit it from the candle on Gilda's tea table. If he could find those precious documents, they would give him a great deal of leverage. From his point of view, López's mistress had too much power over the mariscal. And she was loyal to no one but herself and her gaggle of bastards.

Menenez stopped in front of the window and looked out over the sun-baked plaza. Gilda came to his side and put her small hand on his shoulder. "Do you remember the ball to celebrate Estigarribia's victory at Riachuelo?" he asked her.

She giggled. "The one where all the stuck-up ladies of Asunción were so outraged because Eliza invited the prostitutes. Oh, the looks on their pruny faces! Eliza and I laughed and laughed."

He stared unseeing out the window. Certainly Eliza would have laughed at the discomforted upper classes, especially the dictator's mother and sisters who had snubbed her when she first arrived in Paraguay, pregnant and unmarried. The celebration of that victory ball had been false in every way. Estigarribia and his pitiful Paraguayan flotilla had actually lost the battle, badly. Yet, López and Lynch went on with the planned celebration as if Paraguay had just scored its greatest triumph. Menenez had thought them right to show only strength. An illusion of invincibility would spur the troops and keep the populace in fear of their lives. The government had to look powerful to be powerful.

Though Paraguay's prospects went steadily downhill after that, López never admitted defeat but clung to his iron illusion to the point of becoming unhinged. Now with López madly refusing to yield, Lynch had suddenly come all this way looking for government documents. But what would make such papers so precious?

In total ignorance, Gilda prattled on. "Old Josefina says the snake god Moñái always steals things from villages. Foolish old idiot."

"Be quiet a moment, Gilda. You do not understand. I could be in danger."

"How?"

"That night of the ball, López issued a terrible warning. All the men closest to him had to kiss his hands and swear fealty—like knights in some medieval court. There must have been a thousand candles burning in that room. López sat on a dais wearing his plumed military hat as if it were a crown. 'Beware,' he told us, 'until now I have pardoned offenses, but from now on, I will pardon no one.' The fear in that room was palpable. Faithful as we were, we all knew that if López took offense at any slight—real or imagined—we were dead men." There had been a small, skinny boy at the window, perhaps seven years old, who had stuck his naked legs through the iron grillwork and hugged the bars. He eyed the sweets on the table across the room. That could have been Luis Menenez twenty years earlier. Inside the comandante's chest, the poor boy he had been trembled.

Gilda's hand grasped his forearm. "What has this got to do with Señora Lynch's visiting the Yotté girls?"

"Whatever she came looking for, she trusted it to Yotté and not to me. That means she and López no longer trust me. I have to prove to them that I am not only faithful but also useful. I must find whatever it is and give it to her. Otherwise, she might accuse me of taking it."

"Oh, Luis, you—"

He cut her off. "And if I am in danger, you are too. Do you know how many women have been imprisoned or shot because their husbands failed in battle? We could both die because those documents are missing."

At last she closed her mouth.

"The only way to avoid danger," he warned her, "is to become dangerous."

The incessant bumping and rocking of the carriage made all thought impossible. The roads were a disgrace. Riding, even in as well-built a carriage as this, was bad enough in Europe, but in this backward wilderness rattling along tortured her back made weak by having birthed seven babies.

"I feel like screaming," Eliza Lynch said to von Wisner, who sat beside her twirling his luxuriant moustache between his thumb and forefinger and actually reading a book while riding in this rattletrap at a speed that would terrify a French coachman.

He put a finger between the pages and reached for her gloved hand. "*Ma chère,*" he crooned, "You are overly concerned." His aquiline profile was silhouetted against the afternoon light outside the window.

She pushed away his hand, and with the lurching of the carriage, did so with more force than she intended. "Stop patronizing me, François. This is too serious."

He threw his book on the opposite seat and sighed. "What troubles you, *chérie?*" He sounded more like a priest than a courtier.

"You know very well." Out the window in the woods beside the road, twisted vines choked the trees like the tangled web of deception that strangled her. "How can I tell the mariscal what I entrusted to Ricardo and why? He will see it as betrayal, and you know what he does to traitors."

Von Wisner moved to sit opposite her and leaned forward, taking her hands in his. "You cannot possibly think he would harm you."

"I do, actually," she said, and her stomach quaked. She was used to staging little dramas to get what she wanted, but this was no act. "My only hope is to convince him I did it for his good. Letting him see I no longer share his insane hope of victory would be suicide, even for me."

"Then you must be clever, *chérie*. You are by far the cleverest person in Paraguay."

He meant it as a compliment, but it sparked her anger. "I know people think I control him, that I feed his madness to hold sway over him. They always say the same about men who do ill deeds, that a woman is using her sex to goad him. No woman's influence can be so complete." She wished it could.

François grinned as if he read her last thought, but then his eyes turned sympathetic. "It might be better if you could. As it is, you must use what wiles you have."

She pulled away her gloved hands. "It is too much for me."

Von Wisner sat back. "You will find a way. Practice with me. Pretend I am him." He wrinkled his big hooked nose in that way he had when she knew he was thinking of how inelegant the squat, bandy-legged mariscal looked compared to his aristocratic self.

She fell easily into playing the role. "I did it for both of us, my mariscal," she said to von Wisner's cravat, which was at the level where López's head would have been. "I was sure it

was safe, because no one would suspect Ricardo had the treasure." Her voice shook from the bouncing of the carriage and
from her terror. "There was no time to discuss it. We were abandoning Asunción. I had to see to the safety of the children."
She looked into von Wisner's sympathetic green eyes. "In fact,
that is true, François. The mariscal was so distracted he did
not notice what was missing among all our belongings. He regretted only that we had to abandon my piano."

"I regret that too," von Wisner said. "You see. You will convince him you were relieving him of a burden."

"So he could concentrate on commanding the army and
saving Paraguay."

"Exactly."

"How could I know that someone would kill Ricardo?"

Von Wisner knit his busy eyebrows. "Do you think the
one had something to do with the other?"

The idea had, of course, occurred to her, but who could
have known? Ricardo had sworn he would tell absolutely no
one, and he would never have betrayed her. Suddenly an idea
presented itself. "Yes," she said, more to the thought in her head
than to von Wisner. "I will direct the mariscal's anger against
whoever killed Ricardo. I will convince him that only by finding Ricardo's murderer will we recover our treasure."

※

The scent of the horse. Of the blooming wild orange. Something else. Xandra was suddenly awake. The rain had not come.
The clouds had passed. Her head was in shade, but the sunlight outside the lean-to was strong. She had fallen asleep. What
was that other smell? Leathery, something like fresh-cut wood.
She blinked and lifted her head and screamed before she knew

what she was screaming at. But before the scream faded, she was sure she was dreaming. Tomás! He was sitting on the ground beside the lean-to, smiling at her. She rubbed her eyes. "Are you real?"

He laughed. "Yes."

She sat up. She had fantasized so often about what she would say if she saw him again, but she did nothing but stare in disbelief. Her thoughts in a tumult like the plants in the forest, twisted together, each trying to dominate, none succeeding.

"I am happy to see you," he said.

"Did you come back for the horse?" A stupid question. If he had, he would have taken César and gone.

His shining eyes turned serious. "The day I left, I heard people moving through the forest. I heard a voice, but not yours. I thought I was about to be discovered. Then I realized that if they found me and saw your father's horse, they would know you had harbored me. They could kill you for helping the enemy. I picked up everything and ran into the bush."

"Did someone come?"

"No, but then I thought, what if someone had? Staying here could endanger you after all you have done for me."

She could not read the sincerity of his words. She had seen that look in his eyes before, as if he were having a joke all to himself. He was like the ocean, something she, a girl from the center of a continent, wanted to touch and feel but did not really know. Her thoughts collapsed into confusion again. "So you went away without saying good-bye." She sounded petulant, even to herself. She was doing this all wrong.

He moved toward her and as if he read her mind, he took her in his arms and kissed her with his soft lips, held her, tasted her mouth with his tongue. His breathing quickened as it had when the fever was strongest on him. He put his hands on her back and drew them down over the curve of her buttocks. A melting heat ran through her, and she pressed him hard against her body. But he suddenly stopped, held her away from him and laughed again, but this time his eyes did not dance. They were dark. She had done something wrong. They had taught her how to protect herself from seduction. How was she supposed to know how to seduce?

She dropped her hands. The thought of trying again terrified her. She was foolish in his eyes, pathetic. He was angry. All she wanted was for him to want her, and she had no idea how to make him.

"Where have you been all these days?"

"Looking for food in the forest."

"You could have taken our chickens."

"I would never do such a thing to you." He was indignant. "I stayed away. I told you I was afraid to be found, to endanger you."

"But you came back today."

"I checked almost every day to see if you were here. One day I saw you here with your father. You seemed so sad. But I ran away. I knew I must not let him see me. Then today the horse was gone, so I waited nearby and came back to find you. I have been watching you sleep."

She threw her arms around his neck and kissed him. "I want you to make love to me. Now."

He took her forearms in his hands as if he were going to push her off him but she clung to him. He kissed her and without taking his lips off hers, undressed her. And he did what she asked.

Afterwards he seemed sad. She clung to him and breathed in the spicy, smoky scent of his neck and tried to feel happy.

She was sure he was sad because she made love badly. It had hurt—the way the girls in school said it would but she did not care about that. He had expected her do something she had not done. She could not figure out what, but she wanted to try again. "Tell me how to do it right."

He shook his head. "I did not want to take your virginity. I have done a terrible thing." He pulled her chemise back over her head.

She hugged herself across the chest. "You think I made you commit a sin. Well, I did not." She told him what the padre had said at mass.

He laughed again, and though she did not understand why it was funny, she laughed too. "Good God," was all he said. Then he put his hand under her chemise and caressed her breast, and this time she did not have to ask him and he did not have to tell her how. He showed her, slowly, with his hands and his mouth and his tongue. And afterward she thought she understood why the Bible called making love "knowing."

Her back to Salvador, Alivia sorted a bundle of weeds, separating inedible leaves from a small harvest of herbs that would taste bitter and nasty—like the times they were living through. She pretended to ignore him, but she was never unaware of him—had not been since she first saw him all those years ago. Not even when he was far away in battle. When the news dribbled in that this or that woman's husband had been killed or died of cholera or measles, she always knew he was alive. In the depths of her grief over their boys, she had found moments of comfort remembering the suffusing pleasures of their passion for each other, and the quality of the man who loved her. She had confessed to the padre her guilty fantasies of sex with

Salvador as she mourned the loss of their sons. The padre had told her in the confessional of the belief of the Greeks in the gods of Eros and Thanatos and said that it was natural for people to turn to thoughts of that which brought new life when a dear one died. It had seemed a pagan thing, but the padre said that the pagan beliefs were an attempt by primitive people to explain the secrets of the human heart. She, pure Indian woman that she was, felt she must still be part pagan.

Salvador puttered, as if he could hide from her that he was taking bits of food and hiding them in his pockets. He insisted he ate it himself. But she knew better. The surface of her skin read his thoughts. He took food to someone dear to him, someone kept secret. A pang of regret swept over her. He had always been most aroused when she was ready to get pregnant or when she already had a baby inside her. Perhaps someone else was doing for him what she could no longer do. Manuela, the blacksmith. He would choose her.

She waited for him to mumble his excuses and leave. Then she made a bundle of the rejected grasses to carry on her head, as if she were taking some remedy to a sick villager. She waited out of sight, watching as he went slowly, laboriously between the rows of trees that lined the red road to the village, patiently bearing the agony of walking toward what he loved. Every step he took away from her made a painful pressure in her heart.

When he turned the first curve, she followed, walking as slowly as he did, difficult as it was to hold back. What would she do when he reached the smithy? Should she wait outside for them to begin their lovemaking and then barge in? She knew how he made love. Did he do it the same way with Manuela? Though she could picture them in her mind, she did not want to see it with her eyes. What would she say? If she went right in and surprised them before they began it, how could she accuse them? She should turn back and let it be. But she could not. Her body had become barren with age, but the force of her desire for him was as great as ever. Greater. Had intensified as time went by. She had imagined that when he returned from the war he would not be able to keep his hands off her. But he came back sick and weak. So she nursed him, confident that when his strength returned so would his desire. It had, evidently, but not for her.

Before reaching the village, at the wall of the Yotté garden, he turned to the right, toward the forge, as she knew he would. She kept back, behind a tree, guilt assailing her heart. This was a mistake. How could she spy on him? She was betraying all they had meant to each other. Knowing the truth could only hurt her more, but she could not stop. She could not think how she would explain herself if someone saw her. She pressed her back against the trunk of the tree and waited, counting seconds, until she was sure he had reached the forge, and then she moved, carefully, silently.

To her surprise, he did not go into Manuela's workshop or house but kept along the road. His back bent as he leaned more and more heavily on the cane. If he turned now, he would see her. If he were following me, I would sense him, she thought. But he did not turn.

He stopped at the cross where his father died. She gasped and drew back off the road into a clump of trees, as quietly as she could, hoping the chirping of the insects and the calls of parakeets and plovers would drown out the rustling of the grass under her feet. He cut a branch of oleander and without kneeling down, dropped it perfunctorily across the arms of the cross and moved on. She followed along, keeping her distance, past the stream, where he approached a tree and took from its hollow the honey jar he told her he had broken. A toucan flew down and squawked at him and set her heart thudding that he would turn and see her. But doggedly he went on into the forest to a spot where the great flowering trees formed what looked like canyon walls.

She had to move closer or she would lose him in the dense thicket. She put down the bundle she had been carrying on her head and stealthily as a hunting cat followed until he disappeared behind a natural wall of vegetation. Fearing he would vanish into the jungle, she moved swiftly around the wall and surprised him opening a bolt on the door of a rough-built shed that had been invisible only a few feet away. He turned with shock and fear in his eyes. He gasped and called out her name.

A loud clunk and a human moan came from inside the shed. "What are you doing here?" Salvador demanded.

She did not answer but moved to the door and pushed it open. No amount of suspicion could have prepared her for the sight she saw. A person in chains attached to a beam. Scrawny legs drawn up under the chin of a thin, haggard face. A miserable torn shirt and cloth wrapped around it like a diaper. Dark, dirty hair, hanging lank to the shoulders. She could not tell if it was a man or a woman. It moaned and turned its face away when it saw her. It was a boy, she thought. And then he began to sob, and she knew him. A grip of pain squeezed every drop of blood from her heart. Her body turned to stone.

Salvador came up behind her and touched her shoulder. Without turning, she swung her arm and slammed her fist into his chest. She dropped to her knees at the boy's side. She stroked his arm with two fingers. "Alé? Alé. It is Mama." They stayed like that: her fingers on Aleixo's bony arm, her boy's body convulsing with sobs, Salvador standing perfectly still. Anger seeped into her heart. "Take these chains off him," she commanded. "Take them off now."

"He is violent."

"I do not believe you." But she did. Otherwise Salvador would never have done this to their son.

Aleixo raised his head and looked into her eyes. The hardness of his glance froze her blood. This was her Alé's body, but the creature inside was not her child. He reached out and grabbed her fingers, squeezing them so tight that his grip sent a searing pulse of pain up her arm. Tears flowed from his eyes. He reached around her waist and embraced her. She stretched out her legs and took him into her arms. He rolled himself into a ball as tightly as the chains would allow, in the position of a sleeping newborn child, and held on to her as if she could save him. But she was drowning too. In anguish. In anger. But with a halo of hope. Her boy was alive. Mad. Horribly wounded in his soul. But alive.

His father came and sat on a stool, handed her the pot of honey and some chipa. He unwrapped a small roasted bird, and together they fed their son.

8

Martita Yotté leaned back against the carved wooden headboard of the bed she had shared with her sister since they were small children. She stifled scolding words. They had sat here sharing secrets thousands of times: fantasizing about their futures, gossiping about the girls at school, weeping and sobbing when their parents died. Estella was the person Martita loved most in the world. And the person she most hated. Today she wanted to shout down Estella's pathetic words.

"Josefina said the snake god Moñái steals things from villages," Estella said. "Suppose he stole Señora Lynch's valuables and hid them in the forest. Suppose the god Teju Jagua is guarding them."

Martita raised Estella's chin so she could look her in the eye. "The señora said documents. Do you really think some snake with horns stole some political papers and buried them in the jungle? And that some huge lizard with seven dog heads and fire spurting out of his eyes is protecting the hiding place? Are you crazy?"

"Josefina believes in Moñái and in Teju Jagua. And I do too." She stopped picking at the threadbare sheet and looked up at her sister. "Stop scowling at me. I believe in the Virgin Mary and her son, though I have never seen them. I believe in the old Guarani gods, too."

"Oh, Estella, be logical for half a minute. Señora Lynch would come all this way only for something extremely important. If it was that valuable, Ricardo must have hidden it somewhere no one else would ever find it. Now he is dead. Suppose Señora Lynch decides we have taken her valuables and mean to keep them. What then?"

Estella clamped a hand over her mouth.

"Right," Martita said. "You finally see it. It could mean our lives unless Señora Lynch gets her papers back."

Predictably, Estella burst into tears.

López's latest makeshift capital lay on a small plateau surrounded by conical hills on the outskirts of Villa Rica. There, in a white tent that flew the Paraguayan flag, Eliza Lynch took special pains over her toilette. She chose her emerald green peau de soie gown that would bring out the red-gold of her hair and the paleness of her skin, which always set López on fire. And the décolletage would produce the proper response if all else failed. For the mariscal knew what would be his when she took off the dress. The world at large thought they saw in her beauty what enthralled men. They did not understand her secret weapon. Her beauty was only the beginning of her attraction. It made men desire her at first glance, but what captivated and enraptured Francisco Solano López was what enchained all the men who had been hers: the illusion that what she bestowed when she yielded her body was a rare and incredible gift that he alone was privileged to receive, that he would get only if she found him worthy. Other women looked down on her because she was not married to the man who had fathered her children. But marriage, she knew, would spoil the magic she had worked so hard to create. If she were his wife, he would have an absolute right to enter her secret, precious place whenever he wanted. She would owe him the prerogative, having sold it once and for all for a single plain gold band. She much preferred to force him to earn every single entry.

She dismissed the maid Carmencita and lay on her couch and pleasured herself. This would color her cheeks, set her eyes to sparkling, put the scent of sex on her. Tonight she needed every weapon in her arsenal if she was going to convince López that the arrangement she had made with Ricardo Yotté was for both their benefits—not the act of treason his disordered mind would most likely suspect.

Phrases she had rehearsed with von Wisner during the jolting, jarring ride in the landau flowed through her lips: "No time to consult in the melee of abandoning Asunción," "danger of the materials falling into enemy hands," "the enemy would gloat and make a great noise of victory if they had captured such a prize." She repeated them over and over.

If only, when he had had the chance, López had accepted the terms the Allies had offered, all could have been different. More than a year ago, her heart had leapt when the mariscal had uncharacteristically sought peace with the Argentinean President. Release could have been just around the corner. The Allies agreed to meet him the very next day among the tall palm trees at Yataity-Cora.

But as soon as the enemy accepted his proposal for talks, López had turned suspicious, feared an ambush. She had encouraged him. "It was your idea, my mariscal. They and the rest of the world will now see what a statesman you are."

The look he gave her told her he would stop trusting her entirely if she overflattered him. He, with whom flattery had always been a foolproof tactic. Well, flattery and fellatio anyway.

While he was gone, she had paced her little cottage, concentrating on the joys of escape: the Parisian balls, good wine, evenings at the gaming tables, mornings riding in the Bois with her boys.

López returned from the talks in a rage: the Allies had demanded that he leave Paraguay forever. He had flatly refused. Six months afterwards, he refused peace again, even though the Brazilian commander Caxias offered him a "golden bridge."

Tonight's seduction was critical: her only hope was to recover her own golden bridge from wherever Yotté had stashed it.

She called in Carmencita to pull the laces of her corset as tight as possible and to put the finishing touches on her hair.

She had ordered ham and fresh figs as a first course, then boeuf-en-daube, the last two bottles of good claret, and meringues with crème anglaise. A bit of Paris amid the squalor. China. Crystal. Shining silver. Then, when she had satisfied his craving for her, he would give her Luis Menenez to solve her problem.

☙

At three o'clock the next morning, a rider exited Señora Lynch's tent, left the encampment at Peribebuy on a fast horse, and sped southward toward the once-lovely village of Santa Caterina with urgent orders for the comandante.

Padre Gregorio had spent a sleepless night wondering who Menenez would accuse of Yotté's murder. The priest despaired that it would be the guilty party. Clearly by carrying the body to the belfry, the murderer meant the padre to discover it. The killer meant to implicate him. Why would anyone want to do that? Except for his prickly relationship with the comandante, who resented any authority in the village but his own, the padre was on easy, cordial terms with all his people. Now someone wanted to put the priest at the center of a dangerous investigation.

Rather than toss and turn, at dawn he went out and distracted himself by weeding the tiny vegetable patch he had planted with the precious seeds Alivia had given him. But he had no idea which of the tiny shoots coming up were vegetables and which were weeds. He stood and brushed the dirt from his fingers and donning his wide-brimmed hat walked out into the plaza. He took a place on one of the stone benches under the purple flowering trees. A parrot, which had been perched on a limb above the bench, squawked and flew off as the priest sat down. The jacarandas were fading already, but the orange trees still flowered and perfumed the air with a scent as sweet as his thoughts were bitter.

Untouched by physical battles, Santa Caterina was a typical, small colonial village—invisible from a distance but for the bell tower, built in a fertile valley bordering a steep arroyo, nearly buried in the dense forest growth that surrounded it. The old adobe church with sculptured arches over its windows still showed traces of the gold leaf and vivid colors that had once richly ornamented its façade. Around the square, six short streets of red dirt led off it, each lined with one-story houses of long, narrow bricks, which were held together by coarse mud, and painted white or shades of salmon. They were simple dwellings of two or three rooms, scrupulously clean and furnished mainly with snow-white hammocks. Their high-peaked roofs of thatch or red tile jutted out in every direction to protect the walls and unglazed windows from sudden downpours and the fierce tropical sun. Before the invasion every house had a family. Now many were empty, starting to fall into ruin, heavy vines springing up everywhere. Within the ancient brick walls behind the houses and the church complex, the kitchen gardens so carefully cultivated in past years were choked with weeds. Still, despite the neglect, the sweet garden perfume of tropical flowers hung in the warm air.

On Sundays, in the cemetery next to the church, quiet, sad-eyed women attended scarlet flamboyants, jasmine, and blue and yellow lapacho that shaded the little pink and blue stucco tombs of their loved ones. Most of their dead soldiers had never been brought back. Only the news came—from ragtag messengers passing through, or from the few broken shells of men who had returned to die—to tell the fates of fathers and brothers, husbands and sons they would never have a chance to bury. Those lacking new graves to care for seemed to have brought all their grief to bear, beautifying what graves they had.

Life should have been easy in this rich, warm, and fertile land but was made difficult first by the rule of the Spanish, then of the dictators Francia and Carlos Antonio López, and now López's son, Francisco, and his inexplicable war.

Most Paraguayans had simple needs and tastes. They loved games, music and dancing, horse racing. They prized witty conversation and silly jokes.

Ordinarily, if he came to sit in the plaza they would congregate around him, but even as the sky grew brighter and the sun strong enough to throw soft shadows, no one crossed the plaza. The pale light of a candle shone from the doorway of Alberta Gamara's café, but he would not go there. Since his sermon a week ago, many people had reported—some with glee, some with horror—that Alberta and her cronies were keeping score of which of the old men was having sex with whom and who might get pregnant first. They claimed they needed to record which of the future babies were actually brother and sister, so they would not marry by mistake when they grew up. He had not considered this ramification of his advice. He was a fool. He should go back to his house, but he could not bring himself to be alone with his empty larder, his painful heart, and his prayers to a God who had made this world too difficult and complicated.

To his dismay, the only person who approached him was the very one he least wanted to see.

Luis Menenez carried an expensive-looking piece of paper with a red seal on it. With a flourish obviously intended to make sure the priest took notice, he folded the document and put it in his shirt pocket. "You are abroad very early, Padre," he said with oily good humor. "Perhaps you have not yet gone home from wherever you spent the night. Not seemly for a celibate man." He laughed and gave the padre a conspiratorial look, as if a serious priest should take such a remark as a joke.

"Tell me what brings you out at the hour of the mosquitoes, Señor Comandante."

"Investigating Yotté's murder."

The priest's breath quickened. Another attempt to pry out secrets. He waited.

"As you can imagine," the comandante continued, "the mariscal has taken a great interest in the crime and orders me to investigate with dispatch." He patted the pocket where he had secreted the paper.

The padre hoped the gloom under the trees obscured the fear in his eyes. "That was to be expected."

"My orders include finding some items belonging to Mariscal López that Ricardo had in his possession when he died. When you were alone with the body, did you search his pockets?"

The very idea rankled the padre. "Priests are not in the habit of rifling the pockets of the deceased. I was busy administering a sacrament."

The comandante moved closer. "I did not ask what priests in general do, Padre." He pronounced the last word as if it were a threat. "I asked if *you* had found anything."

"No, nor did I search him." He let his outrage show in his voice. "Josefina and Gaspár prepared the body. Have you asked them?"

"I have interrogated the sisters and Josefina and Gaspár. They know nothing of any valuables on the body when you found it."

"You are sure they are telling the truth?"

The comandante stood. "Gaspár is completely loyal to me, and those women could have no use for the missing items. The Yotté sisters gave Ricardo's jacket to Hector Mompó, who washed it in the river and ruined it. He said there was nothing in the pockets but a handkerchief. He knows he will die in seconds if he lies to me about those documents."

'Oh, is it documents you are seeking? If so, Gaspár, Hector, and Josefina will not be able to help you. They are all illiterate."

"That is why I do not suspect them. But there are many in

this village who can read. And regardless of who has the documents, I will do whatever it takes to find them." Menenez patted his pocket again. "I have all the power of the mariscal behind me." Without a good-bye, he walked away with the light of the rising sun on his back.

9

 Gilda Ana-Luisa León de Menenez, as she liked to
sign her name on missives to her idol Eliza Lynch,
peered over her husband's shoulder as he studied again his latest orders from Francisco Solano López.

"I told you you worried unnecessarily," she said. "The mariscal has put this important commission entirely in your hands."

He put his arm around her waist, pulled her toward him,
and kissed her mouth with more passion than he had felt for
her since the fall of the great fort at Humaitá. "Yes, *mi amor*,
but it may not be so easy for me to carry out these orders. The
mariscal is very vague about exactly what it is that he and La
Lynch entrusted to Ricardo."

She pointed to the paper. "It says 'valuable government secrets.' It must be documents of some sort, as Josefina has been
saying."

He released her and began to pace the dining room. "Exactly what I thought, but how many? Two? A hundred? I will

have to start beating information out of people if I am going to prevail with the speed López demands."

Gilda preferred her husband to be forceful but despaired that he would learn to use subtlety and charm instead of brute force. Ricardo had known how to seduce people into giving him his way. That was how he earned the trust of Eliza Lynch. "The Yotté sisters are your best source," she said, "You are not considering torturing them?"

"Certainly not," he barked.

"I am glad," she said. "Señora Lynch came all this way to console them. It would not do to harm her special friends."

"She came looking for important government secrets." He tapped the back of his fingers on López's letter. A bit of the red wax seal fell off onto the floor. "La Lynch evidently did not find them, so the mariscal has engaged me." His dark mood suddenly brightened. "You can help." He walked into the front hall. She followed him. He took his cap from the hall tree and placed it carefully on his head. "You must find out what you can from those silly girls. They were not at all cooperative with me, but they must know something. Use your womanly wiles."

"I will, but—"

He waved away her objection before she spoke it. "Do as I ask."

Gilda had another idea of how to proceed. "Are you going to turn whatever you find over to the mariscal?"

"We do not know what la Parisienne has hidden here. Whatever it is, we will have to give it over, but we may earn a handsome reward by doing so." He gripped her around the waist and kissed her again. "Go make special friends with the Yotté girls. Bring them food. Get that old hag who takes care of them on your side. Bring her some food too. And while you are at it, ask about that brother of yours. He walks around the countryside more than a man with one foot should want to. Find out what he is up to."

In the little casita Tomás had built in the hours when she was not with him, Xandra untangled herself from his hot embrace. The smell of him that she loved so well was still on her, but so was hunger from having given him half the meager food she had found in the forest. Foraging was getting impossible. Every edible thing within a mile of the village had been picked and eaten, and the hour new shoots emerged, they were taken— sometimes to be consumed on the spot. She had taken César halfway to Caazapá to look for birds' eggs and pineapples and found nothing but a few palm nuts, which they had roasted. All the while when she was chewing on the bitter oily nuts, she was sure the smoke from their fire had given them away, and that at any moment people would descend on them and kill them—Tomás for being an enemy and her for loving him. The sun had burned away the cool of the early morning. Muggy air collected under their thatched roof and stifled her breath.

"What is it?" he asked. He reached for her, but she jumped up from the straw pallet where they had lain together. She put on her chemise and underdrawers and pulled her tupoi over her head.

"My parents are suspicious. I tell them I am coming to take care of the horse. Even my father sees through that."

He started to dress too. "Maybe it is time I met them."

"Are you crazy?"

He looked down at the ground. "I know."

She put her hand on his shoulder. "I wish it too. But something is going on between my parents. Before the war, they were like one person. Since Yotté's death, they never let me hear what they say."

"Do you think they could have had something to do with killing Yotté?"

She stopped dressing. Sweat broke out on her face, more from anger than the heat. "Are you crazy? What would make you think such a thing? My parents? *My* parents?" She wanted to slap him so hard she would knock him down just for thinking such a thought.

"Well," he said as casually as if he were discussing the flowers or the trees, "Yotté was hit over the head and stabbed. That could mean two people were involved." He was buttoning his fly.

"How do you know he was hit over the head and stabbed?" He suddenly looked like a total stranger.

"You told me, after you came back from the funeral." He picked up his shirt and put it on.

"I do not remember telling you." She studied him for a moment. "It could have been one fierce person." Like him, for instance. He was missing the morning they found Ricardo. As soon as the idea came to her, she was sorry.

⊛

Later that morning, in the tiny cabin behind the thick forest foliage, Alivia León let loose the anger and frustration she had kept dammed up for the months since Salvador had returned. They had come to feed Aleixo, but the sight of her child shackled like a mad dog drove her to scream. "Release him. I insist. How can you keep your son chained like an animal?"

Aleixo's eyes followed the words she had thrown at his father, but the boy said nothing. Nor did Salvador.

Too late, she bit her lip against her outburst. She added to the boy's hurt by shouting in front of him. It had been three days since she discovered him closed in this little hovel—thin, silent, looking as if he would spit at the next person who came near him. She had brought him his own proper shirt and trousers of homespun. They hung on his bony body as if he were a little boy wearing his father's clothes. She had made him a pallet with a mattress stuffed with soft old rags to ease his emaciated body. She gave him an elixir of pine she hoped would calm him. It had not. How could anything cure a boy kept prisoner like this?

She looked at Salvador expectantly and waited, playing on him his own waiting game.

At last, he relented. "The boy might have killed Yotté," he said.

The only response she could give was to blink her eyes. Her mouth, her limbs, her mind could not move.

"Alivia?" he said as if her were trying to wake her up. "Did you hear me?"

She exploded again. "How could anyone think that our Aleixo was—" she was going to say "a killer." But she saw that in the war they must have all been turned into killers.

Salvador explained that the boy had been free the day the padre found Yotté's body.

"Whenever I ask," she said, "you refuse to tell me what made him this way. If I am going to understand your actions, I have to know the truth of him."

Salvador winced. "He was mad when he came from the war."

She sat down on the floor and took the boy's hand. "Tell me everything. You have been saying that it would be better for me not to know, but I must. You never gave me a chance to help him when he first came home. I could have tried to cure him sooner. He might be better by now." Even as she said it, she knew that there was nothing on her shelves of herbs and tree saps that could take away the anguish she saw in her son. Time might do that. Might, but not certainly.

Salvador sat down too and took the boy's other hand. Aleixo let them do it. He did not struggle; he did not weep.

"A corporal came to the meadow near our house and kept the boy there until he saw me returning from the village alone. The corporal was deserting with a handful of starving fugitives—all too weak to fight. They had somehow managed to elude the authorities. On their way south, they brought Aleixo home, already mad. They had to tie his hands behind him and bind him to the strongest of them to keep him from being violent to himself or others, or from running away. He believed they were Portuguese who had captured him and were bringing him to Brazil as a slave, the way the traffickers took the Indians in the old days. They left him with me and continued toward their own villages. I hope to God they found some people alive when they got home."

"But what destroyed my son's soul?" she demanded

"The officer told me they were defending a bridge at Ytororo. They had not eaten in three days, not slept for two. They were positioned to fire on the Brazilians crossing the bridge. At first the enemy took a lot of casualties, but then our men were out of shells and had to fight hand-to-hand with lances and machetes. Alé was fighting beside his best comrade—a boy from Caacupé. A Brazilian shell exploded and—" Salvador stopped abruptly. He could not go on.

Alivia looked at him. He was looking into the boy's eyes. They both had been in combat. The father could not speak of the horror the boy had endured. She had not been there, but she could imagine. Blood. Torn limbs. Pierced bellies. Stench.

She took the boy in her arms, his head against her chest. She gripped him to her and wept tears that wet his hair.

Salvador jumped up and paced the small space like an animal trying to find a way out. "Twelve hundred Paraguayans died in that battle. When the few survivors escaped, their own officers took them prisoner for being cowards and not fighting to the death. *Cowards!* When they had stood up to overwhelming odds." He stopped and looked down at her, eyes blazing with outrage. "They brought them to a prison camp where hundreds of people were in shackles. When the corporal saw what their fate would be, he took his men and ran away. Somehow they got here." He crossed his arms over his chest. He would not, could not tell her more.

"That does not tell me why you hid my son from me," she said. She raised the boy's hand and kissed it.

"When he first came back," Salvador said, "he cursed you. 'I want to kill her for giving birth to me.' He said it over and over. How could I let you hear that?"

She let the idea sink in. "How does this lead you to believe he killed Yotté?"

"I am not sure he did, but he has been so ferocious for so long. He seemed capable of it. When you told me about Yotté, I had just returned home from finding Alé had gotten loose. You said that whoever killed Yotté was so enflamed he stabbed a dead body. It seemed it must have been him."

She looked again into the boy's dark eyes, which used to be so full of mischief and charm. There was challenge in them now—the first look from him in these past days that in any way resembled a human thought. "Do you remember how sweet he was on Estella Yotté before he went away?"

Salvador crouched next to her and touched her forearm. "I do."

"I warned him," she said to Salvador without taking her eyes off Aleixo's, "that he must not seduce her, that it was not right to do such a thing to a maiden. He was so beautiful and so engaging, it was hard to imagine any girl could resist him." He took after his father is what she thought, and more tears she could not stop flowed down her cheeks. She turned to Salvador. "He should have made love to Estella. How could that have been worse than this?"

They were silent for a moment.

"Even if the comandante never suspects him of killing Yotté, at best, if he finds him, he will call him a deserter," Salvador said. "If Menenez takes him to López, they will shoot him for that, and I would not put it past my brother-in-law to take us too, for harboring him."

She knew he was right, but she could not stand the idea. They had killed Aleixo's spirit. She was not going to let them kill his body. She thought she had gotten used to the idea that he was dead. Now that he was alive, she would never be able to accept his death again.

"Come," Salvador said at last. "We have to leave him. I told you. If we spend too much time here, he will be found. You go first, by the road. Pretend you have been foraging. I will come home through the forest."

She looked again into Aleixo's eyes, searching for a glimmer of his old spirit. "Every time I leave him here like this," she said, "I betray every bone in my body." His eyes were empty again. She kissed his cheek, which he let her do, and left.

Gilda obeyed the comandante in word and deed, motivated by the thought of a delicious outcome. Whatever La Lynch had entrusted to Ricardo must be something that would make a person powerful or rich. These were the things Eliza Lynch cared about. If Gilda had her way, she and Luis would take whatever it was and escape to Buenos Aires. She pictured a sunny, elegant apartment filled with real French furniture, upholstered in green silk—the color of that beautiful jacket she had seen on Señora Lynch's Hungarian count. She would buy flattering ensembles where everything matched, even the shoes. The theater. The dances. A life such as this had tempted her in dreams evoked by La Lynch's stories of Paris: fittings at the dressmaker; assignations with lovers.

As soon as Luis left, she donned her best sky-blue dress and put on shoes to show she was not a lowly woman who went about barefooted. At her command, Lelia, the cook, packed a basket of yams, rice, cured beef, Ceylon tea, and a packet of precious salt for the Yotté sisters and a smaller basket of manioc, cornmeal, and onions for Josefina. She found Gaspár pretending to sweep her front yard and made him wash his hands and button up his faux military shirt before pressing him into service carrying the baskets to the casa Yotté. On the way, she fantasized about being a noble Parisian woman, returning from shopping with her livered footman carrying her purchases, though Gaspár with his bare legs and crossed eyes hardly made an elegant impression. She deserved much better. If whatever La Lynch was looking for was valuable enough and she found it first, she and Luis would live in Paris.

Gaspár set down a basket and knocked on the Yottés' mahogany front door. When it swung open, Josefina Quesada bid her enter with a gesture of a hand holding a lit cigar. The crone led the way toward the patio, her grandson shuffling behind her. He smelled rotten. Gilda waited until Josefina's back was turned to wrinkle her nose. If anyone in this house knew what Ricardo did with La Lynch's valuables, it would be Josefina. Better not to alienate her.

Gilda found Martita and Estella weeding a pathetic vegetable patch. "What are you doing, my darlings," she exclaimed. "You should not be doing that." She turned and snapped her fingers at Gaspár. "See to it." He put the baskets on the patio table and trundled out to the garden.

Gilda motioned to the sisters. "Come, my dears, and see my gifts."

The girls wiped their hands on their skirts. They looked decidedly rustic.

"We were not expecting you," Martita said. She eyed Gilda's baskets with a skeptical glance.

Gilda handed Estella the larger basket. She gave the smaller one to Josefina, saying, "This is for you and little Pablo," hoping the old lady would leave her alone with the sisters. Josefina took the gift but did not move away.

Estella lifted the napkin covering the contents. "Is this salt?" she asked with genuine awe.

"It is. And this is tea from Ceylon. They drink it in London and Paris. Señora Lynch gave it to me. I myself have adopted the refreshing habit of taking some with cakes in the late afternoon."

"The rice and yams will be helpful," Josefina said, peering over their shoulders.

"The comandante has heard from the capital," Gilda said, certain they would be suitably impressed. These simple village girls would not understand that the capital of Paraguay was a tent in the middle of nowhere. "The mariscal has commissioned my husband to bring your brother's murderer to justice. Perhaps he will soon send us some eggs or a chicken. He usually does when he asks for special work to be done. When we get them, we will share them with you, my dears."

Josefina made a doubtful-sounding grunt.

Gilda refilled the baskets and thrust them into the old woman's hands. "Perhaps you should take those to the kitchen."

Josefina and her foul grandson finally left them, and they took seats at the table. "I know how devastated you must be by the loss of your dear, dear brother," Gilda said once they were alone. "I wanted to come sooner, but the comandante keeps me busy helping with his important work."

Martita and Estella looked at her and said nothing.

Gilda decided to get right to the point. "I wonder," she said lightly, "if you know anything about documents entrusted to Ricardo?"

"You know about Señora Lynch's documents?" Martita asked.

"Oh, yes. The comandante knows all such things."

Estella shook her head. "Señora Lynch said that we must not—"

Gilda felt Martita's foot reach under the table and kick her sister.

"We never saw any documents," Martita said. "We told the comandante Señora Lynch's men came and searched the house."

"They hunted everywhere?"

"They were very thorough, and we looked everywhere again after the señora's visit. We found nothing."

"Well, they must be somewhere. Have you looked in that secret place beneath the carpet under Ricardo's bed?"

A snicker came from behind Gilda. She turned to see Josefina's sneering face and with her that sanctimonious pain in the neck, Maria Claudia Benítez. "Oh, hello," she said to Maria Claudia. "Well, Martita, Estella, I hope you enjoy the gifts I brought you. I will come back soon with more."

Estella touched her hand. "Is there a place under Ricardo's bed?"

Gilda froze.

"How do you know this?" Estella insisted.

Gilda stood up and smoothed the blue muslin of her dress. "I had better go home now," was all she could think to say. Only after she left did she think of other answers to satisfy Estella's question. Of course, she could never have told the truth—that Ricardo had told her about the hiding place when they were in his bed together. But she could have given another explanation: Ricardo offered the space to Luis to hide their own valuables or that she had heard Ricardo tell Señora Lynch about it. At the very least, she could have said that this wind from the north always gave her a headache. Her big mistake was getting flustered and leaving the question unanswered. Gilda did not know how long that sanctimonious Maria Claudia had been standing there. She might have overheard the whole conversation. Suppose news of her liaison with Ricardo got out? The only one who knew was the priest. She had told him in confession and then had broken off with Ricardo once and for all, because he loved not her, but only La Lynch. Gilda had received the results of his intense desire for Eliza. Their lovemaking always began with a few minutes' conversation about his idol, and then he would be ready to close his eyes and enter the only elegant woman he could get his hands on. She was just as guilty in her own way, for when he made love to her she fantasized that she was La Lynch—with that skin, those eyes, that hair, receiving the adoration of men. But not from the fat mariscal with his hairy arms and crooked legs and smelly breath.

She could not fathom how a woman as beautiful as Eliza Lynch could bear his touch. Gilda's imagined lovers were elegant men in Parisian clothes, who offered her jewels and fine wine and whose underclothes were made of silk. At least Ricardo Yotté had had silk underwear.

But the affair had ended before Ricardo lost his life. And now maybe Maria Claudia would spread the word of her adultery.

Gilda dismissed the thought as silly. Maria Claudia was so holier than thou. No one could imagine her gossiping for the fun of it.

No matter how she tried to console herself, Gilda could not still her fear or banish the conviction that she had made a fatal mistake. She did have a headache, and it had nothing to do with the wind from the north.

🍥

Maria Claudia had prayed for the padre all the way to Martita and Estella's house. Something about Ricardo's death frightened him. The comandante had questioned him about the murder. The padre knew something he could not tell her because Ricardo had confessed it. What would it be like to hear the confession of a man who seemed without a conscience? She wondered how the priest, such a good man himself, could bear to hear and hold other people's sins in his heart and find the mercy to give them God's forgiveness. Her own loneliness seemed trivial compared to his solitary troubles.

She would help him stave off the comandante's threats. Martita and Estella might reveal a secret about their brother. If she could tell the comandante about it, he might leave the padre in peace. She vowed to protect Padre Gregorio any way she could.

Maria Claudia was surprised when, on opening the front

door, Josefina said, "Someone is here," in a conspiratorial tone. The old lady said everything as dramatically as possible, as if every thought she imparted was a message from the gods, but this sounded like a real warning. Maria Claudia followed her and her grandson to the patio. The boy moved like a ghost. Alivia said he would die eventually. Oh God, Maria Claudia prayed. Why must the poor child suffer so?

Then she heard Gilda's voice say, "Those documents must be somewhere." And then something about a hiding place under Ricardo's bed. An alarm went off in Maria Claudia's head. She paused in the doorway to the patio. Gilda's back was to them. When Martita saw her on the threshold, her expression remained perfectly calm. It was hard to tell if she already knew what Gilda was referring to. But even from behind, Maria Claudia saw how upset Gilda was with herself.

Without having to ask a single question, Maria Claudia knew she had found out what she came here to learn.

Late the next morning, Eliza Lynch returned from a brisk walk in the relatively cool air of the cordillera and found an envelope addressed to her in a girlish hand, lying on the silver tray just inside her tent. Trembling with hope, she snatched it up and for the first time since the fall of Humaitá, found good news.

Dated the day before, the note said, "Gentle Señora E. Lynch, We send out greeting in the hopes that this letter finds you well. We have discovered the items you seek in a hiding place we did not know existed until today. The trunks are still sealed as you described they would be. We will follow your instructions and not open them or tamper with them in any way. We will tell no one about our discovery. We will prepare

ourselves to leave Paraguay and go to our uncle in Buenos Aires. We hope very much that we will leave soon. Please, kind
lady, help us to leave very soon." It was signed, "Your servants,
Martita and Estella Yotté y Saramiento."

Eliza kissed the paper that carried the happy message. She
had three critical tasks left, all easier than having had to tell
López what she had done with the trunks. She must arrange
the Yotté sisters' departure. She would inveigle the new French
ambassador—an easy matter for a beautiful woman who had
honed her seductive skills in Paris. The most dangerous step
was to prepare dummy trunks filled with rocks and have them
delivered to the casa Yotté. She would need help with this, but
there was no one she could fully trust. She also had to ensure
the real treasure was not found in the meantime. In his last
orders, López had set Luis Menenez to sniffing around. Now
she would have to get the comandante out of the way. He pretended to respect her, but he thought her a whore. She had
seen it in her eyes. She did not trust any man who did not
want to sleep with her.

She quickly penned an answer to the Yotté sisters, warning them again not to open the trunks or to speak of them to
anyone. She hurried to dispatch her orders before lunch.

10

 At siesta time that afternoon, Comandante Luis Menenez emerged from his postprandial nap and went looking for his wife. He found her in the drawing room, sitting at her tea table as she did every afternoon at five o'clock in pathetic imitation of the mariscal's mistress. She gave him a simpering smile, as if she were playing hostess in an English palace. Except she was alone. She poured herself a cup of the Ceylon tea she only pretended to drink.

"Well," he began, "tell me what you have learned from the Yotté girls."

Gilda busied herself with a maddeningly slow and ceremonious preparation of a gourd of maté for him. "They were very pleased with the food, quite amazed by our generosity really." She put the silver-encased gourd down on the tray table and indicated it with an outstretched palm, an exact imitation of La Lynch demonstrating her largesse.

The comandante snatched up the maté, rattling a dish of the tasteless little cakes Gilda insisted on serving. "Stop all this nonsense. Did you find out what Ricardo did with those documents?"

She stirred sugar into her tea as if she intended to drink it. "Oh, Luis, you can be so impatient sometimes. I try to use finesse in such things. We spoke of it, of course. They have not found anything. I told them the mariscal had charged you with finding the documents. I am sure, hearing that, they will take the matter very seriously."

He sucked on the bombilla. The maté was bitter. "Your methods may be subtler, but mine are quicker. The mariscal said he wanted results immediately. I have to show progress before he becomes impatient or I will wind up in chains."

"Ridiculous!"

"No, Gilda. I assure you it is not. I have seen him do enormous, impetuous harm for matters of less importance." He put down the gourd with a thump.

"Luis, I am sorry to have to say this, but Ricardo's sisters cannot help you." She nibbled at a sweet. "If Eliza gave Ricardo something that important, the murderer probably killed him for it. Find the murderer, and you will find the goods."

He considered his wife. What a dolt she was to announce the obvious as if it were a great discovery. "Yes. Of course," he said to pacify her.

"If I were you, I would stay away from the Yotté sisters and catch the killer." She said it as if he could pick out the murderer as easily as picking an orange from a tree.

He grabbed two of Gilda's little cakes and shoved them in his mouth. As usual, conversation with his wife only frustrated and annoyed him. A cleverer woman would have been able to get something out of Ricardo's pathetic sisters. He would see to it that they gave up their brother's secrets.

An hour later, the padre waited in the oppressive heat of the confessional for penitents. He gripped his hands together, desperate to pray but having no idea what to ask of God. He wanted peace in his heart, but there was no peace to be had in Paraguay. The war dragged on. The dictator fought and fell back to fight again, taking position after position and retreating at the last possible moment—to the slow but steady slaughter of what was left of his devastated army. Each time their allied enemies won a battle, they inexplicably held off their pursuit of López long enough to give the Paraguayans time to regroup and make another stand. It was almost as if the invaders did not want to triumph and end the war, but preferred to torture everyone with its death throes.

The confessions the padre had already heard that day disturbed him more than those of peacetime. His flock used to come to him with their sexual peccadilloes, their greed, their petty jealousies. For those sins, he had counseled them, given them absolution, and felt satisfied he had helped them become better people. These days, they berated themselves for their loss of trust in the Lord's benevolence. They saw sin in their feelings of despair, while Paraguay's powerful did not scruple at unleashing evil left and right on the weak and the impotent. The most sinful of all was the man in charge who ruled with absolute confidence in his right to perpetrate horror on anyone he chose. And the priest sinned by doubting God.

A creek of the kneeler outside the box announced another penitent he was not ready to advise. He slid open the grille, and his heart sank further into despair. He could never reveal his weaknesses to her.

"Bless me, Father, for I have sinned," Maria Claudia said and made the sign of the cross. "I have—I have—" she said and then fell silent.

He could not speak without showing his impatience, so he held his peace.

"I have impure thoughts," she said, astonishing him. She had never confessed such a thing before.

"Have you been with a man, trying to become pregnant?" he asked, though he could not think that of her.

"No, Father." Indignation sharpened her usually sweet voice, and despite the dim light of the confessional, he could see it on her face.

"Is there anything else you need to tell me?"

"No. Yes, but not a sin. I need to speak to you about Ricardo's death."

"Wait for me on the patio of my house. We will talk about it when confessions are over." He raised a hand to give her absolution.

"You have forgotten to give me a penance, Padre." She smiled. "Oh, and I forgot to confess another sin: I told a small lie to get someone to accept a gift I offered him."

He smiled too. "Say a rosary for the repose of the souls in purgatory." He raised his hand and blessed her, absolving her sins in the name of the Holy Trinity, but he—the man—could not forgive her the certainty of her faith, which only reminded him of how weak his own was. He wished he were the man she thought he was. He closed the grille.

After waiting to be sure there were no more penitents, he left the confessional and found the comandante standing at attention in the half light near the front door of the church. Menenez held a riding crop in his right hand. He had taken to carrying it everywhere in the last couple of days, as if it were a badge of office, like his hat and his fancy red jacket with its brass buttons and navy blue epaulettes.

The priest approached. "Are you waiting for confession, Señor Comandante?"

"Not at all. I must speak to you." He pointed out to the plaza with the riding crop.

The priest led the way to a bench under a jacaranda tree, but since the comandante did not sit, neither did he. "What is that you want to say?"

"I came to warn you," the comandante said. "I expect you to reveal all you know about Ricardo Yotté's death." He put his hands behind his back and tapped the riding crop on his left palm.

"Much as I would like to help you, Comandante, as I have told you repeatedly, I cannot give you any information. Ricardo's sisters are the people most likely to remember something that would be helpful. I suggest that you bring your questions to them."

"Never mind that," Menenez barked. "Within the next few days, I will make an arrest. You are particularly close to my brother-in-law. He has been acting very suspiciously lately. If anyone knows what he is up to, it would be you. You had better tell me."

The threat prickled the back of the padre's neck. Menenez was right. Salvador had obviously been harboring a secret for some weeks, but he would never betray him. The terrified padre let what words came to mind spill out of him. "My instincts tell me the person most likely to have killed Ricardo Yotté is you, Comandante." The rage in Menenez's face made the priest instantly cower.

But that heat dissipated quickly. Menenez smiled, if one

could call that malevolent look of triumph a smile. "Insanity was not the response I had expected from you, Padre. I would have thought you knew better how to protect yourself. An educated man like yourself. But now it is too late for you to repeal what you just said; you will pay for having thought such a thing." He strode away.

Shaking with rage and fear, the padre slumped down onto the bench and watched him march across the plaza toward the comandancia, the small government building next to his house. When the priest looked away he saw Maria Claudia approaching. He moved over and made room for her on the bench.

"Father, when you did not come to meet me, I came looking for you. Are you all right?"

"Yes. Well, no, not really." He could not admit to her what a foolish thing he had said to Menenez. "The comandante says he is going to arrest someone for killing Ricardo, and I am sure it will be an innocent person."

"Who?"

The padre did not want to worry her with the truth. "He is grasping at straws. I doubt he knows himself."

"But he will choose someone anyway."

"He has been bragging that López personally ordered him to find the killer. If that is true, he will choose someone. He has taken away people before that I knew to be innocent."

"That is what I wanted to talk to you about."

This surprised the priest. "What?"

"I have two worries. I went to see Estella and Martita the other day and overheard a conversation when I entered the house." She gave him a sheepish look. "I hope you are not going to tell me eavesdropping is a sin."

"I doubt you committed a sin, Maria Claudia. You almost never do."

She gave him a strange look, as if it surprised her that he could see into her soul. He was her priest, after all.

"Gilda was there with the sisters. I overheard her say something about Señora Lynch's missing some things. It sounded very important. I think Ricardo was killed for those missing things."

"Mmm. The comandante asked me if we had found anything in Ricardo's pockets."

"It was clear Gilda thought it was something valuable."

"I can try to find out," the priest said. "And? You said two worries."

"This is a bit embarrassing, but Gilda said she knew of a secret hiding place under Ricardo's bed where the señora's valuables might have been hidden. Estella seemed surprised by that. She asked Gilda how she knew. Then Gilda became all flustered, as if she could not admit that she had been in Ricardo's bedroom."

His thoughts flashed on the memory of Gilda in the confessional, vowing once again to break off her affair with Yotté. She had attempted to cut it off many times, but, charming as he was, he managed to make himself irresistible to her. The affair had gone on for a year. She and Yotté had contrived to meet here in Santa Caterina and in the capital since Yotté and the comandante often traveled back and forth. But then, the week before Yotté was killed, he and the comandante had both been away. In confession that day, Gilda had sworn to her priest that she was breaking it off once and for all.

"Should I confess my sin to the comandante?" Gilda had asked through the grille.

"You require God's forgiveness, not your husband's," he had said quickly, fearing the comandante would ravenge his honor if he found out. But suppose she had told him? He might have murdered Yotté despite their being close political allies.

Now the secret of their liaison was out. His lips no longer needed to be sealed, but he still needed to treat the matter carefully. If Gilda and Ricardo's affair became general gossip, others besides himself might conclude that the comandante had killed Yotté. This might be a good thing if it put Menenez in jeopardy with the authorities. But who would come to bring him to justice? There was no rule of law, no order in Paraguay. Only tyranny and chaos. Too many twists and turns confused the matter of Yotté's murder, and danger awaited the innocent around every corner.

Mary Claudia looked into his face. "What occupies your thoughts? Why does what I said trouble you so?"

He stood. "I fear what we have believed: there is no government to try the criminal. What good is finding the truth about who killed Ricardo?"

"I care," she said. "You care."

He looked down at her. She was so thin, but not frail. Where did she get her fortitude?

"And Martita and Estella. They care," she added. She stood and looked up into his eyes. "I think we have to talk to Salvador and Alivia León. It is time for us to start acting like people worthy to raise those children you are hoping for. Otherwise, we will just be bringing more souls into a lawless land of torture and perdition."

He could not deny what she said. So he agreed.

※

The burden of Salvador's grief lay heavier on him. He had thought nothing could hurt more than seeing his dear son so devastated, but Alivia's knowing it somehow made it worse.

He locked the cabin door and followed her into the woods toward home. Over the past few days, they had ignored the danger of being discovered and walked together. No one would believe they were merely foraging in the same place every day. But they could not seem to part when they left their mad son.

They walked side by side, silent in their sorrow. The butterflies still drew their nectar from the flowers beside the stream and beat their wings in the rhythm of lovemaking. The flowering vines still filled the space overhead with their melee of magenta, purple, red, and gold. The spicy scent of the undergrowth still perfumed the air. But none of it lifted Salvador's heart.

"Do you think he seemed a bit better today?" he asked. "Sometimes I think he is getting better."

"Not today," she said. "Not today." She rested her hand lightly on his shoulder as she walked beside him. He could feel her pacing herself—not to go faster than he could. "When he curled up in my lap and wept that first day, I thought it would be the beginning of his healing, that he might be able to give up his madness. But he continues to be so ill that I fear he might never . . ." Her voice trailed off.

"Never be himself again?" Salvador did not know if he had uttered a statement or a question.

"Somewhere inside his tormented body the beautiful soul of our Aleixo still lives," she said. "We must keep trying to help him find it again. I have given him all my herbs. What else can we do but keep hoping."

"Perhaps the padre has some special blessing."

"To tell you the truth, God does not seem to be paying much attention to Paraguay these days." She did not say more.

They came upon a vine of wild melons they had not discovered before, though they had walked this way for many days now. Two of the small fruits were ripe or nearly so. As he cut their stems, Salvador tried to see it as a great good omen.

They left the woods and started across the meadow toward their house. The grass was waist-high, something they never saw when they had had cattle to graze here.

"Look." Alivia pointed across the field toward the house.

In the distance, the padre and Maria Claudia Benítez approached their front door. There was a day when he would have broken into a run at a moment like this. He reminded himself of what the padre had said when he first saw Salvador's injury, after he returned from the war: he should thank God he was alive. He tried to see his life as something to be grateful for.

He reached up and slipped Alivia's hand off his shoulder. "Go ahead. Meet them."

"Xandra is there. I saw her in the doorway," she said, but then she sped away.

By the time he arrived home, he found them sitting on the patio, sipping maté. Alivia was standing at the table, cutting up the riper of the little melons.

Seeing the sadness and pain in her father's eyes, Xandra jumped up and kissed him as if he had come home from a long way. "Thank you for these melons," she said to him, though the fruits were so small that each of them would have but a couple of bites. Her kiss did not cheer him. She gave him the first piece of melon.

It shamed him that he could do so little to relieve the suffering of his family.

Xandra watched them gulp down the not-quite ripe fruit, even Maria Claudia who was usually so dainty. Then her parents and the priest made small talk about whether or not they would have a harvest they could keep, about the spring rains, about anything but what must be on all their minds until Xandra could not stand it anymore. People did not come visiting these days without a purpose. Mostly they came here only if they were looking for a cure for some ailment, or begging food. "I am sorry, Padre, Maria Claudia, but you two must have something to say other than what a dry spring it has been."

Maria Claudia smiled her approval. "I am glad you asked. It is something very hard to bring up." She deferred to the priest as usual.

And he gave her his usual sour look. "Yes, but we must since an innocent person may be in danger."

A laugh escaped Xandra. "Come on, Padre. Hundreds of innocent people have died almost every day for years."

Her father made a disapproving noise, but the priest smiled and held up his hand. "No, Salvador, Xandra is right. This is about the death of Ricardo Yotté." He looked at each one of them as if to make sure he had their attention. "The mariscal has specifically ordered the comandante to find Ricardo's murderer. Menenez says he is going to make an arrest soon. I am afraid he will drag off an innocent person."

Alivia, still standing at the table, took up the empty platter she had used to pass around the melon and held it in front of her chest like a shield. "Who?" She stared at the priest as if she would break the platter over his head if he said the wrong thing.

The heat in Alivia's voice surprised the padre. It was almost as if she were guilty and feared the comandante might know it. "I doubt he knows," the padre said. "He is trying to extort information from me. He thinks I must know something from the confessional. He said it would be on my conscience if the wrong person were executed." He could not bring himself to increase their fear by reporting what Menenez had asked about Salvador.

"Did someone confess it?" Xandra asked.

"Stop it, Xandra," Alivia said as if she were talking to a four-year-old. She pulled up a chair so that they were all sitting in a circle. "Whatever other priests might do, our padre would never betray a sacred trust."

Maria Claudia's hands went to her hips. "Never." She looked to see if the priest would disagree with her on this point as he did on almost everything.

He waved the back of his hand at her. "Listen," he said, looking intently at Alivia and Salvador, "it is time we recovered our society. The people of Santa Caterina must go back to being the civilized people we were before this war. We have to find the real guilty party."

Xandra was flabbergasted. "How can we possibly figure that out? And what would be the point of trying?"

He smiled at the girl's courage to speak her mind. "You are right. It is one death among so many. But this is different. Protecting the innocent is absolutely basic to what it means to be a human being. We have been too docile. Out of fear for our own lives, we have stood by and watched our friends and neighbors perish. I have been the worst coward of all, when I should have bravely stood up against this terror."

They all protested, but he held up his hand. "We have to proceed carefully. I do not want to put any of you in danger, but if we have a chance to save an innocent life, we must try, if we are to call ourselves children of God. Menenez is going to accuse someone. It could be one of us." That was as close as he could come to telling them the whole truth.

"He can mean only me," Salvador said. He wanted to say he would confess to the crime himself rather than see a wrongly accused person go to torture and execution. He wanted to believe this. But he did not trust himself.

"We must find the truth," Maria Claudia said. "Only by

discovering who committed the crime and proving it, can we protect whichever innocent person Menenez might accuse."

"Of course," the priest said. "If we work together, pool our knowledge, we may be able to figure it out."

"Where do we start?" Xandra asked.

"With what we know," the priest said. "Alivia, you examined the body. You said he was not killed in the church."

"I am certain of it," she said. "And the body was dragged, not carried, into the belfry."

"The streaks in the dust and grass stains on the jacket proved that," the padre said.

"And Alivia said that Ricardo had not been dead for long." Maria Claudia offered. They all nodded. Even the priest.

"Do any of you know anything else bearing on the question?" the padre asked.

Alivia spoke up. "We know he was stabbed after he was dead."

The skin on Xandra's back tingled. Tomás. He had said Yotté died from a blow to the head and was stabbed, but she did not remember telling him those facts. Suppose Tomás knew it because the Brazilians had sent him to kill Yotté. Not that she minded Ricardo was dead; he was hateful, even to his own sisters. He deserved to die. And the Brazilians had reason to kill him. Ricardo was very close to the dictator and his consort. But she would never tell anyone about Tomás. He would be killed if they found him, even if he did not murder Yotté.

"Salvador? Can you think of anything else?" the priest asked

Salvador stared at a spot of sunlight on the stone floor of the patio. He could feel Alivia's eyes on him. If he looked up, the others would see that he held a secret. "No, Father," he said and was sure the little tremble in his voice revealed his lie.

Alivia looked away.

Maria Claudia gave the priest an enquiring glance. "We should tell them what I overheard at the casa Yotté." The priest opened his mouth to object, but she stilled him by saying, "If we are ever going to figure out who killed Ricardo, we must be completely open with one another."

This was the Pandora's box Padre Gregorio did not want to open. But Maria Claudia was right, as she always seemed to be. Sharing all they knew was the only way. "Then tell them," he said.

"I am sorry to have to say this about your sister, Salvador," she began, "but she and Ricardo were . . . were . . . together." She explained how Gilda reacted after her accidental disclosure.

"It does not surprise me," Alivia said immediately.

"Nor me," Salvador said, relieved to suspect someone besides Aleixo, though he could not imagine his fastidious sister getting worked up enough to inflict the wound Yotté's head had evidently received.

Xandra was puzzled. "If she was in love with Ricardo, why would she kill him?" She looked into her mother's eyes; they challenged her to think again. She did. "He betrayed her." The thought blurted right out of her mouth. She warmed to it. "He tried to cut it off. That would have made her angry enough to kill him."

The notion startled Salvador. Xandra was right. Gilda was accustomed to getting her own way, practically from birth. Being thwarted always enraged her. He remembered her breaking a precious glass lamp when she was only four years old because she thought her mother had been too kind to a visiting little girl of the same age.

"Or it could have been her husband, if he knew," Alivia said. "To defend his precious honor."

"That could be," the padre said.

"Do you mean the comandante could have killed Ricardo and yet is threatening to arrest someone else for the murder?" Maria Claudia started the sentence in disbelief, but by the time she finished it, she saw it could very well be true. "Yes, I can see he could and most likely will."

"It would be a good way to keep from being suspected," Alivia added.

"He is the law," Salvador said with resignation.

Maria Claudia waited and when no one spoke further, she said, "Does this mean we are going to give up?"

"We might as well," Salvador said.

"No!" The priest's voice was vehement. "Right now, though we have little chance of succeeding, we have to try to get at the truth."

"Tell us what we need to find out," Xandra said

The priest beamed at her. "Many, many things. For instance, Yotté went back and forth to the capital so often, I would not have known if he was in Santa Caterina in the days leading up to the murder. It would be good to trace his steps just before he died."

"Yes, and remember," Maria Claudia said, "Señora Lynch entrusted something to Ricardo that is missing."

"What is it?" Xandra asked. She was frightened again. Suppose it was something a Brazilian would kill Yotté for.

Maria Claudia held out her empty hands. "I came in in the middle of the conversation and pretended not to have heard. I could not very well have asked a question."

"It must have been something important," Alivia said, "if Señora Lynch came all this way to find it."

"Suppose whoever killed Ricardo really wanted to take the señora's things." Alivia was relieved at this possibility and could see Salvador was also. It was what she had told him from the beginning. Aleixo was not the only one who could have killed Yotté.

"What could it have been?" Xandra asked.

"Something very valuable," the padre said. "Menenez practically accused me of stealing it from Ricardo's pockets when I was anointing his body."

"What?" Maria Claudia practically shouted. "You never said—"

"No." The padre ignored her. "I heard a rumor about missing documents."

"Documents?" Salvador asked.

"La Lynch is very involved in running the government," the padre offered. "It could be papers that might influence the outcome of the war."

"So where does this leave us?" Alivia asked.

Salvador took her hand. "We have more questions than answers. But if Ricardo was killed for what La Lynch came here seeking, we have to find out what it was."

A list of missing information began forming in the priest's mind. He held up a thumb and ticked off the first question. "Where was Yotté just before he died? The events leading up to his death must have been dramatic, considering how violent his death was." His index finger joined his thumb. "And of course, what was it Señora Lynch gave him to keep for her?"

"We will have to interrogate the villagers," Salvador said.

"But we will have to be subtle about it," Alivia said. She knew from experience, when she was trying to find out about a sickness spreading through the town: people closed up whenever anyone asked too many questions.

"We also need to find out who Menenez suspects," Salvador

said. He feared if it was him, his whole family would be taken, as was normal in Paraguay under López. Not only the boy, but Alivia and Xandra would be in harm's way.

"I will talk to Estella," Maria Claudia said. "She will be more likely than Martita to open up." Maria Claudia wondered how she would ever find a chance to be alone with Estella. Martita was so protective of her sister that she hardly left her side.

"I will speak to Manuela," Salvador offered. "She is very observant. And anyone who goes to the Yotté house has to pass her forge."

Alivia cut in. "You should talk to Josefina, Salvador. She trusts you. And she understands things better than Manuela. I will go to the café and see what I can glean from the women there. I will pretend to gossip with Alberta about all the—" She hesitated to complete the sentence in front of the priest.

He smiled. "Baby making?" he offered.

They all laughed.

"Yes," Alivia said. "It is a subject they are used to discussing with me. In the process I will ask other questions."

"What about you, Padre?" Xandra asked.

"The padre should not be seen to be snooping around the town," Maria Claudia said with a frown. "Especially since the comandante has already threatened him."

The priest's face and voice carried the full force of his indignation. "I will do my part."

"Maria Claudia is right, Padre," Salvador said. "They must not suspect you of spying. You learn a lot anyway. As long as they are not things you learn in the confessional, you can tell us what you find out."

The priest still looked dubious, but he did not object. He would talk to Gilda. She had told him one secret about Yotté. She might know more.

Xandra knew she was dropping a bomb into the conversation. "I will talk to my uncle," she said. She barely had the words out of her mouth when her parents started shouting their objections. She heard their noise but refused to take in their words. "Listen to me. Listen to me. You never want to listen to me," she said. "I know what he thinks of me, but I can—"

Her mother interrupted. "I doubt you do."

"Yes, Mother, I do. I am sorry to say this in front of you, Padre, but I see the way he looks at my backside."

Her parents tried to interrupt again. She crossed her arms. "Listen for once. I have always been able to see through him; when I was only four years old I knew when he was lying. If he lies, I will know immediately. And I think his—whatever you want to call it—attraction to me will convince him to talk."

The priest came to her support. "I think you can do this, Xandra, as long as you promise to meet him in the square, and during the day, never where you are completely alone."

Though it insulted her that the padre thought she did not know how to protect herself, she said, "Yes, Father," as politely as she could. Her parents sat there looking sour.

"One more thing," the priest said. "We all need to search our minds and souls for any information that may bear on this."

They all gave him wide-eyed stares.

"Like what, Padre?" Salvador ventured. Was the priest asking them to confess their own secrets? He and Alivia could never confess theirs.

"Just things that may not have seemed important at the time but that may have greater significance in the light of Ricardo's murder."

Silence descended for a moment. Alivia broke the spell. "How much time do you think we have before the comandante makes his move?"

The padre shrugged. "He implied he is going to do it soon, but he did not seem like a man who had made up his mind."

Maria Claudia looked alarmed. "Perhaps he is watching you to see whom you talk to."

The very idea chilled the priest's spine.

There was fear in all the faces around the circle.

"Could he know where you are now, Padre?" Alivia asked.

"We should have thought of this. I am sorry that I did not."

"When I talk to him, I will find out if he saw you come here," Xandra said.

Fear prickled the priest's blood. "From now on, he must not see us talking together. We have to meet secretly."

"Where? When?" Maria Claudia asked.

He indicated Salvador, Alivia, and Xandra. "You three can come to the rectory through the woods and the campo without being seen. Maria Claudia, you come to church often enough that he cannot suspect you."

She looked at him with her intense dark eyes as if she needed to defend herself for frequenting the church. "When will we next meet?"

"When do you think?" he asked them all.

"Tomorrow morning?" Maria Claudia suggested.

"Not enough time," Alivia said. "It is already late today. We need more than a couple of hours to get the information. If we seem to want it too quickly, people will think we are spies. How about the next day, over the noon hour. If I know my brother-in-law, he will not be out and about when he can be enjoying one of those sumptuous meals he eats without guilt while the rest of us starve." She patted her empty stomach.

"All right then," the padre said. "We can stay out of Menenez's way until then."

"Day after tomorrow," Salvador said, "just after noon. Be careful."

The priest raised his hand and traced the sign of the cross in the air over their bowed heads. "God protect us all," he said.

"Amen," they said in unison.

※

It was dusk by the time Maria Claudia and Padre Gregorio started back to the village from the estancia León. Ordinarily they would have walked along the road toward their houses, but to avoid the comandante and his spies, they took a path through the forest and across a field toward the priest's back door. "Pretend we are foraging. Maybe we will actually find something we can eat," the padre said.

Maria Claudia walked before him into the woods. The heat of the day was dissipating, but she felt as testy as if it were the muggiest noon of the year. She was ashamed of the resentment she harbored against him. She had agreed to start this project "to save an innocent," as he called it. But it could be dangerous. To him. To Alivia and her family. She was willing to do it for him, yet he rejected every idea she had offered. She finally spoke up after they had walked along in silence for several minutes. "What does it mean 'render unto Caesar the things that are Caesar's, and to God the things that are God's'?"

"You ask the oddest questions."

She ignored this latest barb. "You are so determined about this, as if you were a magistrate in charge of justice in this world instead of a priest saving souls for the next."

"Do you presume to tell me what my role as a priest should be?"

She stopped in her tracks. "Certainly you would interpret

what I said in the worst possible way." She did not care anymore if she offended him. "No matter if I am right or wrong, no matter what I say, you find fault. What is wrong with me? You are so respectful of everyone else. When Xandra offered to see the comandante, which clearly she should not be the one to do, you defended her, acted as if there was value in her every thought, but you never see any value in my opinion." She was whining. She hated herself. She was insulting him, but he deserved it. He always hurt her feelings. Why should she worry about hurting his? She walked on faster and caught her skirt on a thorny tacuara bush and wound up tearing it as she pulled it loose. Seeing the rip brought tears to her eyes that had nothing to do with this silly skirt.

He hung back for a minute and then caught up to her again. "I am sorry if I was rude. I am distraught about everything these days."

She did not want to forgive him. "What makes you think you should take that out on me?" She plowed ahead and nearly tripped on the root of a cedron tree. As if to purposely add to her torture, a swarm of mosquitoes attacked her. She slapped at them and ran ahead to get away.

"Stop," the padre called. "Look here. I told you we might get lucky." He took a knife from his pocket and cut a wild pineapple and handed it to her. It was not ripe. A person who knew better would have marked the spot, left it to grow a bit more, and come back for it. She took it from him. "What have you got against me?" she demanded.

"Nothing. I have become a cranky man." He looked at her through the gloom of the woods. "The world seems so very evil to me these days. This used to be such a benign place. People committed their sins. They confessed, and I gave them God's forgiveness. But generally speaking, what they did was nothing so very horrible. Now. Now? How can I give God's forgiveness? How can I, when I cannot see myself how God could forgive them?" He could not feel God's presence anymore. But he would not say that to her.

She could not bear hearing his doubts, no more than she could stand his rejection.

He drew near her. "Priests are not supposed to be afraid of worldly pain."

"Priests are men," she said. The look on his face told her this was the greatest insult she could have given him.

He walked along for a few steps and said nothing. An uru-tau, the shyest of birds, called its melancholy complaint from a tree off to their left.

What she had said was only the truth. Anger bubbled up in her throat and wanted to fly out of her mouth. She pursed her lips to keep it in but she failed. "And all this doubt you have, is it why you reject everything I say?"

He turned in front of her, blocking her way. "You see things more clearly than I do, and I hate it when you say things I should have thought of."

"I would never—"

He held up his hand. "I know what you would never do."

She wept and hoped the light was too dim for him to see her tears. But it was not.

He reached out and touched her wet face. "I am afraid of losing my faith in God. I am afraid chaos will descend and order will never return. Before this war, I was certain of God, of the rectitude of my own thinking. Every bone and fiber of my body was sure. Now nothing is clear to me. I am afraid of being arrested and tortured. I am afraid of everything."

This made her sob aloud. Not even chicarra crickets singing in the undergrowth drowned her out.

At that moment, Hector Mompó appeared under a cape jasmine tree a few feet away. She nearly screamed when she saw him. He carried a machete and burlap sack and wore a pair of Ricardo Yotté's expensive pants, tied at the waist with a silk cravat. His bony chest was bare. "Good evening, Pai Gregorio, señora," he said with a too-knowing smile.

She held up the pineapple to show him they were foraging. She hoped his rheumy eyes could not see her teary face. She wanted to be invisible.

"I am looking for food for my ladies. Expectant mothers need to eat well. Thanks to you, I am going to be a father at my age." He bowed to the priest. "I hope you are taking your own advice too, Padre. You don't want to be the blessed virgin father forever." His voice cracked when he laughed.

Maria Claudia wanted to slap him for his impertinence, but the padre put his hand on her shoulder and pressed her forward.

"It would be a shame to waste an opportunity to bring new souls to Paraguay," Mompó called after them. "The old Pai Sebastian we had before you sure knew that."

※

Salvador sat on the bed and unbuckled the leather straps that bound his false foot to his left leg. He left his nightshirt on the bedpost and lay down in only his underdrawers. In days gone by, this would have signaled to Alivia that he wanted to make love to her. He had thought about loving her all these months since he had come home, but until now he had been sure he would fail if he tried. He wondered if he could tonight.

Naked, she took her place beside him and put her head on his shoulder and her hand on his bare chest. She was so much thinner than she had been the last time they made love, before he left for the war. Not his soft wife anymore. He took her hand, kissed it, and held on to it. "I am sure it will be me Luis will arrest."

She pulled her hand away and sat up. "Why?"

"He needs someone to blame."

The candle, still lit, flickered on the bedside table. They had always made love in the light.

"How could he risk having the murderer of Ricardo Yotté in his family?" She stretched out again and put her head back on his shoulder.

Salvador stared up at the old wooden ceiling beams. "He is a toad, my brother-in-law." And he was; a fat cucuru. If you let one of them close its jaws on you, you had to kill it to get it off. "I want to find the courage to kill Luis before he can hurt anyone."

"That would only lead to more killing. I have spent my life trying to stop death. Promise me you will never attempt it. You would be the one to die."

He did not answer because he did not want to lie.

"I cannot take care of Aleixo without you," she said. "Promise me."

"I promise," he said, though he knew it was false.

They fell silent. She began to caress his genitals. Desire he had not felt in years suffused him. He kissed her as if her mouth could satisfy every hunger of his body and soul. She moved to straddle him.

"I did not want to bring you this maimed body."

She smiled into his eyes. "I love you; I want you more than ever."

"Do you want to put out the candle?"

"No," she said.

⚘

Under the white tent on the outskirts of Peribebuy, Francisco Solano López held out a brandy snifter to Eliza Lynch. She refilled it with golden brown liquor from a cut crystal decanter. He stared into the glass as if he were trying to read leaves in a teacup. She wondered what her mariscal was thinking.

It had been another day of setbacks. A rider had come at noon to report they had lost the battle for the railroad. Soon, she expected, they would have to move camp again. Though defeat after defeat paraded before him, López never considered capitulating. Because as a child she had desperately needed to believe that dreams could come true, she would have preferred their illusions. But the fear in the eyes of their children obliterated all but desperation for escape.

She sat on his lap. The increased size of his stomach and the widening of her hips after birthing seven babies left less room for her than the first time she had approached him thus, in her bedroom in Paris when she was but nineteen and he twenty-eight. After fourteen years, desire still clouded his eyes.

With a little wiggle, she increased the pressure of the cheek of her behind on his privates. She twisted a bit to make sure her décolleté was positioned for his greatest enjoyment and reached behind her neck to undo the clasp of her pearls. He put his hands on the small of her back and behind her head and pulled her near for a kiss. She turned her cheek, received a peck, pulled away, and stood up with her back to him. "Do you want to undo my dress?" she asked. He reached up and started on the buttons. There were a lot, even for his expert hands.

"You certainly made a conquest of the new French ambassador at dinner this evening," he said.

"He is much more charming than that other fool." Monsieur Laurent-Cochelet, the former envoy of France, and his prudish wife had snubbed her. This new Frenchman seemed altogether more malleable. "I think Monsieur Cuberville will be very helpful. I thought to invite him for lunch tomorrow. Along with François von Wisner, of course. What do you think?"

His fingers were reaching the bottom of the long row of mother-of-pearl. "Excellent idea. If we can get the emperor of France to come in on our side, we might convince the Americans to help us too. You must recruit Monsieur Cuberville to our cause." He undid the last button and stepped back.

She held the front of the dress to her and turned to him. "I will do my best," she said, though she intended to entreat the Frenchman not to help Paraguay to win the war, but to get the Yotté sisters out of the country.

She let the dress drop and stepped out of it, into his arms.

That same midnight, Xandra arrived at the camp in the woods where fireflies winked all around her. The moonlight reflected off dewy leaves and gave a silver cast to César's shiny coat. She reassured the neighing horse with a pat between his ears and threw herself in the arms of a half-awake Tomás. Almost an hour passed before they untangled themselves from each other.

"Xandra," he said, still a bit breathless, "why have you come out at this hour when the jaguars hunt and the forest is full of boa constrictors. You could have walked into the web of a spider whose bite could kill you."

She laughed. "You were not thinking of all that when you kissed me hello."

"Still, you cannot leave now until it is light."

"I have no intention of leaving. I came to apologize for this morning. I was afraid you were angry at me for the way I spoke to you."

"More afraid than of the teeth of *yaguareté?*" He didn't seem to be joking.

She told him the truth. "I thought you might leave me for talking in such a nasty way."

He held her face between his hands. It was too dark for her to see his face clearly, but his voice was determined. "Listen, Xandra. I am not going to leave you. In these past days, I saw that you were not confident of my love. It made you anxious in our lovemaking, and I enjoyed that urgency. But now—I am sorry I did not make you sure of me. I love you. Please do not doubt me. I will never leave you."

She ran her finger along the beard that framed his face. "What would the Brazilians do if they found you?" She had not thought about it while he was sick. But now he was well. "In our army, they shoot deserters."

He put his arm around her waist and hugged her to him. "All armies do that."

She pushed back. The moonlight made his hair look like silver. "Then if they came . . ." She could not complete the thought.

"I doubt they will look. So many died the day I took sick; they probably think I was among them. I would never go back anyway. The war disgusts me. The endless slaughter. My country marches slaves here in chains and then offers them their freedom if they fight. As if they had a choice. So they fight. And for over a year now most of the Paraguayans they have killed have been already maimed soldiers or little boys and old men. Where is the glory in that? I will never go back to the war or to Brazil."

She looked at him in disbelief. "But you have family there."

"Three brothers, much older, who have never taken much of an interest in me. My mother died having me, and my father blamed me. My sister was always nice, but she has her own children now. There is nothing there for me. No. When this is over, I am going to be with you."

She kissed him and held him close. He had said everything she wanted to hear. It quieted her heart.

She told him about how she and her parents and the padre and Maria Claudia were going to try to find the murderer of Ricardo. She toyed with the idea of asking him if he had done it, but she feared what he would say. If he did and she saw an innocent person accused, what would she do? Instead, she told him about La Lynch's missing valuables. "The padre said they are important government documents."

"Mmm," he said. "Señora Lynch cannot be looking for papers. Once Asunción fell, my uncle shipped Paraguay's documents to Rio de Janeiro."

She wriggled out of his arms. "Wait a minute. Your uncle?" He tried to embrace her again, but she would not allow it. "Just who is your uncle?"

He let his hands drop into this lap. "The duke of Caxias," he said apologetically.

She leapt to her feet. "The leader of the invaders?" She was incredulous. "How could you not have told me who you were?" This gave her a thousand reasons not to trust him, but why would the nephew of such an important nobleman want a country village girl like her?

He reached for her, but she slapped his hands away. No

man from such a family could love her. She had risked coming out in the middle of the night. She was an idiot.

He faced her in the darkness. "I love you. I do."

She took his hand and put it to her lips. It smelled of her sex. She asked him the questions she should have asked as soon as his fever passed, but by then she was already in love with him. "Tell me how you got here. Tell me who you are really, Tomás, who told me only that his name is Pereira."

He kissed her hand then, and breathed in the scent of them from both their hands. "My whole name is Tomás Pereira da Graça. My mother was the youngest sister of the Marshal Luís Alves de Lima e Silva, duke of Caxias. He saw to my commission in the cavalry. I came to Paraguay on October tenth of 1866 when my uncle took command of the allied forces. The Argentineans had been in charge. They are hopeless cowards, indecisive, disorganized. They could have captured López by now, if they had any brains or guts."

She did not want to hear about the war. "Tell me about you. How you came to this place."

"I am not sure exactly. I was at Tuyutí, the greatest battle of the war—it was immense. We had more than thirty-five thousand troops in the action—all under that incompetent Mitre—who could not fight his way out of a convent of aged nuns."

She squeezed his hand. "You. Tell me about you."

He stroked her hair and sighed. "Before that battle, a lot of our men had a very bad fever and a terrible flux after months in that miserable swamp around Humaitá. I was to carry messages between General Osorio, the Brazilian commander, and Mitre. I woke that morning feeling feverish, but there was nothing for it; I had to do my duty. All was quiet when Osorio handed me a message to deliver. Then, suddenly, the Paraguayans attacked our entrenched position. When I mounted my horse to take the communiqué to Mitre, I had to circle the battlefield. Howitzer shells were exploding everywhere, men yelling battle cries, screaming in pain, smoke. So much smoke that the soldiers could hardly see what they were firing at. I was riding blind and burning up with fever by then, so weak I could hardly keep my mount. I hung on to my horse's neck not to fall off. I remember taking off my sash and binding myself to the animal. Then, I must have fainted. The horse must have run from the battle. I drifted in and out of consciousness. My horse walked on, maybe for days. In my stupor, I must have loosened the sash. All I know is I woke up when I fell from the horse. He trotted off. I tried to catch him. Then I heard a neigh, and I thought it must be him. I followed the animal's voice until I came here. I stumbled into the shade of your lean-to and collapsed. I thought I would die. Then you found me. I do not know who won that battle."

"The Allies," she said. "An old soldier who brought a wounded boy home told us about Tuyutí—that many, many had died." She wanted to feel sorrier for the dead, but her happiness was enormous—she had found Tomás, and her period was overdue, and if it did not come her loyalty as well as her love would always belong to this golden father of her child.

He stroked her hair. "I cannot understand how López ever imagined in his wildest dreams that he could win this war. He is a canny and sly opponent, but he was deluded. He should never have tried. Once the Allies united against him, what chance did he have?"

She put her head on his chest. "Some people say La Lynch goaded him into it."

He kissed the top of her head. "I have heard that, but I think it is more his blind ambition than her wiles. I saw the Paraguayan fighting forces, Xandra—cavalry without horses, naked troops fighting with knives and rocks, all heart and no weapons, naval battalions in canoes attacking battleships with machetes. And in each battle, López orders them to fight to the last man, and they do. It is madness."

"They have no choice," she said. "Die fighting or be executed for not trying. They fight on the chance they will survive." It broke her heart that her brothers had died in such desperation.

"The only reason Paraguay has lasted this long is because your men are fearless. The generals on both sides are shit."

"My brothers." She finally said it aloud.

He took her in his arms. "I am so sorry," he said. "We were shocked, after the battle at Estero Bellaco, to find children among the dead. López could have surrendered, gotten terms, saved them."

"My father says maybe the mariscal means to outlast the Allies. That if we do not give up, you will get tired and go home."

"Not my uncle," Tomás said. "He will never give up.

In that midnight hour, a mule-drawn wagon stole into Santa Caterina and approached the casa Yotté by moonlight. Señora Lynch had instructed the driver that no one but the ladies of the house should suspect what they were doing. As they approached, the driver prayed that the squeals of the wagon wheels would not wake the populace. Martita Yotté awaited them at her front door.

When the padre came to the door of Maria Claudia's house well before dawn the next morning, his hair was tousled, not neatly brushed and pomaded as when he prayed. The sight of those brown curls in the blue light of the moon confused Maria Claudia's mind and alerted her body. She held the door open only a few inches. Something told her to close it, but she could not move.

He did not take his eyes from hers. "I love you," he said.

She opened the door and let it swing closed behind him. "You have forgotten your hat," some numb part of her brain caused her to say.

He laughed in a youthful way she had never heard before.

She pulled her shawl around her nightdress and laughed too. "That was a stupid thing to say."

He moved toward her, put his hand on her shoulder. "You are never stupid." He leaned over as if to kiss her.

She turned her face away from his blue eyes bright with reflected moonlight and desire. "I am, at this moment."

"I cannot live another day without you." He took her hand and kissed it with passion, breathing in, as if he wanted to take her essence into his body.

He wore black trousers and a plain shirt, not his cassock. He looked like an ordinary young man, and she wanted him in the way of those fantasies she worked so hard to banish in the night. Fantasies that, if entertained, would be a sin and have to be confessed. He was her confessor.

"I have given up trying to resist," he said.

"All those harsh dismissals of everything I said?" It sounded like a condition. She had not meant it that way.

"I wanted to keep you away from me, as if making you dislike me could stop me from loving you. I wanted to show God I could resist you." He dropped her hand, and it fell to her side. "There was no use to it."

"I am afraid," she said.

"Of what people will say? Of the—of the sin?"

"Of losing you. If I let you love me, I will become your sin. One day you will repent and hate me as you will hate your sin. I love much more than your body. I cannot risk that your guilt will turn your love into loathing."

They stood there, frozen for what seemed like several minutes. When she could not stand the silence any longer, she took a tiny step away from him.

He let out his breath, like a soundless groan, opened the door, and disappeared into the shadows.

"I love you," she whispered to the night as it enveloped him.

۞

At first light the following morning, Francisco Solano López drank his habitual brandy to stop the pain in his teeth and took up his pen to write new orders to Comandante Luis Menenez.

At that same hour, the comandante sought out Manuela. Her forge was under a flimsy roof next to her house of mud brick and thatch, on the outskirts of town on the pretty tree-lined road that led past the casa Yotté.

The blacksmith was a handsome, determined, quiet woman of the same short stature as most of the women in the town, although her strength made her seem taller. Her arms and legs were muscular and lithe from her work in the smithy: pumping the foot bellows and wielding the hammers. Not that there was much iron for her to work, apart from the occasional repair of a cook pot or fire grate. She had no metal to make anything new.

The comandante found her sitting on a bench next to her front door, using pliers to pull nails out of an old piece of wood. At the sight of him approaching, she quickly scooped up the nails and thrust them into the pocket of her heavy leather apron, as if she expected him to confiscate them.

"*Hola,*" he said as pleasantly as he could, trying to take a leaf from Gilda's book about charming rather than beating information out of people. He had no idea what Manuela's thoughts were on any subject. Her mother had died long ago in childbirth. She had lost everyone else in the war—her father, her brothers. But she had gone willingly to join the women lancers. Not that any of those bitches actually fought in battle.

"*Buen día, Señor Comandante,*" she said. She glanced in his eyes and then stared at the ground.

At least she was respectful. "I have come to ask what you might have seen."

"Seen?" Her eyes were wide. He had never noticed before how round and pretty they were.

"I am investigating Ricardo Yotté's death. You are the closest neighbor. You must have seen something to help me discover what happened."

"I thought he died in the belfry. People say he was murdered, but I thought he climbed the bell tower to watch for the enemy and fell."

"No, he was murdered." He did not explain.

She offered nothing more.

"Did you see Ricardo come or go from his house on the day he died?"

"No," she said as if apologizing. "I left home early to go to the cemetery before mass."

"Did you see anything unusual in the days before his death?"

"No, señor. Before his death? No, nothing before he died."

"But since?"

"Well, yes." She sounded surprised that he did not know. "Señora Lynch came to console Martita and Estella, in a beautiful carriage with a tall man in a beautiful green jacket. They had lovely gray horses. Matched, they were. We have not seen such horses since—"

"Yes, yes," he cut her off. They were all so enamored of López's glamorous Irish whore and her fancy possessions.

"What about Salvador León? He walks along this road almost every day." It occurred to the comandante that his brother-in-law might be coming to fuck this young woman with the sweet face and soot under her nails. Her lovely eyes betrayed something between confusion and fear. "He goes into the forest," she said. "He must be foraging. I heard there is a tree there with honey in it, but I have not been able to find it. Perhaps Salvador has."

"I will ask him," he said, knowing she was being disingenuous. One did not visit a honey tree every day. One took the honey and left. Menenez walked away convinced that hers was the honeypot his sanctimonious brother-in-law was dipping into.

Maria Claudia left the bed where she had found no rest, washed her face, brushed her hair, and left her house. Agitation drove away any thoughts of the breakfast she could not eat because she had no food. She crossed the plaza toward the church that had been her refuge since childhood, but her steps dragged as she trod on the fallen jacaranda blossoms. The church was his province and not her refuge anymore. I want him, dear Mother, she thought, not knowing if she meant the Virgin or the vague memory of a pale, sickly woman who died along with her baby sister, when Maria Claudia was only six years old. She turned toward the cemetery and the graves of her parents and that infant she had seen only once, but could not forget.

She knelt and talked to her mother's spirit, the way she used to when she was a little child. "Mama, why does my love have to be a sin? I want him. I love him. It does not feel sinful in my soul." She could not say aloud, even to a ghost, her terrible fear: he would hate her now for rejecting him.

She leaned her head against the pink stucco tomb that held all that remained of her little family. Her father, who had loved and cared for her, but who also died before she had finished needing him. A white butterfly alighted on a flower before the grave; its wings had red and black tracings, like the pages of her missal.

A noise startled her into consciousness. She had dozed. She did not know how long. Estella Yotté was walking toward her family's grave nearer the church. Maria Claudia rose quietly, but Estella jumped anyway. The pale, distracted girl gave her an accusing look.

"I am so sorry to have frightened you," Maria Claudia said. "I was saying a prayer for my mother."

Estella nodded. "You are so good at praying," she said. "Please say one for Ricardo." Her request was diffident, like a little girl who had no friends asking someone to play with her.

"Yes, of course." Maria Claudia knelt at the Yotté grave and said a silent Ave, but she thought more of Martita and Estella's parents than of their brother. Their stern father, Don Cecilio, who had sung so beautifully in church, his deep baritone filling up the space over their heads and sounding to them when they were children like the voice of God. Their mother, Doña Antonia, who painted watercolors of flowers in the garden and smiled benignly at the little girls as they played. An elegant mother beloved by a little girl who had no mother of her own. But Ricardo? He mortified her, treated her with disdain, making fun of her plain homespun dresses. When she won an essay contest at school, he gave her a sharp pat on her cheek—a gesture just short of a slap that stung enough for her to see that he meant to put her in her place. When she developed into a woman, he looked at her breasts one day and then into her eyes, and with his superior smile said, "Don't get any ideas about me."

"Holy Mary," Maria Claudia said, "receive the soul of our brother Ricardo into your mercy." She stood and brushed off her knees.

"I have tried to pray," Estella said, "but I cannot stop thinking about the things he did."

The iron taboo against speaking ill of the dead stopped Maria Claudia from agreeing. A few people were entering the church for early mass. The padre would be in the vestry, putting on the chasuble with the lace she had made. His hair would be neatly brushed and slicked down, two shades darker than she had seen it in the moonlight. How did he cleanse his soul to say mass? Everyone in the village went to him for solace and absolution. But he was like her. He had no one.

"Have you eaten?" Hunger had become what the weather used to be, what everyone shared and talked about.

Estella shook her head.

"Let's go foraging. Maybe we can find some pipit eggs."

Estella gave her a sheepish smile. "We have maize and manioc from the señora comandante. I will give you some." She said it apologetically, as if it were a sin to have food.

Maria Claudia had said she would visit the Yotté sisters today, to find out what she could about Señora Lynch's missing valuables and what Ricardo might have been doing just before he died. She had promised everyone at the casa León, before everything changed in the middle of the night. The bell rang inside the church. He was coming out of the vestry now, bowing to the altar and turning to the small congregation that came to daily mass. He would notice she was not in her accustomed place in the second pew on his right, near the statue of Saint Joseph. She wanted to see him, to look into his eyes and apologize again for sending him away. But how could she send such a message to a priest? He would be beginning the kyrie at this moment. Her stomach begged her to go with Estella.

"Thank you," she said. "That would be very kind. Just a little boiled maize." She linked arms with Estella and walked with her back across the plaza.

When they arrived, they found Martita in the kitchen ironing a frock as if she were preparing for a party. "What are you doing here?" she said to Maria Claudia. "We are very busy. We have no time for visits."

❦

Alivia kissed her husband good-bye. He was going to feed their son. She let her lips linger on his. He was hers again.

"On my way back," he said, "I will go to talk to Manuela."

Her skin prickled. She tried to tell herself she would not care if he was making love to the blacksmith. Salvador still wanted her. He had proved it last night.

"Where are you going, Papa?" Xandra asked.

"Foraging," they both answered too quickly. The girl looked suspicious.

"Come." Alivia took her daughter's hand and walked out too. "If we are going to get the information about Yotté, we need to start this morning. Come with me to the village."

Xandra readily agreed. "I want to visit my uncle while he is still at breakfast," she said. "I want to force him to give me a bite of his morning chipa."

"No, you will not!" Alivia said. "You will ask for him and wait in the plaza for him to come out. The padre said you should not go into that house, and so do I."

"I know."

As they started along the road to town, Alivia took her by the chin and looked at her face. "You are different."

Xandra pulled away. "I am the same, only hungrier."

Alivia did not believe her. If there was a man in the village the girl would have taken, she would have sworn Xandra had been with him. This sudden maturity did not come to girls out of the blue. Xandra had always been bolder than was seemly for a young lady, but her father had liked his daughter's spirited ways. She had gained it playing boys' games with her brothers. But the quality of her confidence had changed.

"Who do you think killed Ricardo?" the girl suddenly asked.

Alivia thought only of the mad boy. "There is talk in the village of men who came to the casa Yotté looking for those valuables. Maybe they killed him because he would not give them what they wanted."

Xandra stared at her. "You cannot believe that."

Alivia looked away. "Why not?"

"Because no one who wanted to know a secret would kill the only person able to tell it." She nodded emphatically, satisfied with herself.

Her mother said nothing.

"Besides, if anyone wanted to get a secret out of Ricardo, all they would have had to do is threaten to break his pretty nose. He was not what anyone would call brave."

"You are right about that."

They crossed the stream, sparkling in the early sunlight, reflecting the flowering vines and trees overhead. The hills in the distance were a smoky shade of green. Everything around them was beautiful, except their lives. "This used to be such a happy place," Alivia said.

Her daughter took her hand. "It will be once again, Mama."

They walked hand in hand until they had to separate, Alivia to go to Alberta's café, and Xandra toward the comandante's house on the square.

Alivia kissed her daughter's cheek. "Remember. You are not to go in." The girl's skin exuded a spicy scent. Her mother watched her walk away. She showed no sign of fever. There was no use asking what was happening with her. Alivia knew her. The more interest her mother showed, the less likely she was to offer information. Alivia turned toward the café and called out *"Hola, Alberta!"* as she approached the open door.

In the street before the Menenez house, cross-eyed Gaspár Otazú listlessly scraped a broom at some fallen blossoms. He stared at Xandra's chest as he greeted her. *"Buen día, Señorita León.* What can I do for you?"

She stood perfectly still and waited for him to look up at her face. When their eyes finally met, she said, "Please ask my uncle to come speak with me."

"He has already left," the old man said with a sly smile. "He is a very busy man. And I am too."

"Tell him that I came," Xandra said. "I will return after siesta."

"Do you want to take a siesta with me?" The old man fondled the handle of his broom. "Hector Mompó is not the only one capable of getting a girl with child. I may not have Ricardo Yotté's clothes, but I have my uniform." He touched his lopsided epaulettes and fingered the single brass button on his shirt.

Xandra was about to say something about vomiting when she saw Maria Claudia walking faster than the heat of the morning warranted from the direction of the casa Yotté. She ran to intercept her.

"You look upset," Xandra said.

Maria Claudia eyed old Gaspár and pulled Xandra out of his earshot to a bench under the trees. "I was with Martita and Estella. Martita acted as if I was intruding. She has never been rude to me before."

"Did Estella tell you anything?"

"I had no chance to ask. I met her in the cemetery this morning. She offered me something to eat. When we got to their house, Martita gave me some maize porridge but hardly spoke to me. I felt like a beggar."

"You found out nothing?"

"Just that Ricardo had been away the entire week before he died. He came home in the middle of the night."

"On a horse?" Xandra asked.

Maria Claudia was shocked. None of them had thought of this before. If Ricardo had ridden his chestnut stallion home, where was it? The stable was at the back of the garden. She had not noticed a horse in it, nor smelled one. "I will find out," she said.

"Did you see anything suspicious?"

"No. Martita seemed wary, as if she knew what I wanted."

Xandra bit at her cuticle. "Maybe they will talk to me."

Maria Claudia pursed her lips and shook her head. "You could try, but I doubt she would tell you anything. Except for Estella, I am Martita's oldest friend. Why would she suddenly shun me?"

Xandra's own thoughts chilled her. She looked around. Gaspár was still in front of the comandante's house, looking at them. She leaned closer and whispered, "Maybe I should sneak into their house and see?"

"No!" Maria Claudia shouted.

Gaspár started to sweep in their direction. Xandra jumped to her feet, took Maria Claudia's arm, and pulled her up. "Walk with me." By the time they were out of earshot, she was hatching a plan. "I can go in at night."

"Xandra! No one would do such a thing."

"I would. How else can we find out what Ricardo had that Señora Lynch came all this way to find?"

"Martita insists she came only to console them. That much she did tell me."

"Oh, Maria Claudia, you are such an innocent. Why would someone as important as Señora Lynch come all this way in the middle of a war to say, 'I'm sorry your brother died'? This is about something she is desperate to have. We will understand the whole thing once we know what it is."

"Yes, but Martita and Estella heard what Gilda said about the hiding place. If Señora Lynch's valuables were under the bed, they will have found them."

"Maybe. But they would have to send a message all the way to Piribebuy, and someone would have to come to take the valuables away. Whatever it is could still be there. If it is, we should find out about it."

"To go into someone's house without permission? You cannot. Besides, their house is not like yours or mine. The front door is bolted, the garden is surrounded by that high wall, and the windows facing the street have bars. How would you get in?"

Xandra pictured the wall: its height, the stucco surface, and the flat stones on the top. "You will have to help me."

"I will not."

"You must. Come on, be a person who does something. All you have to do is stand outside the wall and help me get to the top. I will do the rest."

"We should stick to the plan we made with the padre and your parents yesterday. We are going to meet at the padre's house tomorrow. There could be an answer by then."

"And if not? Will you go with me then?"

Maria Claudia did not say yes, but she did not say no either.

Eliza Lynch sniffed at the armpits of her most seductive afternoon frock of an azure blue lawn that perfectly matched her eyes. The airing the maid Carmencita had given it had cleared away most of the musty smell caused by too much perspiration in the wet heat of this swampy backwater of a country. Even up here in the hills, one risked the complete ruination of one's best clothing despite the use of shields, to say nothing of smelly fires to keep the insects away.

Everything about today's luncheon must be perfect. She

dressed, put some fresh red liana blossoms in her hair, and went to the dining tent to check the table. How miraculous Monsieur Cuberville would think it to dine here in this wilderness at a table unmatched anywhere but in Paris. Her last bottle of champagne was under guard, chilling, in a manner of speaking, in the stream that ran at the edge of the meadow where their tents were pitched. Francisco was away tending to the war, so she would have the new French ambassador's ear all to herself. His eyes too. Von Wisner would be with them, but that would not limit how flirtatious she could be.

She fingered the bright floral centerpiece of orange and yellow blossoms, which matched the colors of the Empire pattern of her Sèvres. "Everything looks wonderful," she said in Guarani to the butler whom she called Guillaume for effect, and whom she had chosen because he was tall and slender and not clumsy.

From outside the tent she heard von Wisner's warning: his voice calling a loud greeting to Monsieur Cuberville. She pinched her cheeks and bit her lips to brighten them and smiled at the flap in the tent. Guillaume opened it. The French ambassador and Colonel von Wisner entered, bowing to her. The butler forgot to close the flap as he ran off across the green meadow to fetch the bottle from the stream.

Cuberville was a typical French bureaucrat, so like the ones who had frequented her salon in Paris: short and dapper, with a round face and small, hard eyes, dainty hands and feet. A dainty male member too, no doubt. Like López's. All the easier to manipulate a man so lacking. His glance lingered on her cleavage as she warmly shook his hand. "It is so kind of you to come." He smelled of calendula and lavender— perfume he must have brought with him from Paris.

"The pleasure is all mine." His smile showed fine white teeth. Every man had one desirable feature. Monsieur Cuberville actually had several, not the least of which was a diplomat's right to come and go despite the war.

She indicated the table and watched his eyebrows rise. "*Quelle surprise,*" he exclaimed, as if his own perfectly clean and pressed striped trousers, snow-white shirt, and spotless calfskin boots were not also miraculous in the middle of this remote and muddy jungle. As soon as they took their places, Guillaume opened the bottle he had carried in from the stream and poured the almost properly chilled wine into her Baccarat flutes. Pretending to believe winning the war was possible, she and von Wisner raised their glasses when Cuberville proposed a toast to "*la victoire.*"

They spoke of Paris and the music in its concert halls. The meal was almost good. The fish, though of indeterminate genus, was edible, thanks to the butter sauce with wild herbs. The beef had been cooked within an inch of mush to make it chewable but was quite tasty. Eliza waited until Cuberville took a spoonful of lovely pineapple meringue and closed his eyes to savor it before she brought up the subject closest to her heart. "Monsieur Ambassador," she said, her voice sweet as the dessert on his tongue, "I wish to speak to you of the plight of two lovely young women who recently lost the brother who was their only protector. I need your help reuniting them with their uncle in Buenos Aires."

Salvador talked to the boy about everything that had transpired, keeping hope alive that someday Aleixo's mind would come back and understand. When the son finally fell asleep, the father slipped silently out of the cabin.

He looked up at the sky. It was well past noon. He would have missed his dinner, if there had been any.

He made his way toward Manuela's forge to ask about Ricardo Yotté's comings and goings from his house on the days before he died, and also to find out if she had seen the boy when he was loose. But before he reached his destination, Josefina approached him on the road. "How is it," she asked without preamble, "that you are always in the woods near here? If I were a suspicious person, I would find it very odd."

Salvador knew better than to offer the excuse that he was foraging. He thought of telling her he had some chickens hidden in the forest, but that would only bring on dangerous snooping.

While he cast about for something to say, she spoke again. "Someone you love is in danger." She turned her back, and Pablo followed her to their hovel.

Her hollow tone chilled his heart. He tried in vain to convince himself that Josefina was not an oracle.

He clumped to the forge, crossing a fallow field on the shortest route. As he neared Manuela's house, he heard her singing to the rhythm of metal hitting metal. Her voice floated to him on a light breeze across the waving waist-high grass. He found her at the anvil, holding nails in her pincers and pounding them straight with a ball hammer. When she saw him coming, she grabbed a cloth and wiped the sweat from her face, leaving a streak of soot along her smooth cheek. Her tawny skin looked golden in the afternoon light. "I am glad you have come to see me," she said softy. "I had planned to come and speak with you today." Her voice had none of the strength of her arms and her hands. She was only twenty, perhaps twenty-one, but she had seen and suffered more than most women ordinarily did in a lifetime of fifty years. She gave him a shy smile.

He smiled back. "Then it seems we both have things to say to each other." He pointed at the bench next to her front door. "May I?"

She looked down at his false foot. The flush of working near the fire deepened into a blush on her dirty, pleasant face. "Of course. I am sorry. I should have asked."

"No, no," he said as he hobbled toward the bench. His hips hurt more than his leg today, and he remembered his movements in bed with Alivia. This ache was nothing compared to the one making love to his wife had removed. "I came to ask," he said once he was off his feet, "if you have seen anything unusual along the road."

She grabbed a crate and sat opposite him. In the distance, the sky behind her was clouding over. "That is what I wanted to tell you." She leaned forward, her elbows on her knees and spoke earnestly. "The comandante came early this morning and asked the same question."

The wariness brought on by Josefina's warning prickled his back again. "What did you tell him?"

She shook her head. "Just that Señora Lynch came in her beautiful landau."

She looked so benign, but fear that she had seen the boy near the Yotté house still gripped Salvador. "What else?" He hated that his question came out sharp and brought a hurt look to her kind face.

"Nothing." She looked around and lowered her already soft voice, though no one could be closer than a hundred yards away. "I did not tell him what else I saw."

"What was it?" He could not keep the demand out of his voice.

"A wagon." She hiked the crate closer and leaned nearer

him. She smelled of peaches and smoke. "It came twice. One day at siesta time, I was lying in my hammock, but not asleep. I heard it arrive. Some men got down and went into the Yotté house. They came out about an hour later and went away again. They took in nothing and brought out nothing. Then, last night very late, they came back. The creaking of their wheels woke me up. It sounded like a wounded cat. I looked out. The moonlight made it clear. This time the men carried four trunks into the house and left very shortly afterwards."

It was not what he had expected her to say. "How big were the trunks?" some vaguely engaged part of his brain caused him to ask.

"The kind people pack when they are going to Buenos Aires or across the big ocean." She said it almost reverently. She was, after all, a girl who would never own such a thing or go to such an exotic place.

The padre said Menenez was looking for documents. Could there be four trunks full of them? "And you did not tell the comandante?"

"Yes," she said, and then, "I mean, no. I did not tell him."

He left it at that. She had already entrusted him with a great deal, given the fear Paraguayans had of betrayal by their friends.

He had to make sure of the question that had been burning him. "Did you ever see a boy coming or going on the road?"

She looked completely puzzled. "Other than Pablo?"

"Anyone else—a little older perhaps?" He was going to add "in raggedy clothes," but everyone wore raggedy clothes these days.

She stuck out her lower lip and shook her head. "Never," she said. "I watch the road a lot. I am alone here, and I am often at the forge, though there is little to do." She pointed to the window of her little house. "My hammock is there, so I can see the road when I am lying down."

She seemed to be trying to reassure him, as if she knew he wanted her not to have seen the boy. But of course the boy could have been on the road, could have killed Yotté, even though, vigilant as she was, she had not seen him. He rose from the bench. His hip was stiffer than ever. He replaced his straw hat as he walked out into the sunlight. The clouds were coming, but they were not here yet. He would have to walk home in the sun.

Her fingers went to her mouth. "I should have offered you a maté." She looked as if she would burst into tears over this small breach of etiquette.

'No, no," he said. "I did not want one. But I would like a little cup of plain water."

She went to the well near the forge and brought him a dipperful, which he drank down. When he gave her back the ladle, she caught his hand in hers, and looking right into his face with her sad, determined eyes said, "Señor León?" Her voice had turned very formal.

"Yes?"

"One day. One day soon, please. I would like you to give me a baby."

12

After siesta that afternoon, the comandante approached that hole-in-the-wall the villagers called the café, as if it were a gathering place for Parisian artists or Venetian poets. Hector Mompó lounged on a bench in the shade. At his age, his new sexual activities ought to have been killing him, but he looked younger every day. The old goat sported one of Ricardo Yotté's fine jackets, which now looked as if it had been sat upon by an elephant, and a fancy silk cravat tied in a silly bow at his neck. He wore no shirt, only his double leather apron, and nothing but silver spurs on his feet.

"Are you sure there was nothing in those pockets?" the comandante demanded.

Mompó hugged the jacket as if he expected the comandante to rip it from him. "Nothing, señor," he said. "You are looking for Señora Lynch's missing valuables, yes?" Mompó nodded gravely.

"What do you know about that?"

Mompó showed his empty palms and shrugged. "Josefina

told us Ricardo had valuables. People think it was papers." He pointed his thumb over his shoulder at fat Alberta Gamara who stood impassively behind him. "We were just saying that Señora Lynch would be looking for gold, and the snake god Moñái probably stole it and buried it in the forest. We are too afraid of *yaguaretés* to be out in the night or we would watch for Plata Yvyguy, the headless dog. He would find the buried gold." The backward nincompoop showed the gaps in his teeth in a stupid smile. "You have a *pistola,* Señor Comandante; you can go out at night. Just follow the dog god. He will lead you to the gold."

"What gold? Ricardo had government papers, not gold."

Mompó looked dismayed. "Why would the snake god steal papers?" he moaned.

The comandante walked away from the ignoramuses, but instead of disdain for their superstitions, he was filled with terror. Gold? Suppose La Lynch had really given Yotté gold to hide for her? How could he find gold if he was looking for documents? López would kill him if he did not find whatever it was and very soon. And in the matter of the murder, he had no idea whom to accuse, except for Salvador. Did Salvador know anything of the missing documents? Or was it gold? If gold, anyone would steal it—not just Moñái.

Menenez stoked his moustache. Urgent as these other matters were, his wife's niece had come looking for him, and he thought he knew why. He would attend to that little hot-head first. He might get some useful information out of her in the bargain.

As the afternoon heat began to dissipate, Xandra rose from her hammock, grabbed a big homespun towel, her tortoiseshell comb, a clean chemise and underdrawers, and went down the path through an orange grove to the stream that ran between her house and the village. There under a thick, fern-leaved paraiso tree was the pool where they bathed and washed their clothes. Josefina, who believed very much in bathing, said that the Spanish, when they first came, hardly ever bathed. They were appalled that the Guarani bathed almost every day. "The Spanish said they came to civilize the Indians," Josefina would say, and she would laugh until she coughed so hard you thought she was going to die from all the cigars she smoked.

As Xandra approached the bank of the bathing pool, a red ibis that had been standing in the water flapped its wings, spraying droplets that glistened in the sunlight. The bird took off slowly, straining to lift its own weight. As hungry as they were, her mother would never let them kill and eat an ibis. She said that anyone who ate its flesh would always be unhappy. It seemed to Xandra that the whole country must have eaten a gigantic ibis.

She alone was happy. Though guilt tinged her satisfaction, she rejoiced. Her thrilling time with Tomás imbued her with joy. However long it continued, she was determined to love him and to take all the love he could give her.

She hung her towel and clean underthings on the branch of a flowering lapacho tree. Rose-colored petals showered down around her. A flock of hummingbirds hovered and drank from its blossoms, their feathers like bright emeralds and sapphires. She took off her sash, her skirt, her tupoi. Ordinarily, she would have left on her chemise and underdrawers, but after a glance around, she stripped herself naked. She undid her hair.

Before disturbing the surface of the pool, she looked at herself. She was not pretty. Her father's uppity sister Gilda had told her the truth. A classic beauty must look fragile—like

Señora Lynch—have a tiny nose, more delicate lips, smaller breasts, paler skin. Tomás said she was beautiful, and if he thought so, that was all she wanted. That and the secret growing inside her. She smiled at herself, and the girl in the water smiled back, though her looks were all wrong.

A breeze kicked up ripples that broke her reflection. The hummingbirds flew to the golden flowers on the opposite bank.

She walked into the water, slipping on the mossy rocks, and swam to the center of the pool. The cool water flowed over her body. Her mother would know soon. She already suspected something. She had kissed her twice before she went to sleep last night and pretended not to sniff her hair. Alivia León was like a dog. She smelled what people could not see. When people came to her with ailments, she put her nose to their heads and necks to figure out what was wrong. She probably knew a girl was pregnant by her smell. But she would not be angry with her daughter; she loved babies too much to reject one of her own flesh and blood. When Alivia León held a baby, especially a chubby one of a few months, she beamed with physical pleasure. Xandra imagined cuddling her own child. It had been so long since she had been around an infant. Her brother Mariano was the last baby she had held. But she could not let herself think of Mariano.

She floated on her back in the middle of the pool and looked up at the blue sky and puffy white clouds, picturing her own baby boy with fat arms and legs and golden hair. She tread water and tried to rub her skin clean. They had not seen soap in more than a year. There was no lye, and after the last of the beef was slaughtered, no tallow—therefore no soap. She swam toward the bank and when the water became too shallow, she stood up and let her feet sink into the slimy mud.

Then she saw him. The comandante. Sitting on his horse, staring knowingly at her.

She dove again, and when she surfaced and looked back, he had not moved.

"Are you going to scream?" His eyes laughed at her.

She did not know what possessed her: She took a mouthful of water and spit it in his direction. "You cannot scare me," she said. Even if he did.

"Come out. Gaspár said you wanted to talk to me. I guessed it was about getting yourself with child. I will be pleased to help you with that."

She laughed. And as soon as she did, she knew it was a mistake.

He got off the horse and strode to the edge of the stream. He held up his riding crop as if he meant to flog her with it, though he could not reach her from where he was. He would never come in wearing those precious boots he was so proud of. "You cannot stay in there forever." His tone was seductive, but his glance was cold and severe.

She felt like telling him that he was too late to father her child, but she knew what she must do instead. "See that towel hanging from the tree beside you?" she said sweetly. "Put it down beside the water and turn your back, please." She kept her tone polite as her father always begged her to do with this pig of an uncle.

He smiled, easily beguiled, and did as she asked. Clearly, he considered himself irresistible. He stood with his back to her, tapping his riding crop in the palm of his left hand.

She leapt for the towel, slipping on the muddy bottom and getting her clean legs all dirty again. She wrapped the towel around her. It covered her from her neck to knees. "Okay, Uncle," she said sweetly.

He turned and looked her up and down and took a step toward her. "Now, *querida,*" he said. "Where shall we begin?"

"I came looking for you, Uncle, because I would like to know what you have found out about who killed Ricardo Yotté."

He looked at her with astonishment. "Well, I wanted to speak with you about that too. But given your current state of undress, perhaps we should begin with first things first."

She pulled the towel tighter and pretended to ignore his disgusting offer. "Ricardo's sisters are friends of mine, Uncle. They have been so sad since he died. We all want to know what happened."

"Stop calling me uncle," he said. "What do you mean all of you?"

"Uh . . . just Martita and Estella and me. Everyone must be curious, Uncle."

"I told you to stop calling me that. What have your friends said about how their brother died?"

Feigning nervous jitters, she was taking tiny steps, causing him to turn and putting herself between him and the horse. "He came home in the middle of the night. He does not seem to have come on his horse. Perhaps Señora Lynch sent him in her landau. What do you think?" She felt caught between wanting to inveigle him into revealing information and the pit of her stomach urging her to escape.

"All very interesting," he said, taking a step closer. "Did they say what Señora Lynch was looking for when she came to visit?"

She hugged her towel closer. "No. Do you know? What is señora trying to get back?"

"That is not your business." He reached out and grabbed the towel.

She slipped out of it and with one bound reached the horse, gripped the saddle, launched herself on to his back, and kicked his sides. The horse charged forward.

The comandante shouted, "Halt, Marengo!" but unlike César when her father commanded him, Menenez's horse kept going. Even a horse understood that Luis Menenez was not the man her father was.

✿

When Salvador heard the horse coming, he looked out across the campo and seeing Xandra's black hair streaming behind her thought she had lost her mind bringing César here. Then he realized she was naked and riding Menenez's stallion.

He snatched up his cane and did his hobbling best to rush to her. She rode straight for him. When she reined in, the horse reared and she slid off into his arms. "*Querida*, what—?" He was breathless. He had not moved that fast in months.

She held him tight and then did the last thing he expected: she laughed.

Her mother came running from the house, and soon they were all laughing, though Salvador did not know why.

"What happened?" he demanded.

"Why are you naked?" Alivia asked.

"I was bathing when he came to find me." She stood there like Venus in a painting. He thought he should avert his eyes, but she was so natural and unself-conscious, she seemed not a woman but part of the loveliness of nature—like the flowers or a beautiful tree.

Her mother kissed her. "Go and dress yourself," she said gently.

Xandra ran, her hair dancing behind her. She could be

Caagüy Pora, the fierce, protective goddess of the forest, he thought. When she had gone, Alivia looked him in the eye, saying more with silence than if she had harangued him.

He put his good foot in the stirrup and pulled himself up onto the horse from the right side. "I will get her things and bring that bastard back his animal." He trotted off, and though he started out full of gall against Menenez, he soon succumbed to the joy of motion astride the beautiful horse. He had not allowed himself this pleasure with César. He had gone to see him just once, when he followed the weeping Xandra down into the arroyo, a place too difficult for a man with a cane. Now he tasted hope. If they outlived this war, Salvador León would ride again, go everywhere, like a comet streaking through the forest, be a centaur. That was what the Indians had thought his Spanish ancestors were when they first saw the Conquistadores astride their steeds. They, who had never seen a man riding a horse, thought they saw one being. He would become that when they were free at last of this terrible war. Salvador the centaur. If they were ever free again.

He rode faster and faster until he found his brother-in-law walking away from the place where he had accosted his own niece. Menenez turned and watched him approach. Salvador then realized he would have to get off the horse and did not have his cane. He would be a cripple again.

He slid down and landed on his good foot, nearly losing his balance as Menenez grabbed the reins and pulled the horse away. He looked with disdain at Salvador's wooden foot.

Salvador wanted to take him by the neck and threaten to kill him if he came near Xandra again. But he knew without thinking it through he would be a dead man if he did. He had betrayed his own soul in the war and had wanted to die but could not. Now, inexplicably, he wanted to live, weakling that he knew himself to be. "I am sorry, Luis," he said in an even voice. "My daughter took it into her head that you meant her harm. I myself cannot imagine that you would risk such a thing. I know my sister and would not want to deal with her if she found out you were sniffing around her niece."

In the hot light filtering through the trees, they looked into each other's eyes. Salvador saw Menenez's hatred, and knew his own glance communicated too much irony and insufficient fear. Fear was the only emotion Menenez really understood: his own fear and the fear he created in others. Salvador thought he should cower. But he could not.

"I will deal with you another time," the comandante said. He mounted his horse and rode away without looking back. Salvador looked around for a stick he could lean on and found nothing. He turned toward home, hobbling without support, pained more that he had not thrashed the comandante to within an inch of his life.

He had hardly taken twenty steps when he saw Alivia bringing him his cane. He held her to him and kissed her with passion. "I am a coward," he said.

"That is absurd."

He could have told her how much of a coward, but he did not. He put his free arm around her shoulders as they walked.

"I think Xandra is pregnant."

He stopped and looked at her. "By whom?" he demanded. She shrugged.

"Not that bastard Menenez?'

"No. What just occurred would not have if he was the one."

"Then who?" He could not imagine.

They walked on, arm in arm.

"I do not care," Alivia said. 'I hope she is." And then after another minute, "I hope she is."

The comandante returned to his office and wished for a squadron such as he had had when Francisco Solano first succeeded his father. In those days, this one-room adobe station had been the command center for the zone. Guardsmen under Menenez's direction brought in recalcitrants and slackers. Now the comandante alone had to carry out López's orders.

He beat his riding crop against the side of his trousers. The slaps became harder when he saw his wife approaching. She had something up her sleeve. Her smart-aleck brother had threatened to tell her about the stupid incident with her niece. As if that little bitch was not asking for it. His best possible course would be to take Salvador for Yotté's murder. But he still had to find those missing items.

His wife crossed the threshold. He turned up the corners of his mouth and greeted her. "What brings you to my humble office, my dear?"

She put her tiny hand in his and smiled. "I had a thought about where you might find those missing papers."

"Really?"

"I just recalled—once, at tea with Señora Lynch, Ricardo recounted how clever people were in creating hiding places for the valuables he was supposed to confiscate."

"Yes. Yes, I know about his war on the jewelry boxes. Get to the point."

She looked as if she might stop speaking, but then she said, "Ricardo mentioned that he had built a cache under the carpet beneath his bed. Perhaps—"

Suddenly, a black-clad rider on a galloping stallion charged up to the door and held out a paper. Menenez hurried to take the message. The rider did not descend but handed the comandante a thick envelope, and sped away in the direction from which he had come.

As with the previous letter, the comandante's name was written in the mariscal's own dangerous hand. Feigning complete calm, Luis Menenez tore open the message. His heart sank. His wife had finally offered useful information, but the mariscal's new orders forced him to postpone taking action on what she said. Menenez was being called immediately to the capital.

෯

Fifteen minutes later, Luis Menenez impatiently watched his wife carefully fold his best shirt and cravat and place them in the dark brown leather saddlebag she had bought him in a fashionable shop in Buenos Aires on their honeymoon. "Hurry, Gilda," he said. "I have no time to waste. The mariscal said I must be there by dawn. Given what the roads are like, riding at night, I will hardly find my way. If there is a storm I will be dead."

Gilda's hands continued their deliberate movements. "You have to take your razor and soap and a mirror, so you can shave before you meet them. You must present yourself well."

He turned his back. "Ridiculous. They have made camp in the hills up in Peribebuy. They will not expect me to look, at six in the morning, as if I am going to a ball. You are holding me up with this nonsense."

She went to his shaving stand and wrapped his shaving things in a linen towel. "Señora Lynch will notice if you are not well-groomed. She puts great store in such things."

"The note said to present myself to the mariscal."

Gilda stuffed the shaving things into a bag and buckled it closed. "She is always involved. You know that."

He agreed but refused to say he feared the Irish trollop. "The command said nothing about la Parisienne." He warmed to a lovely idea. "La Lynch may be losing her hold on him. In the past, she could protect her countrymen from his wrath, but lately the British war experts have been thrown into prison along with everyone else López mistrusts. This may be a private meeting to enlist my help, if he suspects her. Suppose she gave Ricardo something she intends to use against the mariscal to save her own skin? López may want me to find out exactly how she is betraying him."

His wife looked at him wide-eyed. "Could this be?"

"Yes. Now let me get out of here."

She thrust his saddlebag at him. "That must be why he wants you to arrive at such a strange hour."

"He wants to speak to me in secret." He took the bag and strode to the front door. Convinced he was taking a giant step toward his destiny, he strapped the saddlebag to his horse, and made for the north in the waning light of the day.

❦

At ten forty-five the next morning, Comandante Menenez was finally ushered into López's presence. He had arrived, as ordered, before dawn and was left to wait in torment for nearly five hours—during which time he could do nothing but sweat and fail to keep up his hopes. He began his watch freshly shaven and wearing his best shirt and cravat, but by the time he was called, his trousers were rumpled and his armpits soaked. He approached a white tent pitched in a green glen on the edge of a beautiful wood, full of blooming trees and vines.

The scene would have been festive—like the celebration of some charming outdoor ritual to welcome the spring—if it were not for the moaning of miserable, wounded men coming from just beyond the trees, where more than ten thousand of López's ragtag army and his more numerous prisoners were packed into a small town defended only by a single trench incapable of keeping out a family of peccaries, much less the Brazilian army.

Inside the tent, where the laments of the dying could no longer be heard, the outraged comandante found López and his party sitting at a long table covered with snow-white linen, strewn with the remains of a sumptuous breakfast. Their plates had been pushed aside still half ful of eggs and ham. Their high-backed chairs were arranged on the opposite side of the table facing the entrance, as if they were presiding over a gala banquet in their honor. The comandante, who had been offered nothing to eat or drink during his long, anxious morning, bowed to the dictator and his Irish whore who held the mariscal's hand and smiled with her perfect teeth. Worse yet, beside her simpered that womanish Hungarian count, if he actually was the nobleman he claimed to be. He certainly dressed the part.

Menenez hid the hatred and despair La Lynch's presence engendered. "Good morning, Señor Mariscal, Señora." He bowed to each of them. "And to you Señor von Wisner. I hope I find you all in best of health." When the comandante raised his head, López was consulting his gold pocket watch and tapping the toe of his spotless patent leather boot, as if he had been the one kept waiting. Never an imposing figure, he had grown so fat, his skin so gray that it would be hard to take him seriously, but for the burning threat in his small, dark eyes and the certain knowledge that he could condemn anyone in the country to torment and death with a wave of his chubby fingers.

"We are grateful to you for making the long journey," the trollop said. "Your mariscal has something most important to impart to you. Something so confidential he could not entrust it to a messenger." While she spoke she looked at López expectantly.

Luis could not help but eye von Wisner. Why was he to hear this secret information?

López followed Menenez's gaze and raised an eyebrow but did not ask the foreigner to leave. "About the unfortunate death of our dear Ricardo," he said and then picked something from between his front teeth with the nail of his little finger.

The comandante straightened his spine. "I am giving the investigation my full attention," he said. The smirk on von Wisner's face made him want to kill the man.

"That is just our concern," López said with a knowing look to La Lynch. "We wish to alter the direction of your inquiries."

"Alter?" Menenez worked to keep any hint of annoyance out of his voice "I assure you, my mariscal, you can count on me completely. There is noth—"

"Yes. Yes." López's tone hid none of his impatience. His thick sausage fingers stroked his heavy black beard. "We have decided to forego your search for the missing government items, and we wish you to leave Ricardo's distressed sisters completely out of your investigation. Do not disturb them in any way. Señora Lynch wishes to protect them from further pain. You must find Ricardo's murderer with dispatch but without bothering his sisters. Do you understand?"

The comandante understood the words but puzzlement plagued his heart. Recovering La Lynch's missing valuables had been their primary objective. They were dropping the most important part of the investigation. "Yes, of course. Those lovely girls have suffered mightily. I, in fact, just the other day, sent my wife to bring them some of our very best food—to alleviate their pain as best we can."

La Lynch's alabaster hand tightened over the back of López's fat, hairy fist. "You are not understanding me, Menenez," López said, his voice cold and harsh. "I forbid you any contact whatsoever with those girls. And that goes for Señora Menenez as well. On pain of our deepest displeasure. Is this clear?"

The comandante bowed low again, holding his body stiff so they would not see him quake. "I understand completely," he said as firmly as he could.

"Continue your search for Yotté's killer. Bring him to me as soon as is humanly possible."

As Luis Menenez backed away, López looked him in the eye. "We will be aware if you do not comply." This was the best the comandante might expect by way of a farewell from the dictator.

La Lynch waved at him with that small hand that had held the mariscal's throughout the interview. "Thank you for coming," she said, as if to a guest leaving a garden party.

Luis Menenez backed through the tent flap held open by a man in a waiter's uniform, and forced himself to stride confidently across to the tree where he had left his horse. He mounted the beast and turned him south at a gallop.

This was a catastrophe. What was López playing at now? He no longer trusted his comandante, who had never wavered in his support. Under the blazing noon sun, he rode the long distance to Santa Caterina, unable to force aside the insult of having gone such a long way to hear such frustrating orders. That Irish woman was up to something, but he could not think what. Clearly, if López did not want him to look for the documents, they had already been found, probably in the hiding place Gilda remembered too late. With their valuables back in their possession, what did López and Lynch care about Yotté's silly sisters?

The clopping of the horse's hooves on the road beat in his brain. He came to only one clear conclusion: following his orders was his only hope. There was only one person whose arrest could profit him. He could only hope in the process he might get the goods on La Lynch.

13

Late that afternoon, after the comandante had re-taken his post in the comandancia, but had not re-gained his composure, a muggy wind blew in and enervated the padre, who awaited his friends in his sitting room. He opened the shutters of his unglazed window and looking out saw Maria Claudia walking away, across the field between the church and the woods. She was avoiding coming into his house until the others were there. He did not blame her. He had been a fool. Now that he had shown her the part of his heart she did not want to see, she would rather wait out there in clouds of mosquitoes than be alone with him. And how was he to face her when she came in? She would not shirk her duty by stay-ing away completely, but she no longer trusted being alone with him. "Maria Claudia," he whispered her name to the heavy air in his room.

He had said his regular Sunday mass that morning, though his soul felt dead. He was supposed to be in a state of grace to consecrate the host. It had been more than a year since he had seen another priest to whom he could confess. Ever since he had given his flock his fateful counsel, he found himself further and further removed from the certainties that ought to mark his beliefs. He was lost in a jungle of conflict and desire and doubt. Today's mass gave comfort to his parishioners, he hoped, but none to him.

He turned away from the window and did what any Paraguayan would when he had a troubled heart: make tea and hope. He busied himself spooning the yerba maté leaves into gourds. Stimulating and comforting, this tea was the country's most plentiful product. It grew on trees found only in Paraguay, was exported everywhere, and had made the country rich. That they had an ample supply despite the war helped them survive. Those who had survived. Their leaders had used the riches made from exporting maté to buy arms and fight for their own glory. Bastards.

He was thinking about this to avoid thinking of her. How he longed to grasp her to him, to make love to her, to take care of her, to drown his weakness in her strength. He looked out again at her in the distance, tiny and still. Then he saw her wave. He started to wave back before he realized she saluted not him, but Salvador, Alivia, and Xandra. Xandra appeared first and took Maria Claudia's arm, walking quickly, putting distance between them and her parents, who followed at Salvador's pace. The young women's heads inclined to each other, sharing a secret. The back of his neck burned. Could Maria Claudia be telling Xandra what he had done, what he had said?

No, she would never do that. He was certain. Still, when he went to his back door, he worried for the first time in his priesthood whether his parishioners saw him for the sinner he was.

When she came in, she glanced quickly at him and took a

chair at the table, sitting so still she seemed to be trying to be invisible. When she was a child, she used to think these rose-wood chairs in the priest's house were thrones for kings and queens. Even now, if she sat all the way back, her feet would not touch the floor.

He did not allow his eyes to linger on her, yet he felt her presence on his skin. He concentrated on serving the tea. By the time Alivia and Salvador arrived, the hot water had been poured into the maté gourds. They took their places around the table. He sat next to her, knowing that it would make her uncomfortable, but unable to resist.

Maria Claudia was relieved that the padre took the chair next to hers. It would save her having to feel his eyes on her from across the table. "I think I should begin," she said before anyone else had a chance to offer information. She told them of her treatment by Martita and that she had learned nothing new. She refused to look at Xandra, who had spent the whole walk across the campo demanding that they meet at midnight and sneak into the casa Yotté.

"Strange that Martita, a friend, should act that way," Salvador said.

"People do strange things when they have suffered losses," Padre Gregorio said. "Martita has never had to make an im-portant decision in her life. Now, she has to take responsibility for herself and her sister, who is sort of—" He paused.

"Who is sort of dumb," Xandra said with that annoyed face she made when other people were being too polite to speak the truth. "But the answers to our questions lie more in the casa Yotté than anywhere." She gave Maria Claudia a questioning look.

Maria Claudia stuck out her tongue and was glad the pa-dre could see only the back of her head.

Alivia pointed a mother's warning finger at Xandra. "We can do nothing about that."

Xandra pretended to examine the pretty painting of the Holy Family on the padre's wall. She hated that her mother could read her mind.

Alivia pulled her chair forward. "I have been thinking about the way the corpse looked," she said, all business. "I think I can explain the odd way the mud looked on the back of Ricardo's clothing. Suppose it was two people who carried it? If they were not strong enough to hold it off the ground between them, they would have had to let it drag on the ground." She wanted the murderer to be two people, not her mad son, who would have acted alone.

"That could have been a lot of people," Xandra said. "Unlike the rest of us who are starving, Ricardo had plenty of meat on his bones."

"Josefina and Pablo, for instance," Maria Claudia blurted out.

Salvador held out his hands in disbelief. "Why would Josefina kill Ricardo? He gave food to her and Pablo."

The padre leaned forward, careful not to let his arm touch Maria Claudia's. "Josefina would not destroy her meal ticket. Whoever killed Ricardo did it out of hate. We saw that in the stab wounds."

Maria Claudia said, "Who would have been that angry at Ricardo?"

"The comandante," the padre said, half question, half statement.

"Or Gilda." Alivia sounded much more certain, "if her love affair with him went sour."

"Who would have helped her?"

"Gaspár," Alivia and Maria Claudia said in unison.

"She had a reason," the padre said. They all looked at him, expecting him to say more, but he let his face go blank—the way he would in the confessional. Gilda's love affair was known to them now, but his conscience prickled at discussing it openly.

"She would not have," Xandra said. She pushed her chair back from the table, got up and paced to the window and back. "I know her. If she was sleeping with Ricardo, she was just playing both ends against the middle. Paraguay is going to lose the war, right? She wants to end up with a powerful man. Her husband and Yotté were her two choices. Until she knew which would come out ahead, she would not kill either one. And if you ask me, Ricardo was in the better position." Her father looked hurt by what she said. No matter how nasty people were, he wanted to think good things about them.

"I still think Señora Lynch's missing valuables must have something to do with it," Salvador said, changing the subject. "I have some information about that." He looked around at his daughter standing behind him near the window and indicated her chair. She put her hands on her hips and glared at him, but then after a couple of seconds, she sat down. "I spoke to Manuela," he said. He could not look at Alivia. She had accused him of making love to Manuela. And he had not. Yet. "She saw two men deliver four heavy trunks to the casa Yotté. Those trunks could have something to do with what La Lynch is looking for."

"Four trunks? I had heard there are just some government documents missing." Maria Claudia said.

"Was this before Ricardo was murdered?" the padre asked.

"Yes, four," he said. "If they were documents, there were a lot of them. And no, it was not before Ricardo died."

"Still," Xandra said, "if they were involved somehow, those men could have killed Ricardo." Impatience continued to tinge her voice. With documents involved, Tomás could be the killer. If he was, most of what he had told her would have to be lies.

"If they could carry heavy trunks, they would have been able to carry the body without dragging it," Alivia said. What was wrong with Xandra, she wondered, that she kept coming up with impossible ideas?

They all looked around at one another, puzzled as to what to think next.

"I doubt the trunks contain documents," Maria Claudia said. "What could be in such papers to make them so important to Señora Lynch?"

"They could contain secrets," Salvador said, "useful to keep power, to gain it, to blackmail someone."

Maria Claudia shook her head. "Four trunks full of secrets?"

"Maria Claudia is right," Padre Gregorio said emphatically. "How could documents be so critical at this point in the war?"

Alivia held up her hands. "Suppose they incriminate La Lynch and López? When the war is over, people might want to prosecute them with that evidence. They may be trying to keep them out of the wrong hands."

Salvador shook his head. "If it were that, they would just burn them. Besides, López has killed so many. His deeds are well known. I had a passing thought that the mariscal could have killed Yotté because he suspected him of conspiracy. Then I realized he hauls in anyone he wants. He is a madman." Salvador gulped as soon as those last words left his mouth. Not even here among these safe people did one speak such treason in full voice.

He saw fear in their faces too. They all looked around at the windows and doors.

Xandra alone remained distracted by the thought that all

those documents were just the sort of reason Tomás might have come to kill Yotté. She had to find out what was in those trunks.

Moved by fear of being overheard, the others brought their heads closer together.

"Be careful," the padre whispered. "At any rate, I agree. The war is a lost cause. López and the señora must be planning how they will survive. Most likely what is in those trunks has something to do with that."

"The señora must be thinking that way, even if the mariscal is not," Maria Claudia said. "Maybe she gave Ricardo their means of escape."

There was an intake of breath around the table.

"Like gold," Xandra said.

"And the jewels from our statue of the virgin," Salvador put in.

"That must be it," Maria Claudia said. They were all nodding.

Xandra could not believe how simple they were being. "What is wrong with you? Manuela said they were bringing the trunks into the house. If Señora Lynch gave them to Ricardo, the men would be taking them *away*, not delivering them."

This quieted them.

"Perhaps Manuela was mistaken, or I did not understand properly," Salvador said. "Perhaps I should ask her again to be sure." He did not look at Alivia.

"If Ricardo was hiding four trunks of gold," the padre said, "that would be a very powerful reason for a lot of people to kill him. Salvador, go back to Manuela and make sure of which way they were going." The padre did not understand why Alivia gave him a dirty look, or why Xandra threw Maria Claudia such a determined one.

※

Comandante Luis Menenez stood with his back to the wall of the priest's house. Weeds and brush choked what had been flower beds when the padre had had someone to keep nature at bay in his garden. Now, after three years of war, the thicket was dense enough to hide a man in broad daylight. Slowly, trying to imagine himself as the hands of a clock, he made his way around the corner of the building so that he could over-hear the conversation inside.

Gaspár had been out foraging and had seen Maria Claudia cross the campo behind the priest's house. Soon the León family met her, and they all crossed to the priest's back door. Good man that he was, Gaspár had sped to the comandancia to tell his *patrón*. As Menenez suspected, his brother-in-law and the priest were up to something. Gaspár had offered to come and spy on them, but the comandante, though exhausted from his hard ride in the noonday sun, seized the opportunity.

His wife's relatives would never spy for him, but his brother-in-law, the padre, and that overly pious war widow, Maria Claudia, were the only people in the village intelligent enough to outwit a donkey. If anyone could figure out who killed Yotté, it would be them.

The room was silent for several seconds after he approached the window. He was about to conclude Gaspár had been mistaken when that virago Xandra said something that turned his sweat to steam. She suggested that his wife had been sleeping with Yotté. His body stiffened at the insult of such an outrageous lie. He stifled an urge to put his head through the window and bark at her. Then he heard the bitch's explanation for why Gilda would take up such a liaison. The heat of his anger turned to ice. His ambitious wife was capable of just such a betrayal.

He could barely tear himself back from his enraged thoughts to hear what they were saying only six or eight feet from where he was standing. They were discussing who had murdered Yotté—a man Menenez now thought he himself should have killed. But not as idle gossip. They spoke in earnest, like a council of judges with the power to punish a lawbreaker.

His infuriated heart screamed at him to barge in and arrest them all for treason. Or to rush off and kill his wife for betraying him. Or to enter the room and kill all of them on the spot to blot out what they seemed to know, which shamed him to the core.

Somehow more of their words seeped into his boiling brain: four trunks in the Yotté house might contain gold. Those knuckleheads in the café were right. And these sanctimonious upstarts knew about it. While he had been looking for papers hidden in a dead man's pockets, they had found out about trunks that were likely filled with the national treasure of Paraguay. Then his brother-in-law, overconfident as always, blurted out that the mariscal was a madman—a statement that would condemn him to the firing squad. Luis Menenez almost smiled at his stupidity. Even among fast friends, one risked death speaking treason in Paraguay.

He listened intently, but their voices became hushed; he could make out only the sibilant sound of their whispering. He moved closer to the unglazed window the better to catch their words, but that stirred up chattering crickets and calling birds in the thicket that drowned out the voices of the conspirators. *Mierda!* He stewed in his own rage and frustration until their chairs scraped the padre's brick floor and their clearly audible farewells drifted out. The only comment of interest in their good-byes was a name: Manuela. They had gotten information she had refused to give her comandante.

He barely had time to slip around the corner and out of sight before they were on top of him.

※

As they left, the padre said good-bye, taking each one by the hand as he would if they were leaving church after Sunday mass. Until he got to Maria Claudia. He backed away to give her a bit of room, but she was determined not to see rejection in that motion. She had given him reason to think that she wanted him to stay clear of her. But she did not. Not anymore. She smiled and looked into his eyes as she never had before. "*Nos vemos,*" she said.

"Yes, I'll see you," he responded.

Salvador and Xandra went through the church toward the plaza. Alivia headed out to the campo. Maria Claudia skipped to catch up with her. "May I walk with you?" she asked.

"Certainly," Alivia said. "I have some honey I can share. Come to my house."

"Thank you." In the past she would have refused to take food from anyone, but not now. Xandra's words had been ringing in her head all night and all day: "Come on, be a person who does something." Maria Claudia had decided what that something would be.

"Alivia, how can a woman tell when she is fertile? Alberta told me that you explained to her how to avoid getting pregnant by not—er—doing it on certain days. That must mean certain days are better if a girl wants a baby."

Alivia stopped and looked her in the face in a way that

made her blush. "I can tell you, but using your cycle is not fool-proof."

"But if a girl wanted a baby . . ." Maria Claudia let the thought complete itself without words.

"If the baby is meant to be, it helps to try at the right time."

"So tell me," Maria Claudia said as they tramped through the waist-high weeds.

The comandante lounged against a jacaranda tree in the plaza and smelled fear and outrage in his own sweat. He wanted to rush home and kill his wife, scream so loud they would hear him in Buenos Aires. But he held still and watched his wife's niece and his brother-in-law exit the church and embrace before parting like a perfect father and daughter, instead of the miserable gossips and spies they really were.

The girl called out something about wild oranges and sped away across the square. Salvador limped in the other direction. He stuck his hand in his pocket and took out something wrapped in a square of white cloth.

The comandante held his place, almost invisible in the dappled shade, and watched until Salvador was nearly out of sight on the road to the forge. Luis Menenez put on his hat, and feigning a complete lack of urgency, followed.

Salvador made his boringly slow way directly to Manuela's. As soon as he was through her door, Menenez ran as silently as he could diagonally across the field to the back of the house and for the second time that day, took a position next to an unglazed window to listen to the conversation within.

To his surprise, they exchanged only pleasantries and then fell quiet. He heard only the scrape of a chair and rustling noises.

And then a groan of pleasure from the girl. Good God. Salvador was fucking her. His pure and holy family man of a brother-in-law was going around getting bastards. And not just doing his duty as the padre had urged, but from the sound of it, with great pleasure to himself.

Luis Menenez, who had not had sex with anyone for weeks, found himself with an enormous erection, and try as he might he could not think the thing away. Not even by concentrating on how his wife who gave him only matter-of-fact liberty to exercise his marital rights while she was—if that bitch Xandra with her defiant, glistening eyes and heavy breasts was correct—screwing Yotté.

The comandante unbuttoned his fly and in anger and desperation and lip-biting silence, relieved his own urges while he listened to Salvador León and his whore Manuela groan with pleasure on the other side of the wall.

෯

In the drowsy heat of late afternoon, Salvador left Manuela curled up in her black wool hammock. Before she fell asleep, he had whispered to her the question about the trunks and gotten her reply. He dressed and kissed her good-bye. He divided what little food he carried for the boy and left half of it for her. He would have to feed her now. Somehow, he would find enough for everyone. He went and kissed her again on her bare shoulder and left without waking her.

He followed the road, beautiful with flowers, toward the boy's cabin. Manuela was young, her skin smooth, her limbs strong and supple. Yet there had been no lust in their coupling. Desire. Intense pleasure. Gorgeous relief. But they had also reached for something greater than the hunger of their bodies. Their longing was for new life. For him, for her too, he was sure, it felt sacramental.

The golden glow of the setting sun filtered through the leaves overhead. He summoned a ray from the bright sky to bathe her in light as he had seen one shine in a painting in the church in Caacupé. Give her a baby, he prayed more to the sun than to God. With his mind he tried to pull its bright energy down on her smooth belly. He turned to see if he could conjure such a life-giving ray from one of the puffy white clouds that sailed in the deep blue sky.

It was then that he saw Luis Menenez slip behind a tree.

14

Maria Claudia shouted, "No!" so loudly that Xandra clamped her hand over her mouth. Then Maria Claudia did what Xandra never expected her to do. She bit her finger, hard enough that she screamed. And then immediately grabbed it and kissed it and apologized. "Oh, Xandra, forgive me." And then she said what Xandra never expected her to say, "Okay. I will do it."

Now Xandra was the one who was afraid, but she could not show her fear. "Good," she said with more conviction than she felt.

Since the clock in the bell tower of the church was just a face whose internal workings had long since been taken to make ammunition, there was no way for them to fix the hour when they would meet. Already the setting sun bathed the trees of the plaza in a rosy light. They agreed that after bedtime that night, Xandra would go to Maria Claudia's house.

"We will have to wear dark clothing," Xandra said as they parted. It was not something country girls in Paraguay ever had had much of. They wore white, made of homespun with edging they embroidered in red and black. "I will bring you something."

Once home, Xandra had a hard time hiding her jitters while she waited for her parents to go to sleep. They had returned home separately through the forest and looked exhausted. "Where have you been?" Xandra asked them.

"Nowhere," her father answered, but Xandra saw it was a lie. Her mother held up a bundle of grasses that looked like weeds. After they ate a thin porridge of maize and whatever herbs Alivia had gleaned from the bundle, she kissed them good night and went to wait in her hammock until she was sure they were asleep. Then she crept into her brothers' bedroom and in the nearly total darkness felt inside the wardrobe for a pair of her brother Aleixo's trousers and a shirt. She took an extra set of boy's clothes for Maria Claudia, and then crept back to her room and changed. She left by her window and, tortured by the mosquitoes, made her way as swiftly as the dim moonlight would allow to Maria Claudia's door.

Maria Claudia again surprised her by donning the trousers without argument.

"What changed your mind about doing this?" Xandra could not resist asking.

Maria Claudia paused for a moment. "It was what you said yesterday. 'Be a person who does something.' It woke me up, made me see that my life is sterile, that I am turning timid and dry—like an old lady." She threaded the sash from her skirt through the loops on Aleixo's old pants that were way too big in the waist.

Xandra's hands went to her mouth. "Did I say that? I am sorry. Sometimes I say the meanest things."

Maria Claudia looked at her in the candlelight. She was

tying her sash around her waist with a tight knot. "I have spent my whole life praying for things, and I never had the sense to pray for something big and important—only tiny things, and even those God never sent me. If we are all going to starve to death anyway. . . ." Her voice trailed off, as she pulled Aleixo's shirt over her head and posed as if she were showing off. Then she took Xandra's hands. "I am scared to death of this, but I will force myself to do it. The only thing I am going to pray for from now on is courage."

Xandra, who had never thought about courage at all, now prayed for it too.

They looked out of Maria Claudia's front door to be sure that no one was about in the plaza and then, in silence, made their way to the wall of the Yotté garden. Xandra showed Maria Claudia how to entwine her fingers to boost her up to the top of the wall.

"Wait," Maria Claudia whispered. "How will you get me up?"

"Help me get to the top of the wall. I will go in on my own."

"No, you will not," Maria Claudia said, as if she were in charge. "I know the inside of this house. Besides, once you have looked in Ricardo's room for the trunks and are ready to leave, how will you get up the other side of the wall? It is as smooth and high as this side."

Xandra let the notion sink in. "You are right. Get me to the top and then I will reach down and pull you up."

As thin and tiny as Maria Claudia was, hoisting her was easy.

Once they were both at the top, Xandra lowered herself down the other side, scraping the skin on her arms as she let herself drop the last two feet to the ground. She stood close to the wall and tapped her right shoulder. "Reach down with your foot and put it here," she whispered.

Maria Claudia tried, but her leg did not reach. She slipped along the wall in the process and let out a small cry. They both clamped their hands over their mouths and stood very still for a long time, praying with all their might that they had not roused anyone inside. The garden was silent except for the ceaseless trill of the cicadas. The air was damp and cold at this hour. The pale rays of the moon gave them just enough light to see the bushes and the patio table and chairs near the house. A lizard ran into the underbrush and made them almost jump out of their skins. Eventually, they got up the nerve to cross the patio and slip into the house.

Though their hearts pounded, they easily found their way through the parlor and across the hall to Ricardo's room. The latch of his door did not click as Maria Claudia had feared it would, and the hinge did not squeak. Not until many, many days later did Maria Claudia realize the now-dead Ricardo must himself have kept his hinges oiled—since he was in the habit of letting another man's wife silently into this room in the middle of the night.

His bedroom was large, with windows lining the wall opposite the door. The open drapes admitted enough bluish light for them to see four trunks lining the left-hand wall. Xandra went to them and felt around the lids. "I cannot see clearly, but they seem to be nailed shut," she whispered in Maria Claudia's ear. She ran her fingertips over them again. "They are belted with heavy leather straps. It is impossible to look inside them. We came for nothing."

"It is not gold, as we suspected," Maria Claudia said. "The trunks would be hidden away if they contained treasure."

Xandra took the leather handle on the side of one trunk

and hefted it. She could barely lift it an inch. It would take two strong men to move it. "Whatever it is, it weighs a lot." She turned toward the other side of the room. "I want to find the secret hiding place," she said.

She went to Ricardo's big matrimonial bed that stood against the opposite wall. A thick European carpet lay under it.

"Xandra!" Maria Claudia's whisper was soft but urgent. "We have seen the trunks. We have to go before someone hears us."

"One minute. Just one minute." Xandra knelt and put her hand under the carpet. Her fingertips found a depression in the wood floor with a metal ring nestled in it. "There is a hiding place," she whispered over her shoulder.

"Come away, now!"

"Shh!" Xandra rose and started to roll back the carpet. "Here. Roll it back the rest of the way while I pick up the end of the bed."

"Are you crazy?" Maria Claudia's voice shook. "What do you hope to find? The trunks are over there. They are locked, and we cannot open them. *Terminado.*"

"I am just curious. Come on. We are here. We might as well find out."

"You are crazy," Maria Claudia said, but she got down on her hands and knees.

Xandra grasped the underside of the footboard and gave every ounce of her strength to lift the heavy bed and hold it, while Maria Claudia rolled back the rug.

Once the rug was out of the way, Xandra let the heavy bed down easy, got down on her stomach, and reached under to lift the trapdoor as high as the small space under the bed would allow. These hinges did squeal. Xandra held her breath a second and then reached and felt around the hole she had revealed. The space was almost as wide as the bed. Her fingertips discovered another trunk and another. She wriggled further until her head and shoulders were under the trapdoor. She reached in as far as she could. Four. There were four more trunks secreted under the bed. She tried to lift the one nearest her by its handle. It did not budge.

"We have to get out of here. Now!" Maria Claudia's voice carried a note of hysteria. She went to the window that looked onto the interior patio of the house. Silently she returned. "Now, Xandra."

"Yes. Yes." The door squealed again when she let it close.

They rolled the rug back into place, left everything as they had found it, and slipped quickly across the patio to the wall where they had dropped into the garden. Xandra turned to Maria Claudia. "Boost me up," she whispered into her ear.

"Wait," Maria Claudia's voice was as quiet as the rustle of a breeze through the leaves of the orange tree overhead. She pulled Xandra back into the dark corner behind the tree and held her hand in a crushing grip.

Across the garden, on the opposite side from Ricardo's bedroom, they saw the glow of a candle and two ghostly figures in white.

Their hearts thudding, they flattened themselves against the dark wall and hardly dared breathe.

"I heard something. I know I did." It was Estella's voice, petulant and insisting.

The shorter of the two—Martita—raised the candle over her head. "Look. Do you see anything?" She turned with the candle this way and that, making a small circle of light at the edge of the garden near the entrance to the parlor. "Nothing," she said with disdain. "No Plata Yvyguy. No headless dog digging up the garden looking for buried treasure." She lowered the candle.

Estella wrapped her shawl around herself. "I know I heard something."

Martita turned and moved toward the doorway. "You were dreaming."

"I was not asleep."

"We have to rest," Martita said in a loud insistent voice. "We have a lot to do tomorrow." She turned and carried the candle back into the house. Estella followed her.

Xandra held Maria Claudia's hand tight until the candlelight disappeared. They waited another hundred beats of her heart. Only then did they dare to move.

When they were safely over the wall, Maria Claudia laughed softly and hugged Xandra. "That was wonderful," Maria Claudia said.

"I was scared to death," Xandra said.

Maria Claudia was still laughing under her breath. "For the first time in my life, I enjoyed being invisible."

"What is that supposed to mean?" Xandra asked.

"Nothing." Maria Claudia hugged her again.

"There are eight trunks," Xandra said quizzically.

"Maybe the others are just some old trunks the Yotté family has had all along."

"Hidden like that? I doubt it. And they were full of something really heavy. Whatever it is, it is important."

The next morning, Alivia sipped maté and wondered why her husband and her daughter slept so late. She rose and went to the cool springhouse where they used to store quantities of food, when they had quantities of food. Now she had only a few eggs saved over the last several days. She took two. Salvador needed something to restore him and Xandra, if Alivia was right, would need extra food to grow a healthy child. As she walked back to the hearth, a light rain started to fall. It was what they had been waiting for—the water that would start the crop of corn. Their last harvest had been meager because she and Xandra were able to till only about an acre on their own with no ox to pull the plow. The army had taken all the oxen. For nothing, Salvador had told her, since they all died trying to pull cannons and heavy pallets of shot through brush and mud for miles on end, while the women, starving as they were, had to be the oxen on the farms.

Alivia made the usual porridge with some of their small supply of cornmeal. When Salvador finally emerged from bed, looking more rested than he had in years, she cracked one of the eggs into the center of a bowl of hot cornmeal mush, and served it to him with a few grains of precious salt. He gave her a quizzical look. "To what do I owe the honor of this feast?"

She touched his tousled hair. "It is going to be a rainy day—a day to stay indoors and recoup your strength."

He searched her eyes for more meaning than she had intended, but then he savored his breakfast slowly and wiped the bowl clean with his forefinger, licking up every bit. Lightning flashed. The first thick drops of the storm hammered the broad leaves of the rubber plants outside the window. Alivia closed the shutters, but the drumming of rain still filled the air.

While he ate, Xandra came in, full of energy. She wolfed down her special breakfast, thanked her mother with a kiss, and insisted, despite the weather, that she had to go out and care for the horse. Their discouraging words, meant to hold her, just chased her toward the door and trailed after her as she drew a poncho over her head and sped off into what was now a full downpour. That horse, Alivia thought, had something to do with Xandra's lover. But she did not care what. She cared only that her daughter had found someone.

She stood next to the table where Salvador sat and held herself still, hoping with her whole body for his love. In the past, on days like this, if the children were at school and the farmhands all snuggled in their cottages, they would go back to bed and make love slowly to the sound of rain on the roof tiles. Though she could not bring herself to ask for it, she wanted that today, just him as he had always been.

He stood up slowly and walked without his cane the few steps to the tall, dark wood cupboard where they kept the crockery. He reached up to the top and took down his guitar that he had not touched for years. He brought the instrument back to his chair and sat with it across his lap. He took the tail of his white homespun shirt and dusted the guitar. Watching behind him, seeing his broad back as he hunched over the guitar, hearing his voice as he hummed the notes to tune it brought a lump of joy to her throat and anticipation to her loins. This house used to be filled with music, as every house was. And dancing. Paraguay was a country of music makers. Yet it had been years since any of them had heard a song except in church—where they sang with all their hearts to God, who did not hear their pleas to end their punishment. She wanted Salvador's music and then she wanted him.

He cleared his throat, struck a chord, and tapped his foot to a gentle beat. He began to sing. His once-clear, almost an-gelic tenor voice rasped as if it was rusty, but his notes were true. He sang "Navidad," a Christmas hymn. Its melody had always sounded like a love song, and it thrilled her to think he sang because they had broken the dam of his love, and it would flow now like the notes of the song. Her heart sang too, swelling with love for him.

"José! Maria! La luna clara," he sang. *"Venga pastores del campo,"* calling for the shepherds to come witness the birth. The longing in his voice went right up her spine.

Then suddenly her tears of joy turned hot. She saw it. This was not about his love for her. He sang about the birth of a baby. This was the Salvador who loved nothing better than making babies with her. And now? Now? What if this song was about a child of his? It must be that.

A dark pain seared into her throat that had been filled with love a moment before. She put her hands over her ears to block out the passion and beauty of his singing and ran silently from the room to the bedroom where her sons had slept and threw herself on Mariano's narrow cot. She clamped her hand over her mouth to keep in the wailing that made her chest feel as if it would explode. Her body convulsed with the anguish of her lost babies, her damaged, perhaps irreparable Aleixo, her own lost fertility. Salvador sang for his baby, but no baby of his could ever again be hers.

Her heart blackened. Pictures of him making love to Manuela seared into her mind. She did not want to deny him the right to have another son, strong and whole. But she could not banish the poisonous jealousy that had entered her heart. He is mine, she thought, I want him to be only mine. Outside, the storm, straining toward its full force, whipped the vines that grew on the walls of the house and beat them against the shutters.

After a while the music stopped, and the thump of his cane

went to the front door. Out to brave the muddy roads. Toward that woman. She always knew it would be Manuela. He liked his women strong. Alivia bit hard on her knuckles, but she could not make them hurt enough to blot out the searing agony in her heart.

✿

By the time Salvador arrived at the priest's house, he was soaked through his poncho and his shirt. He rapped his cane on the door rather than pulling the cord for the bell. He had come to prepare himself to die, to confess the truth about himself before he did.

The padre looked haggard when he opened the door. Salvador had heard of religious people whipping themselves with chains to punish themselves for their sins. Salvador could not imagine this lively priest doing such a thing, but the padre's eyes betrayed suffering from within.

He brought Salvador to his sitting room. Its few pieces of simple furniture were of beautiful orangewood, rosewood, or cedar. A harp and a guitar stood in one corner. The padre had the only house in the village, except for the comandante and Gilda's, that had pictures on the walls. They had Francisco Solano López, who looked like the pig he was, and that beautiful La Lynch, who was not the dictator's wife. The priest had San Ignacio and Santiago.

Though the day was warm as well as wet, the padre offered him a seat near the fire and gave him a towel to dry his face and a cup of hot maté to warm his stomach. Salvador looked down and saw he had trailed red mud across the padre's tile floor. It looked like pools of congealed blood.

"Don't worry about that," the padre said, as if Salvador had spoken an apology. "Tell me what brings you here on a day like this."

"Padre, I am in grave danger." Salvador looked not at the priest, but into the fire. "My brother-in-law, the comandante, is going to arrest me. I have to run away."

The priest took a step forward and put his hand on Salvador's shoulder. "What makes you think so?"

"I saw him sneaking around behind me yesterday. That could mean only that the government wants me, or Menenez thinks it does."

"How can I protect you?"

Salvador looked up into the padre's kind blue eyes. What could two half-starving men do against the power the comandante wielded? Salvador pulled the towel around his shoulders and hugged it to him. A shutter banged somewhere in the house. He told the priest about Aleixo. "I am afraid he may be the one who killed Yotté," he said at last.

"But that may not be true," the padre exclaimed.

"That will not matter if the comandante finds him. He will take the boy."

"How, if he does not know about him?"

"If Menenez spies on me, he will find Aleixo," Salvador insisted. He looked away from the priest. "It was only by chance that I saw him following me. He has asked Manuela why I have been so often in the area of the forest where the boy is hidden. You know how the government is. They spy on everyone."

"Everyone but whoever killed Ricardo," the priest said.

They shook their heads. Salvador grasped the priest's arm. "I do not trust myself to do what is right."

The padre looked at him, incredulous. "Then you are not the Salvador I have known all these years."

Salvador lowered his head. "I am not. You must hide the boy from me. If I know where he is, he is dead."

Padre Gregorio grabbed a chair and dragged it near. He sat down and looked at Salvador with the concern of a confessor. "My friend, I still trust you. Tell me why you no longer trust yourself." He waited.

After a few moments, Salvador unclenched his fists and felt his body sag, unable to protect himself from his own disgust. He turned away from the priest and gave up his secret. Like vomit. Searing shame poured out of him, and he saw his vile self in the story as he told it.

It was after the Battle of Tuyutí—where the ground was so littered with corpses they had had to tread on dead bodies in their retreat. Their colonel had joined the few surviving of Salvador's platoon with the remnants of another regiment, men from San Pedro they did not know. They had had nothing to eat for days but a few bites of putrid horse meat that Salvador could hardly swallow. With no *caña* or aguardiente for consolation, they were drinking sickeningly sweet liquor they had made from tiny wild oranges. In the middle of night, completely drunk, he had gone away from the others a few yards into a little copse to think of Alivia and masturbate. But he could not come. He had shouted at the top of his voice at his limp penis, "This war is shit. This war is shit. I hate this fucking war. I hate you too, López. I hate you and your fucking war."

He must have fallen asleep after that. In the morning, he awoke, his head throbbing, to kicks at his back and legs. His sergeant took him at knifepoint to the colonel, who said, "You were heard making a treasonous speech in the night."

Vaguely, through the haze of the drunken memory and the blinding headache the alcohol had left, he remembered what he had shouted. He stood in the attitude of salute that he had learned when he first entered the army, with his hands together in front of him. To do the salute properly, he should have been clutching his cap, but he no longer had a cap. He feigned an innocent look, like a schoolboy denying speaking behind the teacher's back. "It was not me."

"Then who was it?" the colonel demanded.

He smiled meekly.

"Do you know?"

He said nothing. He knew how to play this game with the teacher. But instead of the rod his schoolmaster would have used, the colonel gave him the Uruguayana. They sat him on the ground, tied his legs together and his hands behind his back, palms facing out. They put a musket under his knees and bent his legs around it and tied his ankles to his thighs. Then they put a bundle of three muskets behind his neck. With thongs of leather, two sergeants tied the muskets behind his head to the one under his knees, and pulled them tight, forcing his knees up and his head down. They bound him in that position. He felt the bones in his spine crack from the pressure.

"My feet went numb first," he told the priest, "and all I could think was we could have won the battle at Tuyutí if we had those weapons and proper bullets. As the pain grew, I tried to count the sounds I heard, to name and number the insects crawling on the ground under my face, anything to take my mind off the excruciating pain burning in my body. When numbness reached my knees and my hands, all I could think about was the agony.

"They asked me over and over. 'Who shouted in the night? Was it you?' Like a coward, I denied it and denied it. "If it was not you, who? If not you, who? Give the name of the person who shouted treason in the night.' I said nothing. Nothing. Then they untied me; I thought I had beaten them. But the next day they tied me again in the same position and kept me there—it must have been two days. My whole body shook, and I was soaked with sweat. The bastards left me there in the sun and the rain—until I had to give them someone or die of the pain. I swear I did not want to. I could hardly speak; my tongue had swollen in my mouth. My throat was on fire. 'Vargas.' I gave them the name of a man I disliked from the other regiment. 'Vargas.'"

Then they untied him. He was hardly able to unbend, much less walk after days tied to the muskets, so the colonel dragged him with one hand while he gripped his pistol with the other. Through the whole camp until they found Vargas. Without a word the colonel shot the innocent Vargas in the head. "Thank you," the colonel had said and dropped Salvador there in the mud.

The other men beat him. He wanted them to kill him. But they did not. They did something worse: they shunned him. In the next battle, at Curupaity, he ran, charging ahead of the others to try to die. But God knew how to punish him.

"He took my foot and forced me to live," Salvador told the priest. He wiped the tears from his face before looking up.

The padre's expression filled with pity.

"I have received Holy Communion without confessing this sin, Padre. I deserve to go to hell."

"No, Salvador. What you did was not a sin in God's eyes."

"How can you say that, Padre? That poor bastard Vargas is dead—when he did nothing but boast and tease and swagger. He was a son of a bitch, but he did not deserve to die for that. I am evil."

The priest put his hand on Salvador's shoulder. "No. What a man says under torture—" He sighed deeply. "It is the people who inflicted that pain on you who are responsible. A man should not risk death for speaking his mind while drunk. And drunk is what any man would have gotten if he had seen what you saw in the battle the day before." He ran his hand through his hair, and his blue eyes brimmed with tears. "Listen, Salvador. This guilt is not yours. Even drunk, you were right. This war is shit."

"All war is shit, Padre," Salvador said. "It is impossible for men to obey the Commandments in war. I have read of the glories of past wars, but they must all be like this one—full of disease and stupid orders carried out by men too afraid to do otherwise. But I should have been better. I should have let them shoot me rather than give them Vargas."

The padre stared out the window, into the gloom of heavy rain. "Does Alivia know this?"

Salvador threw off the towel. "About the Comandante following me or about the torture?"

"Any of it."

"None. She has suffered enough," Salvador said, as if he were not hurting her more by hiding himself from her. Before the war, they had kept no secrets from one another.

The priest sat down again beside him. "Listen, Salvador. You could not have known that the colonel would kill Vargas. You were not in your right mind."

"It was me, Padre. I did it. And I received Communion without confessing it. I asked God to come into my black soul." He looked at the priest, daring him to disagree.

"I am going to give you absolution, Salvador. We are going to wipe this guilt from you." He raised his right hand in blessing.

"*Absolvo te in nomine Patris et Filius et Spritus Sanctus,*" he said, as if a man could forgive himself such an act, even if God could.

Salvador made the sign of the cross but felt no relief. "Do you see now why I cannot know where Aleixo is? I am a coward. When my brother-in-law takes me to be tortured, I will betray my own son."

The priest looked up at the ceiling in thought for a few seconds. "Neither of you will be here. You will take Aleixo away. To the south. I know a priest in Encarnación. You can stay with him until the war is over. You must go right away, before the comandante finds Alé."

Salvador sat up. "No, Padre, I have just thought of a better solution. I will just confess to the comandante that I killed Ricardo."

The priest's head snapped around. "You did not kill him," he said, half accusing. "No, of course not," he said quickly.

"No."

In their silence, the rain beat hard on the tiles of the roof.

"You will not confess to a crime you did not commit," the priest said. "That would be suicide. You will not condemn your soul like that."

"No."

"You will take the boy away."

"Yes."

"Good. I only wish you had a horse to make the journey easier."

Salvador told him about César.

"Thank God," the priest said.

Salvador stood up. "Manuela wanted my baby." The statement roused a desire in him he did not think possible at a moment like this. "Will you look after her? She has to have enough food."

"Certainly," the priest said, "and Alivia and Xandra too." Then he smiled. "Not that any of them needs much help. Your women are all strong."

"I guess I prefer them that way."

"I do too." A blush reddened the padre's cheeks. "Forget I said that."

Salvador nodded. He grasped the priest's shoulders. "I will take the boy away," he said and a lightness entered his soul and frightened him.

15

Eliza Lynch caught her reflection in her dressing table mirror as she bent to open her jewelry box. She grabbed a pot from the table top and dabbed some cream on the dark streaks beneath her eyes. "Take my gray pearl earrings, François," she said to von Wisner's reflection.

The count gave a shy smile. "They would not look well on me. Gray is not my color. The emeralds now, those would bring out the green in my eyes."

"Stop it. There is no reason for levity these days. None." But she smiled nonetheless. Without him, she would have cracked long before this. She said this to herself, but deep in her gut she knew nothing would break her.

Though she feared López would miss the gray pearls, she put them and the emeralds, into a red velvet pouch. "I am serious, François. You must go to Buenos Aires with Dr. Stewart and the French ambassador to make sure they do as they promised. Take these with you." She tried to hand him the earrings.

Gently, but firmly, he pushed her hands away. "I have told you, Eliza. I am not going to leave you."

She touched his hair. He was her island of normalcy amid the chaos. Except for Juan Francisco, who would not leave his father's side, her boys were safe in Cerro León with McMahon, the United States minister. She longed for the joy and purity of their love. In the eyes of her children she saw the adoration that truly satisfied her soul. She had always craved the worship of men because she used their desire to get what she needed. That was quid pro quo. But her children gave her unsullied affection, looked upon her with the eyes of saints in paintings worshiping the Virgin. If only Juan Francisco would go with her, she would leave. When she tentatively suggested it, he immediately called any such plan a betrayal of his father. So she stayed to protect her boy. "I wish I could see my babies," she said. "I did not expect to feel this way about children. I thought that like my mother, I would consider them—" She broke off. She did not allow herself to think about her mother that way, much less reveal such thoughts to von Wisner.

He put a hand on her shoulder. "The end will come very soon—one way or another."

She folded a pretty green shawl that still carried the faint scent of the jasmine perfume she used to wear to balls in Asunción. She stuffed it into a satchel she had been packing for von Wisner to take to the Yotté sisters. She hoped he was right, that it would not be long now. But she had hoped that for too many months to believe it.

⁂

In Santa Caterina that siesta time, murky clouds gathered as the trusted friends entered an unused, windowless storeroom in the church. The air was dusty, but cool as a cave. Thick doors and walls separated them from prying ears and eyes. The comandante had been following Salvador, which meant the spies would all be out, trying to earn a few crumbs from his table or to save their own necks by giving him information.

The room contained only an old Spanish carved wood table. They dragged chairs in from a side chapel. Maria Claudia lit the small pitch-dark space with stubs of altar candles. The padre had brought a few precious scraps of paper, a pen, and ink and placed them before him.

The padre had decided they must meet once more before Salvador left with Aleixo. They needed to try to finish the work they had begun. If they could prove who killed Ricardo Yotté, Luis Menenez would have to arrest that person and would have no reason to pursue Salvador.

When they were all seated, the priest began. "We must tell one another the whole truth," the padre said. "Lives are at stake."

In the small circle of light made by the candle, Xandra's arms showed the scrapes she had gotten climbing the Yotté garden wall. Her suspicious mother eyed them and the scab on Maria Claudia's forehead above her left eye. Alivia would find out soon enough where the little injuries came from. "Whose life specifically?" Xandra demanded.

The priest held up his hands. "We will come to that," was all he said.

Maria Claudia took some pleasure in being the first to speak. She watched the padre's kind blue eyes flicker to disbelief and then admiration as she reported her and Xandra's midnight foray into the casa Yotté.

"Holy Mother of God!" Salvador exclaimed. "Where do you

get your nerve, Xandra? I have no doubt you were the perpetra-tor of this." But there was a hint of pride in his expression.

Alivia gave Salvador a sour look. "Eight trunks! What could it mean eight, not four?"

"We have no idea," Xandra said. "I could not open any of them. They were bound tight with thick straps and very heavy."

"I am not sure if I should feel impressed or horrified by your audacity," the priest said. Maria Claudia smiled at him.

"Manuela confirmed seeing men carrying four trunks into, not out of, that house only last week, well after Ricardo's death." Salvador was careful not to look at Alivia when he spoke. "I can only think those four must contain things Señora Lynch sent to the Yotté sisters."

"Why Señora Lynch?" the priest asked.

"Who else has trunks of things to give away?" Salvador asked in return.

"But what is so heavy and why is it still locked up?" Maria Claudia asked.

"Exactly," Xandra cut in. "All those trunks have something to do with Ricardo's death."

"Yes," said Salvador. "Very odd that Señora Lynch sud-denly took an interest in helping those girls. She has always been much more interested in helping her own countrymen. I saw her myself at the siege of Humaitá—when the mortars were exploding—walking in the battlefield to encourage her countrymen, but never ordinary Paraguayans."

"Suppose Solano López himself sent those men to kill Ri-cardo," Alivia said. "You know the gossip about Ricardo and the señora. López could have had him killed out of jealousy."

"We have been over this," Xandra said. "Those men would not have had to drag the body."

"And López would not need to conceal it," Salvador said.

"And why did the murderer bring the body into the church?" Maria Claudia asked.

"I think we should make a list of all the people who could be suspected," the priest said. He took a paper from the center of the table and dipped his pen into the ink.

"Gilda and whoever would have helped her," Alivia said. "If Ricardo was breaking off with her—" She did not have to finish her sentence.

The padre wrote Gilda's name on the paper, though he knew from her confession that Gilda had broken off with Ricardo, not the other way around. "Who would have helped her carry the body?"

"Anyone to whom she promised a chicken leg," Xandra said in disgust.

"Should we consider Josefina?" the priest asked. "I hate to believe she can be—"

Alivia stopped his thought. "Certainly it could have been Josefina. We said that the last time. Ricardo took away all the boys. Look what going to war did to Pablo."

The padre wrote down their names.

"Menenez," Salvador said, "if he knew his wife was putting the horns on him with Yotté."

"Or to get rid of his political rival."

"But he would have been able to carry Ricardo." Xandra said.

Salvador waved his hands at them. "Wait," he said urgently. "For all we know, the people who carried Ricardo into the church did not kill him. Suppose the comandante bashed him in the head and made someone else carry his body into the church."

"And made them stab him in the chest?" Xandra was incredulous.

Maria Claudia raised her hand like a girl in school. "Or stabbed him himself out of rage. The comandante is certainly capable of rage."

Xandra slumped back in her chair. "So it could have been anyone."

The priest put down his pen. "We are getting nowhere."

Silence retook the room.

Maria Claudia held out begging palms, pale in the candle-light. "I still ask why anyone would carry a dead body into the belfry. That is important."

"Oh, stop. The padre is right." Xandra's voice was filled with exasperation. "This is a useless guessing game."

"I am afraid that is true," the priest said. "We cannot solve Ricardo's murder. Besides, we have something more important to speak of." He touched Salvador's arm. "It is time to reveal your secret."

A lightning jolt of tension ran through them. Alivia rose half out of her chair and gave her husband an accusatory stare. Xandra's fists went to her hips. Maria Claudia studied the priest as if trying to read the secret in his face.

Salvador swallowed hard. "I have—we have—Alivia and I have been hiding Aleixo."

Xandra stared in disbelief and then beamed. "He is alive? Alé is alive?"

Her father took her hand. The sadness in his expression wiped the smile from her face. "Yes, *querida*. Alive, but—"

"But what?" Xandra demanded in that merciless way of hers.

"He is ill," the priest said.

Alivia stood now. "You have seen him, Padre?"

The padre shook his head. "I wanted to go and bless the boy, to see if the sight of the priest who used to play bolas with him and his schoolmates might calm him, but Salvador pointed out that any strange activity might bring in the spies."

"God help us," Maria Claudia whispered.

"What?" the priest asked her.

"That we live in a place where a priest cannot go to bless a sick person without risking lives."

The padre touched the back of her hand. "That is why we must take action."

"Action?" Alivia demanded.

Salvador reached out to her, but she slapped his hand away.

"I want to see him. I want to see my brother," Xandra said.

"Now is not the time, *querida*," her father said, his voice as gentle as hers was sharp.

"Tell them your plan, Salvador," the padre said.

Salvador took Alivia's elbow and pulled her back into her chair. He explained the plan to escape with Aleixo. "But the comandante is watching me closely now." He looked directly at Alivia. "The padre suggested this."

"When will you leave?" she asked.

"As soon as I have some food for the journey. We cannot expect to find much along the way. I am going to have to take the horse, *querida*," he said to Xandra.

"When you need César, I will bring him to you."

"Not yet. Your mother and I will prepare everything without drawing suspicion. I will let you know when. Probably tomorrow, after dark."

"In the meanwhile, what will we do about Ricardo's death?" Maria Claudia asked.

"I am afraid we must put that aside until Aleixo and Salvador are safely away," the priest replied. "What can I do to help?" he asked Salvador.

"Pray," Salvador and Alivia said in unison.

The priest looked up at the crucifix on the opposite wall—the most famous image of torture and death in the world. The men who had tortured Salvador were no better than the thugs who had done that to the Son of God. Worse, really, for the men who were now torturing people in Paraguay called themselves Christians and had the benefit of the teachings of the Prince of Peace. Bastards. Bastards. And some of them were priests.

The padre raised his hand to bless them but felt like a fraud. What did his beliefs mean, if they could not inspire goodness?

López's face told Eliza Lynch everything she needed to know. "The Brazilians have crossed the river from Santa Elena to San Antonio," he said.

"I will be ready in half an hour."

He grabbed a decanter and splashed brandy into a glass. "We will go up to Cerro Corá." He gulped the liquor.

A thought that had nagged Eliza for a month now resurfaced: what role did all the brandy he took for his toothache play in his madness, his wrong choices? She decided the question was irrelevant. Escaping with as much wealth as possible was the only answer at this point. "There is good news," she said.

He looked at her expectantly. "The trunks?"

She nodded emphatically. "They left Santa Caterina at first light."

His eyes filled with relief. "What does Menenez know?"

"I cannot be sure. So far, he has not tried to take them."

"He would be a dead man, and he knows it."

"Can we make sure?" She let the hint hang in the air.

"He will not disobey a direct order." He downed the brandy and took up his pen. She read the note over his shoulder. He shoved the paper into an envelope and sealed it, then heaved himself out of his chair and went to the flap of the tent. He handed the missive to the guard outside. "Take this to the co-mandante of Santa Caterina without delay. And bring me a bottle of brandy."

෪

As they filed out of the little interior room, Maria Claudia saw pain in the padre's face and could not tell the cause. They all had too many reasons to grieve. Try as she might, she could no longer quiet her heart with reason or pretty thoughts of a heaven hereafter.

She waited behind while the others went out through the back door into the campo. She and the priest watched the three figures crossing through the high grass in the fading light, Xandra running ahead, Alivia walking too fast for Salvador, who struggled to keep up.

The padre faced her and gave a quizzical look. She reached toward him. "Take my hand," she said. When he did, a pulse ran from their touching palms through her veins. "I love you," she said, looking right into his warm, serious eyes. "Come to me."

She let go of his hand and turned away, but he held her fingers, kissed them, and only then released her hand.

With one backward glance, she slipped out, back through the dim church that smelled faintly of incense and candle wax. She took holy water at the front door and blessed herself, feeling surer of what she was doing than when she left the church as a bride, barely three years ago.

෪

From the doorway of the comandancia, Luis Menenez watched Maria Claudia cross the plaza toward her house. That thin, prayerful woman held no sexual interest for him. Her being in the church meant nothing; she never went anywhere else. But she could be coming from some new palaver with the priest and Gilda's relatives. For now he preferred to let them continue their collusion, to see if they uncovered something he had not.

He had toyed with the idea of accusing Gilda of cuckolding him with Yotté, but clearly that would worsen his current difficulties. He would get rid of Gilda when the war was over. He told himself delaying was prudent, not weak. He slapped his riding crop hard against his left palm. Here in this hateful heat, he was trapped in a stagnant swamp of indecision that grew more fetid the longer it stood.

He needed to be a man of action but though he still commanded this village, only the most ignorant and docile still gave him his due. He used to make them quiver and shit their pants just by looking at them the wrong way because he stood in the place of López. But the dictator had become remote, a power fading into the mountains of the north. Only through me is he really a threat anymore, Menenez thought. And he is much more of a threat to me than to anyone else in Santa Caterina.

He threw his riding crop on the table, clasped his hands behind his back, and faced the door. The sight of Josefina approaching across the plaza further frazzled his nerves. That harpy knew more than he about what was going on under his nose. The last thing he needed was a tirade of her silly predictions and interpretations, always delivered with such drama. In the old days of Spain's power, the Inquisition would have burned her as a witch. She dragged that grandson of hers everywhere, like a badge of everything people were not supposed to think concerning the war. He should arrest her for fomenting antigovernment feelings. Or maybe for Yotté's murder. That would get rid of her and placate López. She might be guilty. That fierce look in her eyes might not be only an act to impress the villagers with her spiritual powers. She was sixty if a day, but wiry, still strong. She could have killed Yotté and dragged him into the church. Why not? This eternal nursemaid to the Yotté family, more than anyone in the village, could have caught Ricardo off guard and bashed him. The comandante picked up his riding crop and stood tall as the hag dragged her half-dead grandson through the open doorway.

"*Buen día, Señor Comandante,*" she said. The impassive boy at her side blinked at coming in from the bright sunshine. She dragged her bony finger across the table and looked at the dust, the papers, and the pair of muddy boots scattered on the bare brick floor. "Gaspár cleans like a man. Get Luz down the street to clean for you. You could pay her in food. She is stupid, but she would do a better job than this." She looked at him as if such a remark merited a response.

The comandante was on the verge of telling her this was none of her business when a terrifying thought occurred to him. Perhaps this crone was a spy for López. It made sense. Yotté could have recruited her. Everyone talked to her. It would be easy for the rider who brought messages to the comandante to meet her near the casa Yotté on his way in and out of the village. She may have come to check on his progress. He could not speak. He wanted to be the dangerous man he used to be. Instead he was mortified to fear an old woman.

"Do you wonder why I am here?" she finally asked.

"I thought you would get around to telling me," he said as pleasantly as he could.

She gave him her customary knowing smile. "Your wife made a condolence call on the sisters of Ricardo."

López's threat about not bothering those Yotté bitches rang in his blood. "Well, er—we are all so saddened by what happened," he finally blurted out.

"Yes. Yes." She waved one of her claws at him. "While your señora was there, she mentioned some missing valuables." She looked at him expectantly.

Fear prickled the hairs on his back. "Yes?"

She looked at him for far too long. He could feel her assessing his nerve. He held her gaze, though it turned his stomach to fire. She smiled, showing her teeth, brown from her constant cigars. "I wondered if you know anything about them."

His scalp froze. She was a spy. This was a trap.

She held up a crooked finger, like a duenna warning a suitor off the girl whose virginity she protected. "You are our comandante. You are supposed to know everything that happens in the village, no?"

He bristled. "My concerns are none of your business," he snapped

She showed him her ugly teeth again. She put her hands on his desk and leaned toward him. The triumph in her eyes told him that he had made a dreadful mistake. "I apologize for disturbing you," she said knowingly. "*Vaya con Dios, Comandante.*" She made what should have been a blessing as well as a farewell sound like a threat. Then she took her putrid grandson's empty sleeve and left the building.

The sweat his body had somehow suppressed broke out on the comandante's chest. Where did she get her nerve? She must have López's power behind her. He should go after her, tell her he was about to make an arrest. But. There were too many "buts." He had to make a move. He paced the small space of his office. Terror completely inappropriate for a man of his position chilled his neck, while the rest of him dripped with sweat.

He jammed on his hat and strode off toward the house of Luz. She was stupid, and he never asked her to dust his desk, but she did let him fuck her in return for scraps from his table. Before he was halfway across the square, one of López's Monkey Tails, mounted on a beautiful black stallion, charged into the plaza, handed Menenez a message, and without a word or a salute sped away through the gathering dusk.

16

In the dark of that cloudy night, the priest arrived once again in ordinary clothes at Maria Claudia's door. When he tried to speak, she stopped his lips with hers. She took his hand and led him to her narrow bed. Alivia had told her to look for a thick liquid that would indicate she was fertile. She had found it yesterday and today. Now, when he kissed her, some of it escaped its warm secret place and trickled down her thigh. He touched her there and groaned.

She put her arms around him and let their passion consume her. No thoughts, no decisions, nothing but the heat and taste, the spicy smell of his hair and ecstasy of being one with him.

The storm of their hunger for each other did not diminish until dawn.

As a weak gray light began to illuminate the walled garden outside her bedroom window, he raised his head and spoke. "I must—" was all she let him say before she put her fingers to his mouth.

"You must leave me before the sun rises."

He took her hand and kissed it over and over again.

She rose and drew her old linen sheet around her. He dressed quickly and walked arm in arm with her to the front door. The still sleeping village lay perfectly quiet, the roofs of the houses along the street were silhouetted against a slight lightening of the sky. He kissed her good-bye.

"I love you," she whispered to his retreating figure.

He turned and reached out a hand toward her and then disappeared into the gloom of the street.

※

In that same predawn light, Xandra slipped out of her bedroom window and sped toward Tomás. She wanted him to be innocent, so she would not have to hate every Brazilian for Aleixo's condition. Her parents would not allow her to see her brother. They said it was for fear of the comandante and his spies. But she pictured what the war had done to Pablo. She could not bear that her brother might be like that.

In the gray light, sweet-smelling ferns dangled over her. A roar to her left stopped her. It could be a jaguar or just a big-eyed howler monkey. At midnight it would have been the cat; during the day the monkey. She listened. Birds chattered in the branches nearby. They would have flown from a jaguar. She moved on.

Salvador awoke at that same time. He rolled two ponchos and a machete and tied them with a cord. He gathered some chipa, a couple of hard-boiled eggs, and two wild oranges. Terrors in the night had convinced him not to wait until sunset. They would leave this morning.

He worried he would be seen taking the boy through the forest, that Alé would overpower him and take the machete.

God only knew what he would do if he got his hands on a weapon. Salvador could not run away if foragers or snooping spies saw them on their way to get César. Rather than bring the boy to the horse, he would have to risk bringing the horse to the boy.

Leaving Alivia asleep, he went to awaken Xandra and ask her to fetch the horse, but she was not in her bed. So he set out alone for César, hoping he and the boy could still be on their way before full daylight broke.

❦

In the quiet of their bedroom, Gilda pleaded with the co-mandante: "López said they are breaking camp again and he wants Ricardo's murderer by nightfall today, but listen to me, Luis. Forget that last message. If La Lynch is so keen to get those four trunks, they must contain the treasure of Paraguay. The only intelligent thing to do is to take them and get out of the country."

"Very tempting, my dear, but I think the treasure, if it is treasure, is long gone from here. I have to arrest your brother Salvador for Yotté's murder."

Disbelief was all he saw in her eyes. "Impossible. He is too righteous to have done such a thing."

Menenez held out his latest orders from López. "He says he wants the murderer today without fail, or I must present myself in place of the killer. We know from the padre's description that whoever dragged Yotté's body into the church was not strong enough to carry it. Salvador's missing foot puts him into that category. And we know he hated Yotté because he took Mariano for the army. I can tell López these things. They will convince him I have the right person."

Her thin lips disappeared into a grim line. She stood up

and paced the room. "Arresting my brother would cast suspicion on our whole family. Remember what López did to Mercedes Martínez."

Her words stopped him. She had a point. Mercedes Martínez had been the wife of a brave colonel. During the evacuation after the defeat of Humaitá, Martínez and his few remaining men had held out against the attacking Argentineans so the bulk of the Paraguayan army could escape. For three days, Martínez had refused to surrender. On the fourth day, after almost all the men from Humaitá had made it across the river, delirious with hunger and out of ammunition, he gave up. Instead of praising him as a hero, López had cursed him as a traitor and arrested his wife.

"Yes, yes," he said, "but people also can prove their loyalty by showing their willingness to betray their relatives."

Gilda's dark lashes flickered. "Okay, so you save your life, but what then? When the war is over, we are going to be just as poor as everyone else!"

"And powerless," he said, hating the thought.

"López is the past, we have to look to the future, and without Salva—"

He waved his hand to shoo away her words. "If I fail to bring in Salvador by nightfall, *I* will be in the past." As soon as he said it, a blinding thought occurred to him. "Wait. Stop. You are right. Salvador has the land. When the war ends, if he and his sons are all dead, the land will be ours."

He watched the triumph of such an eventuality dawn on her, but then a great banging at the front door disrupted their thoughts.

They pulled on dressing gowns and ran to answer. Hector Mompó stood on their doorstep, wearing one of Ricardo Yotté's

French shirts, his leather apron, and nothing else but his silver spurs. He held up a string of small fish. "I have been over toward Valenzuela," he said breathlessly, "to find food for the mothers of my children." He gave them a rakish grin, but his weathered old face quickly turned serious. "A man there told me the Brazilians are only a few miles away and moving in this direction."

The comandante held his face neutral. "Did he say how large a force?"

Mompó shook his head. "An army," he said.

"Traveling how fast?"

He raised his bony shoulders. "He said some of them were mounted. An hour or two away? I ran to you as soon as I heard."

"This is good information." The comandante forced the words to come out evenly.

"What will we do to defend our women and our food from the invaders?" Mompó asked, as if such a thing were possible.

"I will decide. For now, go home and wait for your orders. Do not spread this news and frighten people before we have a plan. Do you understand?"

Mompó nodded. The comandante handed him a few small coins.

"This does not change our plans," the comandante told Gilda when the old man had gone. "We will end this war in possession of the estancia. I will arrest your brother. In the meantime, we cannot let panicked villagers prevent me from doing what I must. Go and calmly tell those fools to take whatever they have and hide in the forest. They should move toward the northeast, toward San José."

Gilda donned her bonnet and shawl before she went out,

as if she were some proper English lady going out for a morning stroll in Regent's Park.

⟨⟩

By eight that morning, the plaza buzzed with news of the im-
pending invasion. The señora comandante did her best to control the villagers' reactions, but to no avail. Once people heard
that the original source of the news was Hector Mompó, they
went to him for the full story. Each time he told it, the number
of invaders became greater, the swiftness of their arrival increased, and the devastation they were likely to wreck grew
larger.

At the door of the church, a group of eight or ten women
wept and demanded advice of their priest. Having spent the
last two hours sitting on the edge of his bed contemplating
how he would abandon his priesthood and take Maria Claudia
out of the country, the padre was totally unprepared to counsel them. When Gilda came to the church steps, she could not
shout loud enough to be heard over the clamoring women.

Mompó appeared with his things slung over his stooped
shoulders. "Come. I know a good place. Go get your things.
Meet me in the plaza in five minutes."

He turned and ran to knock on the doors of the houses on
the other side of the cemetery. Gilda marched toward the forge.

"Yes," the padre said to the women on the steps. "Hector's
plan seems wise. Bring what food you have and blankets."

As they turned to go, the priest stopped Fidelia, a girl of
about eleven. "Go to Maria Claudia's house. Ask her to come
to the church. I need her help."

He watched long enough to be sure that child would obey
him. Then he went into his house to pack his own meager belongings.

As Salvador approached the clearing, he thought he heard Xandra speaking to the horse. He felt a pang for his poor, lonely daughter. He stopped to rest from the pain of walking and heard another voice, soft but masculine. He moved slowly, silently, like a hunter stalking a peccary, until he was close enough to hear their words. "But sometimes they get better," the man's voice said. He had an accent. Brazilian. Were there others in the area? Was this a single enemy? What was he doing with his daughter? Salvador had no weapon but his machete. He moved forward as quickly as he could without drawing their attention.

"I want to see my brother." Xandra's voice was angry but not fearful, as if she were talking to a friend. "They say they are afraid he will be discovered. But they are afraid for me too."

Salvador sidled to the edge of the clearing. He saw no one. The horse neighed, Salvador quickly slipped behind a tree.

"Whatever happened to your brother—"

"Wait, I heard something," Xandra interrupted.

Salvador held his breath.

"Birds in the underbrush," whispered that Brazilian voice. He went on talking.

Salvador moved slowly around the tree, making not one sound. They were inside the chicken coop. It was larger than it had been the last time Salvador was here—that day when the padre told the women to get pregnant. Alivia believed Xandra was with child. Salvador's blood flashed hot. By this Brazilian bastard!

He abandoned his cane, unwrapped his bundle, and grasped the machete. He rushed the lean-to, brandishing the weapon.

"Papa!" Xandra screamed.

A tall, lithe figure of a man clad in white breeches and a loose white shirt flashed past him. Salvador swung the machete but missed. The man vaulted the corral fence and leaped onto the horse.

Xandra ran to her father and blocked his arm as he raised it to throw the machete. "Stop!" she shouted.

The Brazilian kicked the horse with his bare heels. César charged forward.

"Halt, César!" Salvador shouted, still holding the machete over his head.

"Run, César! Go, go!" the girl screamed.

The horse hesitated but obeyed the girl.

"I am not your enemy!" the man shouted over his shoulder as the horse jumped the fence and galloped off.

Gasping for breath, Salvador lowered the weapon and glared at his half-naked daughter. "Cover yourself," he growled.

She did the one thing he could not stand for her to do. She burst into tears.

17

Gilda left off warning the villagers. A few sentences to three or four of them had set off a wildfire of words. Women with bundles small or large on their heads, a few with young children by the hand, were already marching toward the woods north of town.

Gilda glanced over her shoulder to be sure Luis was not watching and turned her determined step toward the casa Yotté. In addition to threatening him with death if he did not bring in Yotté's murderer by the end of the day, López's latest communiqué reiterated that the comandante must not disturb the Yotté sisters. Why? It could only be to protect the treasure that still must be there. Unlike her husband, she was brave enough to ignore López and go after it.

"Oh, Luis," she mumbled to herself. She had begun their engagement by imagining that his ambition would carry them to glory. Now he would be lucky if he saved his own pathetic life.

She had a bolder plan. Paraguay's gold must be in those

trunks, which no one would have found if she had not told them where to look. "Oh, Ricardo," she whispered. "If only you had loved me more than La Lynch." More than any man, she wanted that gold.

She opened her parasol as she left the shade of the plaza and took the road to the Yotté house. She froze in her own footprints. A wagon stood at the front door. Two trunks already weighed it down. Two men struggled down the broad front steps with a third, obviously very heavy, box.

✿

The little girl awakened Maria Claudia by pounding on the door with her sandal. "The padre wants you," the breathless child said. "We are running from the Brazilians. I think the padre wants you to run away with him." She sped off.

In the street, several neighbors hurried toward the plaza with bundles on their heads. She rushed to her bedroom and quickly threw on a tupoi, a blouse, and skirt. She rolled her mirror, her mother's tortoiseshell comb, and her father's Bible into a poncho. She took her old patched linen sheet that still smelled of their love and folded it in too. Her mind immediately went, as it always had, to prayer. She should ask God for forgiveness. She felt no contrition. Only joy. She placed her hand on her belly. Whatever magic was happening there, she prayed it would bring her his baby. If God was as good as she had always been taught, he would give her a child.

✿

Salvador hobbled along as quickly as he could toward the cabin where Aleixo was hidden. They would have to walk out. Without the horse, they would be lucky if they got six leagues before the comandante caught up and killed them both.

He had left Xandra waiting for her lover to return. As if he would. Brazilian bastard. She had told Salvador of the soldier's promise—the promise all men made when all they wanted was for a girl to open her legs. He wanted to kill the man who had done that to his daughter. And stolen his horse. The girl, of course, would not see sense, and Salvador had no time to convince her. He had to take his son away before the comandante discovered him.

As he clumped through the forest, he began to hear people coming from the direction of the village. Foragers, he thought. But then he realized they moved too fast to be hunting wild pineapples. They were coming directly toward him. Had the comandante enlisted them to find him? He tried to outrun them, though a child of three could move faster than he.

Saturnino Fermín, the plume on his battered hat bouncing wildly, ran by, followed closely by three women, one carrying a little boy on her shoulders. "Brazilians. They are invading Santa Caterina. Run away!" they called out as they kept going.

Fools. They must have seen Xandra's one Brazilian soldier and imagined a regiment was attacking. He continued, but in a few seconds another group came through. Had they all gone mad? "It is only one soldier," he tried to tell them.

"No, Señor León," one said. "The comandante told us to hide."

"Come with us," said another. "You have a machete. We may need that."

"I will have to tell my family," Salvador said. He pretended to turn toward home until they were out of sight. Then he made for the boy. The closest way would take him near the road past the forge. He would risk being seen, but he could not move fast enough to go around. He prayed the comandante was too busy organizing the evacuation to come after him and his son. But he doubted the comandante would ever put the villagers ahead of his own ends.

※

Luis Menenez loaded his pistol and saddled his horse. He shoved food into a gunnysack with his pitiful store of six shotgun shells. He took their table silver and what was left of his wife's jewelry in case he needed to bribe someone up north. He slipped the shotgun into the holster attached to his saddle and grabbed a coil of rawhide rope with which to bind up that son of a bitch Salvador. López wanted Yotté's murderer today. The comandante's first problem was where to look for his bastard brother-in-law. If León knew about the Brazilians coming, he might save his juicy whore of a blacksmith before he took care of his old, dry wife. No, he was too good of a man for that. He would do the right thing and protect his wife. The estancia was the place to look.

※

While Xandra waited in the lean-to and began to despair, Maria Claudia hurried toward the church. In the middle of the plaza, she came upon Rosaria, Alberta Gamara's three-year-old granddaughter, sitting under a tree alone and crying.

She picked up the girl and ran with her toward the priest's—toward Gregorio's house. The child's dress was damp, and when Maria Claudia put her down to knock on the door, she saw a stain on the back of the child's white homespun dress. The baby had peed herself while sitting on the ground. The mud made a stain, like a stain Maria Claudia had sometimes gotten on her petticoats when her period came during school. Wait. Wait. Her mind flashed with the answer. That was it. The red mud. It looked like blood.

When the padre came to the door, she thrust the child into his arms. "We have to go to Alivia," she said.

He agreed. "Perhaps the news of the invasion has not reached the estancia."

"Not that," Maria Claudia said. "It's the mud. It looks like blood."

18

 Gilda pretended to visit the forge to warn Manuela about the invasion, but in reality her eyes focused on the cart drawn by two strong bullocks now leaving the casa Yotté by the north road. Four heavy trunks, trussed-up with leather straps, trundled off with her hopes.

After warning Manuela away, she hurried to find Luis and make him overtake the wagon and steal back the treasure of Paraguay from that Irish whore.

To her consternation, her house was deserted. Fear froze the skin of her back when she found the secret drawer in her desk open and her jewelry gone.

※

Alivia León examined her shelves of herbs, leaves, and gums: vanilla beans, polo de vivar, polo de barracho, içea roots, but nothing among them could help her. She now needed the cure so many had come seeking, an elixir she knew did not exist in this world—a cure for a broken heart. In her mind, old love songs warred with rage. Over and over in these last hours she had told herself Salvador had a right to beget a new son, but her black jealousy would not lift. When he announced he would take Alé away, her heart hollowed with a miserable conviction that her husband and son would disappear forever.

When she heard hoofbeats approaching the house, she pasted a smile on her face for the husband she had been imagining she would never see again, whom she loved and desired, but who did not love and desire her. She moved quickly to the front door but instead of Salvador astride César, she saw Luis Menenez slide from his horse. Her bowels quaked at the sight of the shotgun on his saddle and the pistol in the holster at his hip.

"Where is he?" he demanded without greeting.

"I do not know. You can search the house. He left at dawn. I swear it." She blessed herself to show that she was telling the truth.

Menenez smirked and astonished her by believing her. He mounted his horse and galloped off.

She gripped her hands together as if in prayer, but no god could help her. God had abandoned Paraguay. Then she saw Maria Claudia running toward her, with the padre following several paces back and carrying Alberta's granddaughter Rosaria.

"Look at the back of her shift." Maria Claudia was breathless. She took the baby from the priest and held her to show Alivia the back of her dress. "See." She pointed to a red stain.

"This could be very bad," Alivia said, "a baby her age bleeding there." Some horrible possibilities occurred to her, but she could not speak them.

"Not blood. Mud," Maria Claudia said, as if that were greatly significant. "They left her under a tree in the plaza. She peed herself."

Alivia lost her patience. "Salvador is in danger."

"Has he gone?" the priest asked.

"Just a little while ago." Tears fell from her eyes. "Did you see Menenez riding away? He is looking for Salvador. Armed with a pistol and shotgun."

The priest thrust the child into Maria Claudia's arms. "Where did Salvador go to get the horse? I will go after him to warn him."

"The hiding place is deep in the forest. You will never find it by yourself," she said. "I will go." She started running in the direction where Salvador had gone when he left the house. "Find the comandante. Delay or distract him," she said over her shoulder.

"What about Aleixo?" the priest shouted.

"He is safe where he is for now," she yelled back to them without stopping, hoping that what she said was true.

"The Brazilians are invading Santa Caterina," Maria Claudia called after her.

Alivia quickened her pace. Dear God! She prayed it was true and that the Brazilians would stop Menenez. And prayed she could still find her children's secret place where she had not been since her boys were little. She stumbled over roots and fallen limbs, imploring God to get her to Salvador in time.

Maria Claudia began to move back toward the town. The padre hurried beside her, carrying the child. "What are you trying to tell us about the mud?"

"I thought I saw mud on Martita's and Estella's clothing the day you found Ricardo's body, but it was blood, not mud."

He stopped in his tracks. "What? Martita and Estella killed Ricardo?"

"I am sure of it," she said without slowing down. "It explains everything."

"Two people, each too weak to carry the body alone," he said.

"Martita had a big round spot on the front of her skirt."

"All the blood from the head that Alivia spoke of." The baby had fallen asleep on his shoulder despite bumping along as he hurried.

"That is why Martita has been so cold to me. She is afraid I know."

"It does explain a lot."

"I want to go to them and find out," she said.

"We have to find the comandante first. We have to save Salvador and Aleixo if we can."

"And Martita and Estella?"

"We will go to them after we deal with the comandante."

"Deal with him?" The hatred in his tone froze her spine.

"Hurry," he said. "I wish we could do something with this child."

Maria Claudia's mind was in such tumult she could barely blunder along at his side. "We have no choice but to take her with us." In her heart, his statement about Rosaria turned into one about the child that could be starting within her. She had not looked past the point of wanting it. Every sinew in her wanted the baby. But did she want him to end up with a baby he did not know what to do with? He no longer a priest?

She did not know who she was anymore. Innocent Fidelia

who had come to her door that morning had said, "I think the padre wants you to run away with him."

She had watched him for years, so good, so helpful to the old people, so gentle with the sick and dying, so funny and lively with the children. How could she take him away from all that? Make him into a husband. Make him into an ordinary man.

A stitch in her side stopped her and doubled her over, breathless from running in the heat of the sun.

In a few steps he stopped and turned to her. "Are you all right?"

"Just winded. Go ahead without me. Leave me the child."

"No," he said. "I am not going anywhere without you."

"We might find the comandante faster if we separated," she suggested.

He looked into her eyes. "No." It was final.

"How can we possibly stop the comandante, if we do find him?"

"We have to try."

"Yes," she said.

"I love you," he said without looking at her. The child was drooling in her sleep, leaving a wet spot on the shoulder of his cassock.

19

Comandante Luis Menenez, from his vantage point astride his tall stallion, scanned the roads and peered into the trees on either side, searching for a glimpse of his brother-in-law. When he arrived at Manuela's house, the fire still smoldered in the forge, but there was no sign of Salvador's whore.

Gaspár Otazú came shouting through the woods. "I saw a cart coming this way, drawn by two stout horses. It must be the Brazilians."

"Armies send cavalry ahead, not carts," the comandante said. "Have you seen Salvador León? I have to find him."

"Good idea," Gaspár said. "He can help us kill those Brazilian devils." He licked his lips, hungry for a fight at his ridiculous age.

"Have you seen him?"

"No, Comandante, but I saw your señora. She is looking for him too. Is she helping you to find him?"

The statement confused the comandante. He had told Gilda to warn the citizens, not to go after her brother.

A frightening thought speared him: Gilda could be López's spy. All those intimate visits with La Lynch. She could have been reporting on her own husband. "Where did you see her?" he snapped at Gaspár.

"In the plaza, a little while ago."

Menenez wheeled his horse to the left and then to the right. Gilda was out of his control and could harm him. He should stop her before she put them both in jeopardy. But he had only today to deliver Salvador to López.

His mind was made up for him by a glimpse through the trees of a figure in a white shirt, barely visible, but surely from the pace and the stumbling way it hurried, it was Salvador.

"Find my señora," he told Gaspár. "Take her to the forest near the estancia León, where those tall palms rise above the other trees. I will return tomorrow and meet you there. Keep her with you and protect her. If you do not, I will kill you when I find you."

Once he saw the fear in the old man's eyes, he pointed his horse in the direction of the figure in white disappearing into the trees.

＠

"The trunks will be here very soon," Eliza Lynch said to Francisco Solano López. "You go ahead. I will wait for them and then follow."

He gave her an inquiring glance, tinged with suspicion.

"Leave Maiz with me," she said, knowing that at this point López trusted only Father Maiz, who had at first stood up to him but later led the torture squad.

He nodded. She followed him out of the tent.

Two silent stalwarts in Monkey Tail uniforms boosted their corpulent dictator into his saddle. Her firstborn sat tall and handsome astride his beautiful chestnut stallion, like a page in an epic poem about knights of old. Her heart melted at the sight of him. Then it solidified and crumbled. He would go with his father. Every time they retreated, they had fewer soldiers to defend them. All the Brazilians had to do to find them was to follow the trail of bodies of executed traitors and the wounded who expired.

López would die rather than surrender. But what of her dashing and dutiful son?

Live, please live, her mind called after him, while first at a canter and then at a gallop, he disappeared into the trees.

Then her bright eyes turned to the south. If those accursed trunks arrived soon, she could follow her boy.

&

Xandra heard movement coming toward her as she waited in the hidden clearing, hoping for Tomás to return. But this was not a horse but something smaller, moving too fast to be her father. Perhaps Tomás had met her father in the woods, given him the horse, and had now returned to her. She ran toward him.

"Xandra?" Her mother's voice.

"Mama?"

They met under a yellow flowering acacia tree.

"Where is your father?"

"Gone to Aleixo." There was too much fear in her mother's eyes. Her mother who seemed to fear nothing.

"He took the horse?" Alivia looked over Xandra's shoulder. Xandra could not answer.

"Well?" Her mother's demand was sharp, almost threatening.

"No," she said tentatively. "He did not take César."

"Why not?" An accusation in the question came like a slap in the face.

Xandra did not reply. "Why are you afraid?" she said instead.

"The comandante came for him with weapons."

"Already?"

"What happened to the horse? They have to go quickly. Maria Claudia says the Brazilians are invading the town."

"Oh, my God!" Xandra took her mother's hand and started to run toward the village. "Come, Mama. Quickly. Take me to where Aleixo is. Hurry."

The comandante reined in his horse before he neared the figure fading deeper into the forest. His quarry was going not to the forge but somewhere else, with a determination that betrayed desperation. He decided to let his brother-in-law find his precious thing, whatever it was, before he bound him and dragged him off to his death. He dismounted and tied the horse to a tree off the road where no one would see it. Then, stealthily, he easily picked up Salvador's trail and closed in on him.

20

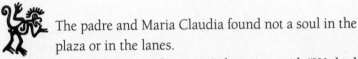 The padre and Maria Claudia found not a soul in the plaza or in the lanes.

"I pray Salvador escaped in time," the priest said. "We had better get away before the Brazilians attack."

Maria Claudia started walking in the direction of the casa Yotté. "Let's look for Martita and Estella."

The padre followed her. "They would not stay at home with the enemy practically upon us."

"It will take only a minute to see."

"You want to find out if you are right." He smiled at her, a sunny smile that had nothing to do with the predicament they were in. "Quickly, then. When the Brazilians get here, there will be chaos."

"Just one look." She had to get to the bottom of Ricardo's murder, as if solving it would take away all her doubts. Which was stupid, but she was angry at herself for not seeing the truth sooner.

"The Brazilians will not hurt a priest, especially an Argentinean. I will protect you."

When he pounded on the Yotté's' front door, the child stirred. They waited a moment in silence, but no one answered.

She tried the latch, but it did not open. Unlike the other houses in the village, which had doors at street level, the casa Yotté had three steps up to the entrance. When she turned to look at him, she noticed tracks in the dirt of the road, which had been softened by the recent rains. Two sets of shallow tracks coming from the north and two sets of much deeper tracks, one going north and the other south.

She pointed to them. "Two wagons."

"Or one that went away and came back and went away again?"

"I want to look inside. The sisters could be hiding in the house."

"This rich house is the first place an invading army would take over."

"Martita and Estella would not know that," she said. She had not known it. "You have to boost me up to the top of the wall. I will show you how."

He gave her that sunny smile again. "I know how. I was a boy before I was a priest."

And a man before you were a priest, she thought, picturing the love they had made.

"Maybe I should be the one to go in," he said.

"I am not sure I can lift you."

They went to the spot where she and Xandra had scaled the wall. She opened her rolled-up poncho and laid it on the ground so he could put the sleeping Rosaria down on it.

She took off her sandals and put her foot in his intertwined hands. She leaned forward and kissed him on the mouth. He held her foot and looked into her eyes. She saw love in him, love that thrilled her heart but one that a voice within her told her she ought to have refused. "Boost me," she said.

When she reached the top, she dangled her legs over the other side and held on with her hands to lower herself as she had seen Xandra do. But she could not hold on and with no one to catch her she scraped along the rough stucco and fell. She cried out despite herself.

"Maria Claudia, are you okay?"

She stood and brushed the dead leaves from her arms. The skin on her legs burned like fire. "I'm fine."

At that moment a kind of distant thunder started up, coming from the south of town.

"Can you hear that?" she called.

"The Brazilians," he said. "Come out. I will take you away."

"Take the baby into the forest. I will find you."

"I will not leave you."

The rumble from the south continued to grow louder. Suddenly there was shouting from the other direction. "Padre! Padre!" Manuela's voice called out.

"Come back out, Maria Claudia," his voice demanded. The baby started to cry.

"I will," Maria Claudia called and ran to the front door. The casa Yotté seemed deserted.

By the time she reached the hall and swung open the heavy door, the padre was on the top step clutching the crying baby, and Manuela, breathless, was reaching his side.

"Saturnino Fermín," she gasped, "climbed a lapacho tree to see how close the Brazilians were." She looked in the direction of the hoofbeats. They could not see the approaching horde, but they could tell it would not be long before they arrived.

Manuela snatched the baby from the padre's arms. "Saturnino fell from the tree. He is dying, Father. He wants to confess before he dies. Come with me. He needs you." She took a few steps away and looked expectantly over her shoulder and back to the Padre and Maria Claudia in the doorway.

Padre Gregorio looked pleadingly in Maria Claudia's eyes. She read his thoughts instantly and knew at once what her soul demanded. "Go," she said.

"Now," Manuela insisted.

Maria Claudia saw the grief in his eyes. She slammed the door between them and threw the bolt with a sharp clank.

⚘

Salvador had no choice. Knowing silence would have served him better, he swung the heavy hammer again and again to break the chain that manacled Aleixo to the cabin wall. Salvador sweated and smelled his own stink. The stink of rushing through the humid jungle, the stink of the pain that came with every step, of anger that his virgin daughter had been seduced by a Brazilian bastard. Rage that the son of a bitch had taken the horse and terror that he would not get the boy away in time.

The boy flinched with each blow to the chain, as if he feared his father would bludgeon him. Finally the link broke, and the boy was free.

"I am going to take you away from here, my son," Salvador said quietly.

For the first time, the boy responded to what his father said. He stood up. Salvador stopped and considered this. He looked into Aleixo's eyes and saw a spark of life. "We have to hurry. Take this." He tried to hand the boy the rolled-up poncho, but Alé did not take it.

Salvador wrapped the boy's arms around the bundle. Alé

held on. A few links of chain still dangled from his wrist. "Thank you," his father said gently. Despite his pain and rage, Salvador's heart lifted. "We must move quickly." He rolled up the boy's blanket. He grasped his cane and put his other arm around the boy's bony shoulders. "Come, my son," he said.

He opened the door to see the comandante's smiling face and the muzzle of a pistol pointed at his heart.

ℛ

Eliza Lynch pulled her spring-green lawn dress over her head and turned to let Carmencita, the only one of her girls who had not run off or died, do up the buttons. She had walked in it in their lovely camp among the orange groves after the dreadful battle of Tuyutí. The dress had elicited adoring glances from the English engineers. She chose it today because it matched the leafy jungle where she might have to hide from the relentless enemy. An hour ago, a horseman had arrived, sweaty and exhausted, to tell her the trunks would be here at about this time. Her ploy to keep Luis Menenez from discovering them had worked. He had been kept busy following his useless instructions.

"There, my lady," Carmencita said as she finished with the buttons.

Eliza heard the wagon and stiffened her spine. She would follow López to protect her darling Juan Francisco, he who had prepared the decoy trunks with his own hands and had not betrayed her to his father.

21

Gleeful to have two prizes to offer López, the comandante marched Salvador and the boy toward the horse. With the rawhide rope, he tied father and son together and bound the other end around his own waist. "When I heard the hammer banging on metal," he said, "I thought you were banging your blacksmith whore." He laughed at his own joke.

Salvador spat at him, but the spittle landed on his sleeve. The comandante rubbed it into the boy's face and laughed the harder. "*Vamanos, amigos.*" He mounted his horse and headed north with the man and the boy trotting along, arm in arm, beside him.

❧

Maria Claudia slumped against the door she had slammed on the padre's pleas. She bit back moans of anguish lest he hear them. Her throat ached, and her eyes burned.

"Hide," the priest called from outside. "In the place under the bed. I have to go, but I will come back for you."

She did not respond. After a few seconds, she heard them run off, baby Rosaria's cries fading into the distance, the sound soon overwhelmed by the swelling rumble of hoofbeats and the shouts of soldiers coming from the plaza. The Brazilians had entered Santa Caterina.

Her remorse should be for her beautiful, flower-filled town, so picturesque and tranquil in days gone by. Tormented for years by the war. Now engulfed by it. But her inner grief broke her heart, even as her loins longed for new life.

And him? She could not let herself keep him. He was a priest. Needed by everyone, for the things no one but a priest could give. She could not figure out if she wanted him as much as she wanted his child.

She listened to the quiet within the house. The place must be deserted or someone would have heard her voice and come to find out what was happening.

"*Hola*," she called, just in case. She crossed the hall and entered the central patio. "*Hola*." No one responded.

This house had been the scene of her childhood fantasies of perfect family life: a wealthy father; an elegant mother; an older brother who would grow up and introduce a girl to his handsome friends; sisters to share all her secrets. What secrets did Martita and Estella share? Had they killed their brother? What did those wagon tracks mean?

It would be a while before the Brazilians found this house on the outskirts of town. Martita and Estella must have run off to the forest.

Questions gnawed at Maria Claudia. She made for Ricardo's bedroom and gasped when she saw the disarray. The bed had been moved from its position over the hiding place. The carpet was rolled back and the trapdoor left open, leaving the empty hole exposed. All eight of the trunks were gone. Those tracks

out on the road, were they of wagons taking the trunks to Señora Lynch? Why would anyone take gold and jewels to such
a place as they must be heading? The whole Allied army was
on this side of the river. The mariscal and his lady must be
running for their lives. One would always want to keep valuables away from danger.

In Martita and Estella's room, she found their wardrobe
ajar and empty. A large photograph of the stern-looking Don
Cecilio and the impassive Doña Antonia that had hung on the
wall beside their bed was missing from its frame. Odd bits of
clothing were strewn on the bed and the chair, but the bulk of
their belongings were gone.

Maria Claudia picked up a grayish homespun skirt and
examined it. It had been washed, but the ghost of a stain on
the front remained. Blood did this, not mud, as every girl,
once she got her first period, knew. Mud stains came out of the
hems of petticoats that had been dragged along wet roads on
the way home from parties, but blood from an unexpected
period or a murder victim's head remained, sometimes forever.

A cough behind her startled air into her lungs and every
ounce of it back out into a scream. She spun around to see Josefina and the pathetic Pablo staring at her from the doorway. She
dropped the skirt.

"You did not know, did you, the day Ricardo died? You
have just realized, right?"

"Earlier today I figured it out," Maria Claudia replied.

"I told Martita you did not know, but she would not believe me. Estella believed me. But they have always been that
way. Estella accepting too much and Martita too little."

"Where have they gone?"

"To the big river. That tall man, the friend of Señora Lynch,
took them in a wagon at dawn. The French ambassador has a

boat going to Buenos Aires this afternoon. One of the mariscal's foreign doctors is going too. They are saved."

"Which one killed Ricardo?"

Josefina pursed her lips and shook her head, her habitual signal that she knew but would never say.

"The eight trunks?" Maria Claudia asked.

A pounding on the front door and a shout in Portuguese stopped their hearts and their mouths.

❦

Alivia and Xandra entered the belfry from the campo behind the padre's house, stole into the church, and then out the side door and into the graveyard. They hid behind the thick foliage and magenta flowers of a bougainvillea vine that grew over the church doorway. Alivia blessed herself. This was the door used only when grieving relatives followed coffins out of the church for burial.

Peering through the leaves, they saw Brazilian soldiers dismounting and fanning out to sack the comandancia and the comandante's house on the other side of the plaza. For now they seemed to be ignoring the church and cemetery. Xandra became agitated at the sight of them. "Where did Papa hide Aleixo?" she whispered.

"In the forest, beyond the forge." The thought of the forge plagued her soul. Yesterday, in her grief and anger, she had wished harm on both Salvador and Manuela. She now promised God she would forgive her husband anything, welcome Manuela's baby, if only he would let Salvador live.

"Would I be able to find it?"

"I will show you."

Suddenly Xandra dashed between the graves toward the plaza. "Come," she shouted over her shoulder. "Quick!"

Alivia followed. "Stop. They will see you," she said as loud as she dared.

The girl flew toward the horses under the trees. She let out a loud whistle and shouted, *"Venga, César!"* Their horse, whom Alivia had not recognized among the others, raised his beautiful head.

Xandra untied him and launched herself into the saddle. "Hurry, Mama."

Alivia ran, grabbed the girl's extended hand, and hiked herself up behind Xandra, who kicked the beast hard in his flanks as she turned him toward the road to the forge.

⚘

Padre Gregorio ran with Manuela to where Saturnino Fermín lay unconscious beneath a lapacho tree, his tricorn hat lying beside him. Alberta sat next to him, smoothing his thick white hair and murmuring. The padre thrust the child into Manuela's arms.

His priesthood had cracked apart in his desperation to help his people, then evaporated in a passion he had failed to control. Now, though his legs had carried him to his duty, his heart hovered on the doorstep of casa Yotté where the woman he loved, whom he was sure loved him in return, had had the courage to lock herself away from him. Here lay Fermín, needing absolution only a priest could give to see him to his God.

The padre dropped to his knees, and others gathered around as he blessed himself and began the prayers for the dying. He spoke to God of the repose of Saturnino's soul, and though he could never pray for what his heart and body longed for, he prayed for the safety of the woman who seemed to have slammed the door on his love.

22

"Is there a way out the back?" Maria Claudia whispered, though the din the Brazilians were raising at the front door certainly drowned out what transpired inside.

Without a word, Josefina took her hand and Pablo's empty sleeve and pulled them through the house to the rear patio. She pushed them through a thick stand of huito bushes heavy with red flowers. Behind the laden branches, she pulled several bricks out of the wall that protected the property. They crawled through to the fields behind the village where the cattle used to graze.

"Where did the wagon go that took them to the French ambassador's ship?"

"To Villetta." Josefina gripped her arm with her clawlike fingers. "You will not hurt them." It was a question and a statement. And from the malice in the old woman's eyes, a threat.

"This is not about that."

"What is it about then?"

"They were always my best friends." She peeled Josefina's

fingers off her arm. "Take Pablo into the forest before the Brazilians get him, and when you see the padre, tell him where I went."

❧

Xandra kicked the horse's sides. "Go! Go!" she shouted in his ears. Her mother held on so tight she could barely breathe.

If César came into the village with the Brazilians, Tomás was there too. He had rejoined the invaders. She wanted to go back and find him, to see if he really meant to protect her as he had shouted he would when he ran away from her father. He should not have run. He should have stayed and helped save her father from that son of a bitch Menenez.

Still she galloped toward Aliexo. She longed to see him, though her mother said she would not recognize him.

If she did not turn around now, she might never see Tomás again. He would go away and one day remember her only as that Paraguayan girl with the big breasts, a diversion until even a Brazilian would see his duty and go do it. He would never know the child of their love.

"Go to the left here!" her mother shouted over the squawking birds and the clopping of César's hooves. "Through those trees."

Xandra slowed the horse to a walk. Vines hung from the trees and caught in their hair. "Where?"

"In that thicket." Her mother slid from the horse and ran ahead. "Come on foot. *Hola, Salvó!*" she shouted through cupped hands. She disappeared into a wall of vines. Xandra followed.

A cabin built of vertical logs blended in almost completely with the trees. The door stood open. Her mother stared in.

"Mama? Is Papa there?"

Gaspár Otazú emerged. "Gone, *querida*. Don Salvador called

you that. *Querida*." He smiled, gap-toothed and malevolent. "The comandante took him."

Alivia grasped Xandra's shoulder and groaned. Xandra reached around her mother's waist and supported her. "Where did that bastard take my father?"

"To López, of course," Otazú said, and gave another ugly smile, this one filled with false sympathy.

"Why are you here? What is your part in this?" Alivia demanded.

The old man stood at attention and took off his cap in a mock military salute. "I am the mariscal's eyes in the village," he said with enormous pride. "I make sure the comandante carries out his orders."

Alivia threw off Xandra's embrace and rushed at him. "What does López want with my husband?" she shouted. She grasped his tattered military shirt and shook him. He put his hands around Alivia's neck and began to choke her.

Xandra leapt at him, peeled his hands off her mother, and shoved him into the cabin. An iron hammer and a machete lay on the floor. She snatched up the blade and wielded it over his head. "Which way have they gone?"

He crossed his arms over his head, as if his skin and bones could protect him if she decided to split him in two. "North along the stream," he gasped out.

She knocked him to the floor with a punch to his chest and ran out carrying the machete. She slammed the door behind her. "Can we lock him in?"

"Yes." Her mother closed a clamp on the door and threaded a bolt through it.

Xandra grabbed her mother's hand and pulled her back toward the horse. "Listen, Mama," she said as she mounted. "I am going after Papa. You must do as I say. Go back to the village.

Find the Brazilian captain Tomás Pereira da Graça. Tell him to come and help me. He can capture the comandante of this sector."

Alivia looked up at her as if she were praying before the statue of Santa Caterina in the church. "Keep yourself safe. Please come back to me, Xandra."

She smiled at her mother, grateful she did not try to stop her. "Just be here when I get back. I will need your services next June," she said, and gripping the machete she wheeled the horse toward the stream that led to the road to Peribebuy.

Maria Claudia moved along the garden walls behind the houses to her own bedroom window. She stole in like a thief and threw off her clothing, wet from the sweat of heat and terror. She pulled on the boy's trousers and shirt that she had worn the first time she had climbed the wall of the Yotté house with Xandra. She quickly braided her hair and took her father's old straw hat from the peg next to the front door. She cracked open the shutter on the front window and peered out into the sun-drenched street, deserted and eerily quiet.

She shoved her braid inside the crown of the hat, turned the latch, and walked out into the blazing light.

At the end of the street, she pressed her back against the front of Luz Martinez's house and listened intently to men's voices coming from the square. In this most silent part of the day, she heard them clearly, laughing and chatting, but their lively Portuguese was barely comprehensible. When a sudden commotion drowned out their voices, Maria Claudia screwed up her courage and poked her head around the corner.

At the far end of the plaza, Alivia León ran toward the invaders and they toward her. Maria Claudia stepped out, thinking she should speed to Alivia's aid. But when Alivia began to speak to them, they listened and did not threaten her.

Maria Claudia seized her chance and ran to the horses under the trees. She chose a small mare with a sword hanging from its saddle and walked it away from the crowd at the other end. Mounting astride, as she had seen Xandra do, she urged the beast along the Camino Jesus Maria in a direction she had never gone, toward Itá, where she could pick up the road to Villetta and the river.

⚘

As soon as Alivia heard the name Tomás Pereira da Graça, she knew he was Xandra's lover. She did not know whether he knew he was going to be a father. The girl seemed sure he would come to her aid. But she always feigned complete confidence when her doubt was strongest.

When Alivia approached the Brazilian soldiers and asked for him on a matter of great urgency, the looks on their faces confirmed that her daughter's lover was a high-level officer. They immediately scattered to find him. Then Alivia realized where he would have gone and found him herself, as she expected, on the road to the estancia. He dismounted.

The two soldiers who accompanied her spoke to him in Portuguese. She understood a bit. When they referred to her as the "mother of your lady," he smiled and bowed and said in grammatically perfect, if heavily accented Spanish, "I have come to protect Xandra and your esteemed family. I found César gone and thought it must have been Xandra or her father who took him."

Alivia told him urgently where Xandra went and the danger of her mission.

He turned to the soldiers who had accompanied her. "Run

to the square and get horses and four other men. I will meet you there. We have no time to lose." They broke into a run.

Tomás turned to Alivia. "Please, my lady, I am sorry to put you in any danger, but I am afraid I must ask you to show me the way. I do not know the land. My men and I will protect you, I assure you."

"I will gladly come," Alivia said, "but we must hurry."

Tomás leapt into the saddle and pulled Alivia up in front of him. This man and Xandra were in love; Alivia wondered that such a miracle could happen between enemies in the midst of all this misery.

When they reached the plaza, they gathered six of his men, already mounted. Alivia pointed the way, and they galloped past the forge and followed the stream Xandra had taken in pursuit of her father.

Salvador leaned more and more heavily on his son. Whenever they could, they jogged along the bank where the footing was surer. In spots a dense mist rose from the water. Salvador saw that on the pretense of steadying himself, his son was breaking branches as he went along, as the children used to do to make a trail when they played in the forest all those years ago. "Thank you for helping me," he murmured after the boy broke and left dangling the branch of a blossoming orchid tree.

"Shut your mouth," Menenez snapped. The sun had passed its zenith and was beginning to cast shadows toward the east. "This is taking too long. Much as I enjoy watching you wince with each step, we have to get there by nightfall." He slid off his horse and drew his pistol.

Salvador felt the boy stiffen under his arm.

With the weapon in his left hand pointed a couple of

inches from the boy's heart, the comandante untied the knots holding Aleixo's wrists. "Untie the ropes from your father's waist," he commanded.

The boy stood impassive.

"He does not respond. He never does," Salvador said. "He was driven mad by the war."

"Shut your trap," Menenez growled.

Salvador turned his back and said, "Untie my hands, Luis, and I will do whatever you say. Do not hurt the boy."

When his hands were free, he unbound himself from Aleixo. His son startled him by looking him directly in the eyes. The father saw intention in that glance. He leaned over and kissed the boy's cheek and whispered, "Not yet."

Menenez shifted the pistol to his right hand and slapped Salvador with the back of his left. "Don't dare try anything."

The boy's fists bunched, but his father held his gaze.

The comandante threw the end of the rope to Salvador. "Tie the boy's hands in front of him," he said, "and then tie the middle of the rope to the girth of the saddle."

Salvador did as he was told.

With the gun pointed at the boy's head, the comandante checked the knot. "I am glad to see you are not stupid enough to try any tricks," he said with a grim smile when he was satisfied. "Now tie the other end of the rope around your own waist."

When Salvador had done that and Luis had checked the knot, he passed the pistol to his left hand again and held it to the boy's head while he mounted the horse. Without moving the weapon, he ordered Salvador to mount the horse behind him.

Salvador saw the chink in his plan. If they moved ahead in this way, a point would come where he could knock the comandante from the beast, and if his son would respond, they could overpower Menenez, tie him up, take the beast, and escape, despite the threat of the gun. If the boy would respond.

He stared at the boy, hoping to get him to look up, but the physically powerful comandante held the reins in his right hand, with the pistol in his left pointed at the boy's head. The boy dared not move. "You cannot get the best of me," he said over his shoulder. "Your half-dead son will be all dead if you move a wrong muscle." He spurred the animal, and Aleixo had no choice but to run alongside.

The boy's eyes met his father's, and for a second Salvador saw in them the soul of his true son: Aleixo, the daring boy who would chase down a peccary and laugh when he had to scamper up a tree to escape it. Still could he now, damaged as he was, help his father defeat Menenez? How long before the weakened boy lost all his strength from being forced to run like this?

The call of a *carpintero* caused the child to turn and glance behind them. With his head, he signaled his father to look.

Along the bank of the stream, about thirty yards back, through the tatters of fog that rose from the water, Salvador caught a momentary glimpse of César—unmistakable with that distinctive white blaze on his black face and one white leg like a stocking. The Brazilian had stolen the horse. Whoever was riding him now was hidden in the foliage along the bank. Salvador could not see who—no, it had to be Xandra. No one else would have used the signal of the woodpecker's call. She was moving along the bank of the stream, keeping up with them. The boy slowed his pace and dragged on the rope, pretending to stumble. Then he fell and nearly dragged the horse over on himself.

At that moment his sister let out a whoop, like a warrior in their childhood games. Menenez growled, but as he pointed the pistol at Aleixo, Salvador kneed his elbow. The shot went into the trees.

The comandante reined in the horse and leapt down, dragging on the rope and toppling Salvador from the beast. By the time Salvador regained his footing, the comandante had the boy by the throat with the pistol pressed against his temple. A machete grasped in her hand, Xandra rode up at a gallop. She groaned when she saw her brother cowering under the gun.

"Get down from that horse," Menenez barked.

She obeyed. He seized the machete and flung it into the bush.

"This will do very well," the comandante said. "Now, we can travel at a proper pace."

Without moving the pistol from Aleixo's temple, he got Xandra to tie her father and brother together. Once they were mounted on César, he switched the pistol point to Xandra's head, ordered her up on Marengo, and bound her hands behind her back. He mounted behind her and bound her to him around the waist. With the muzzle of the gun at the back of her head, and the reins of both horses in his other hand, he spurred his stallion. In a few miles they would reach the high road to Peribebuy.

☙

As her mare jogged along a deserted road through the forest, Maria Claudia's heart beat with fear that riding a horse astride like a man might bring on her flux and take away her hope of child. "I need you, my baby," she said aloud as if talking to the soul of a child hovering nearby, who might enter her body if it heard her voice. And what would happen to her on the road all alone? What if she never found Martita and Estella? She was afraid to go and afraid to turn back. She kicked the horse to make it go faster.

The road passed through a palm grove and then a low area covered with small lakes where herons and curlews called good morning to one another. She felt alone in the great world, but instead of the loneliness of her ordinary life, in this completely new place she felt as if she could go on and on to the other end of the world. Flowering trees of spring were everywhere around her: pink, magenta, yellow, and purple. Her country, not seeming to notice how its people suffered, bloomed with riots of flowers, just as Paraguay was going down in defeat. Or, perhaps, these trees saw the sadness around them and displayed their beauty to comfort their countrymen.

And her? Never had she felt so alive. Her body was not unlike these trees, sad for loss, but full of hope that she, like they, would bloom and bear fruit. She snuffed out the voice inside her that told her to go home.

Soon the road left the canopy of the trees and curved across a plain dotted with cypresses. A tall, red outcropping of rock loomed near Itá. The houses on the outskirts of the town were all empty. About halfway to the river, she stopped to rest for a moment at a once-lovely estancia next to a steep arroyo and a waterfall. She called out greetings, but this property looked as if it had been deserted for some time. In the yard were two scarlet termite hills, the height of her head, which no landowner would have allowed to grow so close to his house. The whitewashed stucco of the buildings was covered with black mold.

She drank from the well and found a small, bitter wild orange on a tree near the barn. At her feet, blue butterflies, the color of Gregorio's eyes, alit on a fallen orange and with pulsating wings, sucked the juice. She whispered a prayer for the people who had lived here and continued quickly on her way. The wagon had to be traveling much more slowly than a rider on a horse, but she was not sure how long ago it had started out.

She did not understand what she was doing or why. Well, she knew one reason: she needed to get away from him, if only for a little while. She loved him, and she knew that he loved her. But was that love strong enough to break the bonds of his priesthood and sustain him without his vocation? Was she strong enough to bear leaving him?

Padre Gregorio Perez. He had told her years ago that, growing up alone with his mother, all he had ever wanted to be was a priest. When he was only five, his father had been killed, run down by a speeding horse cart, on their own street in Buenos Aires—Avenida San Martín, where all the houses had glass in the windows.

She was a wanton. Her grandfather would curse her from the grave if he knew she had seduced a priest and wanted nothing so much as to bear his bastard. If she had a son, he would be barred from becoming a priest like his father.

As she cantered on, the sun burning the back of her hands as she held the reins, she worried again that riding like this would ruin her chances of a baby. Did the padre know? Did he know that her loving him had become as much about his child as it was about him?

The air changed around her as she neared the river, from the clearer mountain air in the hills to an atmosphere infused with moisture and light. Here people jammed the road. A few had carts with household belongings stacked up. A burro plodded along, his back piled high with firewood, led by three women, thin and pale, dressed only in tattered white tupois, moving like wraiths toward the water. Another younger woman about Maria Claudia's age, also pitifully thin, clad only in a poncho cut from an old blanket, puffed on a cigar. She did not look up as Maria Claudia trotted by.

An old man with a pockmarked face waved a battered straw hat. "You, boy," he called from the side of the road. His chest bore a large wooden cross on a string around his neck. It took a moment for her to realize that he called to her. She waved and kicked the horse to press on, but they were slowed by the gathering throng.

"Stop, boy," the old man called. "Where did you get that horse? It has a sword. I see it."

She turned the animal to the other side of the road, out of the crowd, and kicked its flanks until she got up to a gallop.

When the road turned south along the riverfront, her eyes followed the flight of a *tujujú*, a crane so large it seemed impossible it could fly. Suddenly she spotted the wagon lumbering along ahead of her. Martita and Estella sat inelegantly in the back on the trunks, and held gauzy white parasols over their heads.

She trotted up behind the wagon, keeping her face shaded by her big straw hat. Next to the driver sat the handsome, slender man who seemed always to have been at Señora Lynch's side. He held a huge tan umbrella over his head and mopped his brow with a lace-trimmed handkerchief.

Estella looked half asleep, swaying with the movement of the cart. Martita wore a glove on one hand and bit the cuticle of her bare thumb. "You are sure the boat will not leave without us, señor?" she asked of the man under his tan umbrella.

"Do not worry," he said in elegantly pronounced Spanish. "Madame Lynch gave strict instructions. Monsieur Cuberville and Dr. Stewart will not let the boat leave without you." He patted the box on which she sat as if he were patting her shoulder to reassure her. Then he said something to the driver of the wagon, which Maria Claudia could not hear.

She nudged the horse to walk up beside them the better to listen. As she did, the driver slapped the reins on the mules that pulled the wagon and the elegant man pulled a pistol from the sleeve of his beautiful green jacket and pointed it at Maria Claudia.

※

Xandra looked over at her brother riding César in front of their father. Besides being bound at the waist, Salvador's arms were around Aleixo and their four wrists were bound together with Salvador's hands holding the reins. In that position, they would have to move as one person. Alé's gaunt face was hardly recognizable. His arms, once muscular and lithe, had thinned so that the bones of his elbows were more prominent than his upper arms. Of all of them, César had come through the war the best off.

The comandante's pistol was now stuck into her back. Any wrong move on her part would mean her life. But César could certainly outrun Marengo. If the horses got into a race, the rope that bound her uncle to her father and brother might break. The comandante was heavy enough that perhaps, if the rope held, he would hold the saddle and Salvador and Aleixo would be dragged off. What would the comandante do in such a case? Shoot her? But what good would that do him? Her father and brother might get away, while he found himself bound at the waist to a dead woman. Not even her Uncle Luis would be stupid enough to put himself in that position.

She had to do something. Her father would never risk

harming her. If no one made a move they would all wind up in the moving prison the mariscal dragged around in his wake. Tortured. Dead, anyway. Better to die fighting.

Her head pounded like the hooves of the horses on the road. Get him to drop César's reins. Maybe she could do that. And save her father and her brother. And herself too, if she was what her brothers had called her—*Afortunada*. She took a deep breath and held it. "Help me, blessed Mother," she whispered in her heart. Then she threw her weight sideways onto the reins that stretched from César to her uncle's hands as she shouted, "Go, César! Go!"

César charged. She and Menenez fell on to the rope. It broke. The gun went off. Marengo stumbled and crashed to the ground. She and her uncle, still bound together, lay sprawled half on, half off the horse.

"Bitch," her uncle barked. "I will kill them and you." The gun went off again. On top of her uncle, she turned her head and sunk her teeth into his arm through his shirt. He yelped. "You miserable *puta*," he growled. She butted him in the nose. He started to bleed and soon there was blood everywhere, coming from her uncle's nose and from the horse. One of the shots had gone into the Marengo's head. She twisted again and bit Menenez on the hand. He tasted as bitter as he was.

"*Mierda!*" He dropped the pistol. She rolled and twisted and butted any part of his body her head could reach, keeping him from retrieving the gun.

"Cunt," he grunted and grabbed at her face.

The disgusting taste of him still in her mouth, she bit him again.

From a few yards ahead, her father shouted, "Halt, César!" The beast's hoofbeats stopped and then came back toward them.

"Son of a bitch." The comandante tried again to reach the pistol lying a few feet away. She strained with all her weight on the ropes to pull him back. He rolled on top of her.

Marengo shuddered beneath her. The big stallion was dying. Her uncle's hands closed around her throat. She struggled, tried to gasp for air. Nothing. Her chest ached for breath. She stopped struggling.

A shot rang and whizzed past her ear. The hands fell away from her throat. She choked and retched. The comandante's eyes stared in shock as his last breath left his body.

The pistol was in Alé's hand. He and her father were still bound together. Aleixo looked into her eyes. "*Bastardo.*" He mouthed the word more than said it.

She looked down at herself. She was covered in blood. But she did not hurt.

"*Querida?*" Her father's voice shook.

"I am okay, Papa."

Her father managed to untie her hands and unbind her from her uncle's body. She was freeing the rope around his and Aleixo's wrists when they heard several horses galloping toward them.

Around a curve of the road, she saw her mother riding with Tomás. They both shouted. Her mother jumped from the horse and ran to her. "My darling?" She touched the blood.

"It is not mine," she said and wept. "It is not my blood," she told Tomás.

Maria Claudia threw off her hat. "No. Stop. It is Maria Claudia." The driver reined in his mules; she did the same with her horse. Estella shouted her name. Martita hid her face in her hands and doubled over.

"Do you know her?" the elegant man with the pistol asked. Estella nodded. The man pointed the pistol at Maria Claudia again. "Get down and get in the back," he ordered. Her body, numb with fear, obeyed.

He took the sword off the horse's saddle and put it under the front seat and then tied the horse to the back of the wagon. He waved the gun in the direction of the port. "Keep going," he ordered the driver. "They will not be happy if we delay them further."

Maria Claudia sat on a trunk, gripping its leather strap to steady herself as the wagon rumbled forward. Her legs and back were stiff from riding the horse such a distance. The box had the words "Stewart" and "Scotland" painted on it, and some other words that Maria Claudia could not understand.

"What are you doing in boy's clothing?" Estella asked. She and her sister were dressed in white lawn dresses, gripping their pretty parasols, as if they were going to an elegant picnic or a tea dance.

"The Brazilians were invading Santa Caterina when I left."

The man in green put his pistol away and said, "You see. It is as I said. We did not have a second to spare. We were lucky we got away." Maria Claudia was not sure if he was talking to the driver or to the Yotté sisters.

Martita lifted her head and leaned toward Estella. "I told you she knew it was us," she said, barely audibly to her sister. She put her face back into her hands.

Maria Claudia looked at the man in green, but he was facing ahead again and talking to the driver in Spanish. She switched to Guarani and whispered, "I did not know until this morning."

Martita's body sagged. Estella took Maria Claudia's hands. "I didn't mean to do it," she said.

"Why did you?" Maria Claudia asked.

"We were in the garden early that morning," Estella said. "He had told us the night before that he was leaving Paraguay. That the war was lost and our country would never recover. He was going ahead to Buenos Aires and then to Paris, to prepare for Señora Lynch. He made it sound as if they were going to live together."

Martita let out a sigh that turned to a growl. "He was a fool. What could a woman like La Lynch have wanted with a man like him? She seduced wealth and power. He had neither, except for what was connected to López. She used him."

Estella looked imploringly into her sister's eyes and said, "I did not sleep all night. At first light, I went out to try and plant some beans. His leaving us meant we would starve. He came out and made fun of me. I begged him to take us too, or we would die. He said we would be a burden, that he needed to take care of the señora and her children.

"He turned to walk away. I went crazy. I was holding a spade. I crashed it into the back of his head. It was awful." Fat tears ran down her cheeks. "As soon as I did it, I screamed and screamed how sorry I was, but he just lay there. The blood was everywhere. He never got up. Martita and Josefina tried to wake him up, but he was dead." She grabbed Maria Claudia's hand and squeezed until pain seared into her joints.

Maria Claudia untangled her fingers and moved next to Estella on her trunk and put her arm around her. Estella buried her face in Maria Claudia's neck and sobbed.

Maria Claudia looked into Martita's eyes. "What about the stab wounds?"

"I did that," Martita said, "with a knife from the box of garden tools. Though he was already dead. To show Estella that I was killing him too. He deserved to die." Her eyes hardened.

"It was him, you know, who betrayed our father to López. He endeared himself to the mariscal by betraying his own father to prove his loyalty. They took our father and shot him. Our father wanted to go to Buenos Aires where our uncles had taken their families. But Ricardo would not go, and Papa would not leave without him. Instead of obeying, our brother reported our father as a traitor. When they shot Papa, Mama died of a broken heart. I stabbed him for that." There was not a shred of remorse in her voice.

Maria Claudia prayed in her heart for all of them. *This* was the family she had envied as a child.

Martita's eyes challenged her. "If you figured it out just this morning, why did you come after us? Surely you do not hope to bring us back to justice."

"I wanted to know why." It seemed a silly reason. "And I had to get away from the Brazilians," she added. Maybe she needed to run away from the padre and nothing more. "Why did you take his body to the belfry?"

Estella lifted her head. "We hoped the padre might still be able to save his soul. He was mean to us, but we wanted to save his soul from hell."

Mean, she called him. Not evil. As the wagon creaked along, they sat in silence, Maria Claudia and Estella holding on to each other; Martita stiff and grim-faced.

They reached the quay. A paddle wheel steamboat flying an American flag was anchored at the pier. It had two tall smokestacks in front and two decks surrounded by white railings. The words "Southern Cross" were painted on a two-story circular enclosure at the rear. Behind the charming American boat, a three-masted frigate and four ironclads, all flying the Brazilian flag, floated at anchor. The river had a dank, foreign smell.

Señora Lynch's elegant friend hailed four men who waited

at the gangplank. Six American soldiers stood guard on either side. The driver brought the wagon to where they stood.

"May I help you down, ladies?" one of the men asked in a pleasant American accent. He wore gray and black striped trousers and a black frockcoat. His elaborate whiskers hid his face, but his handsome eyes were bright blue, the color of the padre's. He lifted Estella and Martita to the ground and bowed to each of them as he placed her on her feet. He looked Maria Claudia over. "Your maid has chosen a very practical outfit for the journey," he said and winked at her.

"She is not—" Estella started to say, but Maria Claudia handed her her parasol with a curtsy and cut her off. "No need to apologize, my lady. I am sure the gentleman did not mean it as a criticism."

"No, indeed, mademoiselle." He offered each sister an arm. "It was actually very intelligent to wear boys' clothing. Now that they are close to victory, the Allied soldiers are getting pretty raucous. But you are safe now here with us. I am, however, afraid I must hurry you along. Time and tide wait for no man. And not even for lovely ladies."

The three other men who met the carriage were helping the driver carry the trunks up the gangplank. A man they addressed as "doctor" directed them to a cabin on the lower deck.

Maria Claudia followed the sisters toward the ship. If she walked up the gangplank now, this American would continue to assume she was their maid. He might let her go with them. It would mean the end of her life here. How much did she love the padre? Enough to go away? Too much to stay and ruin his priesthood? Enough to break both their hearts?

At that moment a small, dapper man appeared on the deck of the ship and hurried toward them. He seemed so delighted that for a moment, Maria Claudia thought he was going to embrace the sisters. Instead, he rushed right past them to the man in green. "François, is everything here?"

"Oui." He launched into a hushed and conspiratorial French. After a few sentences, he pointed at Maria Claudia and whispered something.

She hurried ahead to Martita, who was already halfway up the gangplank, and still holding the arm of the flirtatious American. "Please, señor," Maria Claudia said, "may I have a word with my lady?" She pointed to Martita.

Estella went ahead with the American.

"Martita," Maria Claudia said, "please take me with you."

Martita gave her a suspicious look. "So you can tell people what Estella and I did?"

"Never," Maria Claudia said with all her heart. "Everyone is starving here. I saw people along the road; you must have seen them too, just lying there, dying, maybe already dead. I just want to have a life of my own. They think I am your maid. They will let you take me. I will cause no trouble. I promise. I promise."

At that moment, the little, dapper Frenchman came up to them and bowed. "I am Monsieur Cuberville, the French ambassador," he said. "I am pleased to make your acquaintance." He spoke to Martita. "I am informed by Colonel von Wisner that it is imperative that we take this person with us," he said, pointing to Maria Claudia. "If the colonel says she must go, I cannot leave her." He stretched out his arms and shooed them up to the deck, away from the last trunk, now coming aboard. From the way he held out his hands between them and the porters, Maria Claudia could tell it was the trunks he was protecting. At last he looked into her eyes. "I cannot let you leave, mademoiselle." Deep inside her seething heart, she felt relief not to have a choice.

Martita took Maria Claudia by the hand out of earshot of the others. "If you ever do anything to hurt Estella, I will kill you."

"I never would. You know I never would."

"Very well. Come then. I will give you some proper clothing. You are a disgrace dressed as you are."

The ship's men had pulled up the gangplank. The man in green stood on the shore and watched as the sailors cast off and hauled anchor. The ship slipped its mooring and its engines rattled to life. Great puffs of acrid, black smoke rose from the stacks at the front. The great paddle wheel at its stern churned the water and helped the current carry them south. The men on the Brazilian vessels saluted as the big American paddle wheeler left port.

The air grew cool as the vessel began to move. Maria Claudia stood with Martita and Estella at the rail, looking at the lush banks of the eastern shore. She had always heard people say they blinked back tears, but closing her eyes, even for a second, made hers flow. She forced her eyes to stay open to see her country as it passed in all its beauty and devastation.

The broad and limpid river was lined with dense forest where tall palms jutted up above the line of the other treetops. Just south of Villetta, great white water lilies with bloodred hearts choked the shoreline. Their huge pads had turned up edges and looked like large serving platters at a banquet. A blue-headed jacana bird with a bright yellow beak alighted on one of them and drank from the river. Farther along, three ghostly women on the bank cast fishing nets and caught nothing, did not notice the alligator nearby with his white underbelly turned toward the sun setting over the trees of the Chaco on the western shore. Around another bend, the shore turned marshy and a chorus of animal and insect voices sang of the coming of evening. Four enormous rubicha vultures circled over a deserted village, reminding Maria Claudia that little boys and old men of Paraguay were still dying for a lost cause.

The American with the twinkly eyes came and showed them to a cabin. He bowed to Maria Claudia. "I apologize for giving you no choice," he said. "The French ambassador said it would not be safe for you to stay." Though he spoke sincerely, Maria Claudia knew the French ambassador was worried, not about her, but about La Lynch's trunks. At the door of their cabin, he said, "Get yourselves gussied up, ladies. We will dine with the captain this evening."

After he left, Maria Claudia went back out to stand alone at the white railing and watch Paraguay slip away from her. The trees and the water lapping at the bank took on a golden hue as the sun sank behind her.

When she was a child, she had thought, as those around her did, of Paraguay as the center of the world—the way the ancients had seen the earth as the center of the universe. Only Gregorio, her personal Galileo, opened her mind to the world he knew outside her country. She was going into that world, though she had no idea what would happen to her. Her heart twisted, fearing that she would never see her once benign and always beautiful country again. Martita and Estella could seek out relatives. She had no one in Buenos Aires, but many Paraguayans had fled there. She could make herself known to them. She had been married. Those who had left the country as the war started would never know that any baby she carried did not belong to Fidel Robles. She was a war widow. That would be all they needed to know.

The last rays of the sun turned the water crimson and the pink flowering trees along the shore to flame. "Good-bye," she said to them and returned to the cabin, where a man was delivering three boxes that contained Martita and Estella's things, including a yellow muslin dress that Maria Claudia wore to dinner that evening, where she ate roast beef and soft, delicious bread and thought about how it would nourish her and make her baby strong.

None of the young women ever saw the four trunks again.

23

 In the next year, while the sun still baked the red roads and the sweet perfume of tropical flowers hung in the air, the Allies occupied the capital. The duke of Caxias put a Paraguayan, Cirilo Antonio Rivarola at the head of a provisional government. Solano López fought on in the mountains of the north. Thousands more Paraguayans died. The last to go down fighting was the mariscal himself, who took a spear, or some say a bullet, in the chest. *"Muero por mi patria,"* he is said to have uttered before he expired. Some people said López died not for, but with his country. His son Juan Francisco also died in vain. Several chroniclers claim Eliza Lynch buried them with her own hands before she took her remaining children to Europe.

War had destroyed the lives of tens, some say hundreds of thousands of ordinary people who had wanted nothing more than their families and friends, enough to eat, music, and a bit of laughter to help them survive the trials that life on Earth entails. In the end there were not enough left of the living to properly count the dead.

Rumors circulated that in desperation, López and Lynch had thrown four trunks of treasure over a cliff in the north and forced the men who had carried them to jump after them, so that no one else would know the place. Hundreds of Paraguayans and foreigners set out to find it. They discovered many likely precipices, but there were only rocks beneath. Not one precious jewel or golden ingot was ever found.

It is documented, however, that Eliza Lynch undertook a long and arduous lawsuit in Scotland against the brothers of Dr. Stewart for the return of her fortune. Her efforts were fruitless.

Paraguay might have disappeared entirely, taken over by its neighbors, had it not been for the bitter rivalry between Brazil and Argentina. Fortunately, neither of them was strong enough to claim the whole of the devastated country. Though diminished by 25 percent of its territory, Paraguay was allowed to survive. But barely. The future was as dark as the depths of the forest on a moonless night.

Though it would take more than a century for the country to recover, in the immediate aftermath of the war, in small groups and in little pockets, the Paraguayan people outlived the devastation, among them the citizens of Santa Caterina, who were aided in their survival by the presence among them, whenever his duties allowed, of Tomás Pereira da Graça. He protected the women and children of the village from the barbarous behavior of the Allied soldiers, which was inflicted on the defenseless elsewhere. He and the padre sought to bring as much normalcy and joy to Santa Caterina as possible. The villagers struggled to survive the want left by their country's defeat but considered themselves more fortunate than the vast majority of their countrymen. Late that following summer, they had a good harvest of maize and manioc to nurture the tight knot of neighbors who remained.

When Xandra and Tomás were married, his father in Brazil disowned him and his brothers mocked him in condemning letters, but his sister sent him, at great expense, one hundred heifers and a prize bull. A herd grazed again at the estancia León. In their small island of sanity amid the chaos, Alivia was very busy. During the next June alone, eight children were born. Padre Gregorio baptized nearly thirty babies within the year, one of them Claudia, the daughter of Xandra and Tomás. Josefina saw it as a great good omen that on the day after Xandra's confinement, Tomás and Aleixo killed a carpincho and provided a feast for the whole village. With peace, the women of Santa Caterina also had the luxury of growing and weaving cotton to make clothes for the newborns.

One day in late June, the girl Fidelia came to the estancia at siesta time to call Alivia to Manuela, who was in labor.

Without waking Salvador, Alivia took her satchel to the forge and with Fidelia's help, made up the birthing bed with thick sheets and blankets. She held her heart calm by saying the prayers her mother and grandmother had taught her, asking God to bless her hands and the mother and baby she was about to help. The prayers had always been a way to keep her nerves steady for whatever happened during a birth. On the day the comandante had taken Salvador, she had promised God she would be a forgiving woman today. She prayed she would be able to keep her vow.

She took the heavy linen sheet, the same on which she had lain to give birth to her children and on which the infant

Claudia had been born only three weeks before, and put it on Manuela's bed.

When she and the girl helped Manuela from her hammock to the bed, she forced away the little black thought brought by the soft, smooth skin she felt when she took Manuela's arm. The water broke between the hammock and the bed. Like all first-time mothers, Manuela gasped when the fluid ran out of her body. "Do not worry, my dear," Alivia said. "This just means your child is very near."

"Get a mop," she ordered the girl, who ran out and returned to clean the worn brick floor.

Alivia prayed her grandmother's prayers. Manuela became to her, not her husband's lover, but a mother whom she was privileged to help with the miracle of birth. When the little head, covered with black hair appeared, Alivia made the sign of the cross on its crown, and with Manuela's last push, wept to see that Salvador had a new son. Then another miracle took place. Seeing the child's face, so like her Juan at the moment of his birth somehow, because the boy was Salvador's, he seemed also to be hers.

To celebrate the harvest the following fall, the padre, Tomás, and the soldiers erected a platform in the plaza and on the night of the full moon, with torches lit, the village women thanked the soldiers for their protection by performing the bottle dance, in which they placed a bottle filled with water on their heads and twirled and danced intricate patterns of steps without spilling a drop. In their turn, the Brazilians staged hilarious, gaudy amateur theatricals with men dressed as women wearing pineapples for breasts and their heads piled high with garlands of flowers from the forest. When Tomás joined them as the most glamorous of the "women" and waltzed with the shortest of the men, the audience roared so loud that all the babies sleeping in their mothers' laps woke and howled, which only made everyone laugh the more. The mothers gave their babies their breasts to comfort them and Salvador and Aleixo took the stage to sing a plaintive, sweet father and son duet.

As the old Guarani believed they could, the souls of those who had perished during the war did not immediately fly off to the heavens, but they stayed near and when Salvador and Aleixo sang a lullaby to the babies, they smiled.

HISTORICAL NOTE

What you have just read is fiction based on historical fact. When it comes to the truth about the causes of and the enormous toll taken by the War of the Triple Alliance, also known as the Paraguayan War, reports that purport to be factual differ wildly. This is especially true as it relates to whether Francisco Solano López undertook a defensive or offensive position in engaging in the war and about the role Eliza Lynch may have played in spurring him on. The best source in English I have found to make sense of it all is the balanced and masterful *To the Bitter End* by Chris Leuchars. No matter what source one consults, however, one fact is universally clear: the war devastated the Paraguayan nation and caused unspeakable hardship among its generally docile and peaceable people.

※

Seldom has aught more impressive been presented to the gaze of the world than this tragedy; this unflinching struggle maintained for so long a period against overwhelming odds, and to the very verge of racial annihilation.

—Captain Richard F. Burton,
Letters from the Battle-fields of Paraguay, London 1870

ACKNOWLEDGMENTS

Thank you with all my heart to:

David Clark, love of my life, huckleberry friend, intrepid fellow traveler, who drove a rented car all over Paraguay alone with a woman who couldn't speak Spanish. Kerry Ann King, my beautiful daughter, who inspires me always with a clear image of what a strong woman looks like. Steve Strobach, who first told me about the War of the Triple Alliance and its aftermath and stunned me with the story. I owe my interest in South American history to him and his lovely wife, Naty Reyes. Toni Plummer, sensitive, supportive editor, par excellence, who treats my work with such respect that she inspires me to do better. Adrienne Rosado, my astute agent and champion of my work. Robert Knightly and Kaylie Jones, fellow writers who are always generous with tremendously helpful advice. Jay Barksdale and the staff of the New York Public Library Research Division, the most amazing and beautiful place to research and write. Support your local library!